# The
# Handsome Man's
# De Luxe Café

## By Alexander McCall Smith

# *The Handsome Man's De Luxe Café*

ALEXANDER McCALL SMITH

Little, Brown

LITTLE, BROWN

First published in Great Britain in 2014 by Little, Brown

Copyright © Alexander McCall Smith 2014

The moral right of the author has been asserted.

A CIP catalogue record for this book
is available from the British Library.

Hardback ISBN: 978-1-4087-0433-2
C-format ISBN: 978-1-4087-0434-9

Typeset in Galliard by M Rules
Printed and bound in Great Britain by
Clays Ltd, St Ives plc

Papers used by Little, Brown are from well-managed forests
and other responsible sources.

MIX
Paper from
responsible sources
FSC
www.fsc.org    FSC® C104740

Little, Brown
An imprint of
Little, Brown Book Group
100 Victoria Embankment
London EC4Y 0DY

An Hachette UK Company
www.hachette.co.uk

www.littlebrown.co.uk

This book is for Alan and Sally Merry

## Chapter One

# The Women of Botswana
# Now Fly Aeroplanes

Precious Ramotswe, creator and owner of the No. 1 Ladies' Detective Agency, friend of those who needed help with the problems in their lives, and wife of that great *garagiste*, Mr J. L. B. Matekoni, felt that there were broadly speaking two sorts of days. There were days on which nothing of any consequence took place – these were in a clear majority – and then there were those on which rather too much happened. On those uneventful days you might well wish that a bit more would happen; on days when too much occurred, you longed for life to become a bit quieter.

It had always been like that, she thought, and always would be. As her father, the late Obed Ramotswe, often said: there are always too many cattle or too few – never just the right number. As a child she had wondered what he meant by this; now she knew.

Both sorts of day started in much the same way, with the opening of her eyes to the familiar dappled pattern made by the morning sun on the ceiling above her bed, an indistinct dancing of light, faint at first, but gradually becoming stronger. This intrusion of the dawn came from the gap between the curtains – the gap that she always intended to do something about, but did not because there were more pressing domestic tasks and never enough time for everything you had to do. And as long as curtains did their main job, which was to prevent nosy people – *unauthorised people*, as Mma Makutsi would call them – from looking into her bedroom without her permission, then she did not have to worry too much about their not meeting in the middle.

She woke up at more or less the same time each morning, thought for a while about getting up, and then rose, leaving Mr J. L. B. Matekoni still deeply asleep on his side of the bed, dreaming about the sort of things that mechanics, and men in general, dream about. Women, she felt, should not enquire too closely as to what these things were, as they were not the sort of things that women liked very much – engines and football, and so on. A friend had once said to her that men did not dream about things like that – that this was just what women *wanted* men to dream about, while men, in reality, dreamed about things that they would never reveal. Mma Ramotswe doubted this. She had asked Mr J. L. B. Matekoni one morning what he had dreamed about and he had replied: 'the garage', and if this were not proof enough, on another occasion, when she had woken him from the tossing and turning of a nightmare, he had replied to her question about the content of the bad dream by saying that it had all been to do with a seized-up gearbox. And then there was Puso, their foster child, who had told her that his dreams were about having a large dog that chased away the bullies at school, or about

2

finding an old aeroplane in the back yard and fixing it so that it could fly, or about scoring a goal for Botswana in a soccer match against Zambia, with the whole stadium rising to its feet and cheering him. That, she thought, settled that. Perhaps there were some men who dreamed about other things, but she felt that this was not the case for most men.

Once up and about, clasping her cup of freshly brewed red-bush tea in her hand, she took a walk around the garden, savouring the freshness of the early-morning air. Some people said that the air in the morning had no smell; she thought they were wrong, for it smelled of so many things – of the acacia leaves that had been closed for the night and were now opening at the first touch of the morning sun; of a wood fire somewhere, just a hint of it; of the wind, and the breath that the wind had, which was dry and sweet, like the breath of cattle. It was while she was standing there that she decided whether the day would be one in which things might happen; it had something to do with the way she felt when she considered the day ahead. And most of the time she was right, although sometimes, of course, she could be completely wrong.

On that particular morning as she walked past the *mopipi* tree she had planted at the front of the garden, she had a sudden feeling that the next few hours were going to be rather unusual. It was not a disturbing premonition – not one of those feelings that one gets when one fears that something is going to go badly wrong – it was more a feeling that something interesting and out of the ordinary lay ahead.

She remarked on the fact to Mr J. L. B. Matekoni as he sat at the kitchen table eating the brown maize porridge that he liked so much. Puso and his sister Motholeli had already eaten their breakfast and were in their rooms preparing to leave for school. The school run that Mma Ramotswe had become so used to was now no longer necessary, as Puso was of an age to make his own way there – the school was not far away – and he was also able to help his sister with the wheelchair. This gave the children an independence that they both enjoyed, although departing on time could be a problem when Puso had some boyish task to complete – the catching of flying ants, for instance – or Motholeli had at the last minute to find another pair of cotton socks or locate a book that needed to be returned to the school library.

'I have a feeling,' announced Mma Ramotswe, 'that this is going to be a busy day.'

Mr J. L. B. Matekoni glanced up from his porridge. 'Lots of letters to write? Bills to send out?'

Mma Ramotswe shook her head. 'No, we're up to date on all of those things, Rra. Mma Makutsi has been busy with her filing, too, and everything is put away.'

'Lots of clients to see, then?' He thought of his own day, and imagined a line of driverless, impatient cars, each eager for his attention, their horns honking to attract his notice: cars, in his view, were quite capable of all the human emotions and failings, including a lack of patience or restraint.

Mma Ramotswe had looked at her diary just before leaving the office the previous day, and had seen that it was largely empty. 'No,' she answered. 'There are no appointments with clients. Nothing this morning and nothing this afternoon, I think.'

He looked puzzled. 'And yet it's going to be a busy day?'

'I have that feeling. It's difficult to say why, but I am sure that this will not be a quiet day.'

Mr J. L. B. Matekoni smiled. People talked about the intuition of women, but he was not sure that he believed in it. How could women possibly know things that men did not know? Was their hearing more acute than men's, so that they heard things that men missed – as dogs or cats might pick up frequencies audible only to them? He thought not. Or was their eyesight more acute, so that they saw clear details where men saw only indistinct blurs? Again, he thought not. What we knew, we knew from our senses, and the senses of women were no different from the senses of men.

And yet, and yet . . . As he returned to his porridge, Mr J. L. B. Matekoni reflected on how there had been so many instances in which Mma Ramotswe had shown a quite uncanny ability to notice things that he himself had simply missed, or to know things about others that most people – most ordinary people, or men, to be specific – would not be expected to know. He remembered how, while out shopping with her a few weeks earlier, she had whispered to him that a woman walking towards them was probably one of Mma Potokwani's cousins. He had cast an eye discreetly over the woman and wondered whether he had ever met her in the company of Mma Potokwani, but decided that he had not. How, then, could Mma Ramotswe tell?

'She was carrying one of those bags that the orphans make in Mma Potokani's craft workshop,' said Mma Ramotswe. 'That's the first thing I noticed. Then I saw the shoes that she was wearing. They were very unusual shoes, and I had seen them before – when they belonged to Mma Potokwani. She must have passed them on.'

He had dismissed this as fanciful, but several days later, when he had gone out to the Orphan Farm to attend to one of the vans, on a pro bono basis of course, he had remembered the incident and asked Mma Potokwani whether she had any cousins visiting her. She did. And had she passed on an unusual pair of shoes to this cousin? 'As it happens,' said Mma Potokwani, 'I did. But let's not waste time talking about these small things, Rra. Now there is something wrong with the spare van too, and I was hoping that you would have the time to look at that one as well.'

He had sighed. 'I am always happy to help you, Mma Potokwani,' he said. 'But there are places called garages, you know, and they are there to fix vehicles. That is their job. Perhaps you might try in future to—'

Mma Potokwani did not let him finish. 'Oh, I know all about garages,' she said lightly. 'But I would never go to one of them – your own garage excluded, of course, Rra. Ow, those garages are expensive! You drive onto their forecourt and straight away that's two hundred pula. You get out of the car – that's another fifty pula. They say, "Good morning, Mma, and what can we do for you?" That costs seventy-five pula to say, and so it goes on. No, Rra, I will not go near those places; not me.'

Now, as he finished the last of his porridge, Mr J. L. B. Matekoni reminded himself that the one thing he felt certain about when it came to women was that you could never be sure. If Mma Ramotswe said she had a feeling about something, then it was perfectly possible that her instinct was correct. So rather than say, 'We shall see, Mma,' he muttered, 'Well, you're probably right, Mma.' And then he added, very much as an afterthought – and a hesitant afterthought at that – 'Who knows, Mma, what will happen? Who knows?'

When Mma Ramotswe arrived at the office that morning, Mma Makutsi was already there. Grace Makutsi, wife of Mr Phuti Radiphuti and mother of Itumelang Clovis Radiphuti, had recently been made a full partner in the business. It had been a long road, one that stretched from her first appointment as secretary in the fledgling agency, to assistant detective, to the vague, rather unsatisfactory status of associate detective, and finally to partnership. It had been a road that started in distant Bobonong, in the north of the country, in a home that housed six people in two cramped rooms, and from there had led, through much scrimping and saving by Mma Makutsi's family, to the Botswana Secretarial College. At the end of her course the road had climbed sharply uphill to the glorious mark of ninety-seven per cent in the final examinations – a result never before achieved at the college, and never since then equalled. But even that distinction provided in itself no guarantee of a life free of struggle, and for some years Mma Makutsi had been obliged to endure an existence of parsimony and want. Mma Ramotswe would have paid her more had she been able, but the No. 1 Ladies' Detective Agency made no money at all, and there was a limit to how generous a loss-making business could be. There would have been no point, she thought, in giving Mma Makutsi a bigger salary and then having to close the business down after a month or two when it went bankrupt.

Mma Makutsi understood all this. She was grateful to Mma Ramotswe for all she did for her, and so when her fortunes changed dramatically on her marriage to Mr Phuti Radiphuti, she made it clear that she would not give up her job, but would continue to work at the No. 1 Ladies' Detective Agency. As a partner in the business, her devotion to the enterprise became even more intense – hence her new habit of arriving earlier than Mma Ramotswe on most mornings.

To begin with, her baby son, Itumelang, accompanied his mother into the office, sleeping contentedly in his carrycot while she got on with her work. Now, however, he had become more wakeful, and consequently more demanding, and this meant that he was left at home with the woman from Bobonong who had been employed as a nursemaid.

'I am very happy with my life,' said Mma Makutsi. 'I find professional satisfaction in my work, and at the same time I have all the pleasure of running a home. It is a very good thing when a woman can do both of these things.'

'Yes, we women are doing very well in Botswana,' agreed Mma Ramotswe. 'We don't have to sit out in the lands all day. We are running businesses now. We are building roads. We are flying aeroplanes. We are doing all the things that men used to think were not for us.'

For a moment, Mma Makutsi pictured Mma Ramotswe at the controls of a plane. It would be hard for her to keep the aircraft level, she thought, as her traditional build would make it far heavier on the side on which she was sitting. It would be possible, she felt, to adjust the controls so that the wing on her side came up a bit, but she still imagined that landings would be a bit heavy, and bumpy. Of course it would be quite a shock if one were to get into a plane and see that Mma Ramotswe was in the pilot's seat. It would be rude to refuse to board the plane in such circumstances, and one would simply have to put a brave face on it and hope for the best. Perhaps one could hide one's surprise by saying something like, 'Oh, Mma Ramotswe, I did not know that you had taken up flying. This is good news, Mma. This is a big victory for women.'

Coming into the office first, Mma Makutsi took it upon herself to have the early-morning cup of tea – as distinct from the mid-morning and late-morning cups – ready for when Mma Ramotswe arrived. This cup was an important one, as it enabled the two women to consider their plans for the day ahead. There might have been no scientific connection between drinking tea and getting one's thoughts in order, but that was the way it seemed, at least in Mma Ramotswe's opinion. Tea brought about focus, and that helped.

'So,' said Mma Ramotswe. 'What have we today, Mma Makutsi?'

'We have tea to begin with,' said Mma Makutsi.

'That is very good.'

'And then . . . well, we have nothing, as far as I can see, Mma.' Mma Makutsi paused. 'Unless, of course, something turns up. And it might. Sometimes there is nothing at eight o'clock and then at ten o'clock there is something.'

'I have a feeling there'll be something,' said Mma Ramotswe. 'When I was in my garden this morning I had a feeling about that.'

Mma Makutsi, looking down at the surface of her desk, moved a pencil from one place to another. 'Yes,' she said pensively. 'There might be something. Later on.'

'You think so, Mma?' asked Mma Ramotswe.

Mma Makutsi waited some time before answering. Then at last she said, 'I am expecting some news, Mma. It might come today.'

Mma Ramotswe knew better than to ask exactly what this news might be. Mma Makutsi sometimes liked to shroud her affairs in mystery, and did not always respond well to direct questioning. So she simply said, 'I hope that you get your news, Mma.'

'Thank you, Mma. When you are waiting for news, it is better to get it. It is not easy not to get news that you're waiting for. Then you think: what has happened about the thing that I'm waiting to hear about? Has it happened, or has it not happened?' Mma Makutsi stared at Mma Ramotswe as she made these remarks. The light caught her large glasses and danced, in shards of gold, across the ceiling.

'And if you don't hear anything,' she continued, 'then you can spend the whole day worrying about it.'

'This news of yours,' said Mma Ramotswe, trying to sound as if the matter under discussion was barely of any interest at all, 'will it come in a letter, or . . .'

'No,' said Mma Makutsi, shaking her head. 'It will not be in a letter.'

'Or a telephone call?'

'Yes, it will be a telephone call. It will be a telephone call from my lawyer.'

This could hardly be ignored. 'Your lawyer, Mma?'

Mma Makutsi waved a hand with the air of one who is accustomed to having a lawyer. Of course she might have a lawyer now, thought Mma Ramotswe, but she would not have had one all that long ago. Yet she did not begrudge Mma Makutsi the satisfaction of having a lawyer after having lived so many years without one, even if she had no lawyer herself, now that she came to think of it.

'It is nothing very important, Mma Ramotswe. Just a little ...'

Mma Ramotswe waited.

'A little personal matter.'

'I see.'

Mma Makutsi rose from her desk. 'But we should not be talking about these things. We should perhaps be going over that business plan I drew up, Mma.'

'Ah, yes,' said Mma Ramotswe. 'The business plan.'

Mma Makutsi had drawn up a business plan when she had seen one that Phuti Radiphuti had prepared for the Double Comfort Furniture Store. Of course the two businesses were as chalk and cheese in terms of turnover and profit, but Phuti had told her that every concern should have a plan and she had volunteered to do the necessary work.

Mma Ramotswe took the sheet of paper passed to her by Mma Makutsi. The heading at the top read *The No. 1 Ladies' Detective Agency: Challenges Ahead and Options for the Future.*

'That is a very good title,' said Mma Ramotswe. 'Challenges and options. I think you are right to mention those, Mma: they are both there.'

Back in her seat, Mma Makutsi accepted the compliment

gracefully. 'It is forward-looking, Mma. You'll have noticed that.'

Mma Ramotswe glanced down the page. 'And there is this paragraph here that talks about enhanced profit. That is good, Mma.'

Mma Makutsi inclined her head. 'That is the objective of every business, Mma. Enhanced profit is what counts. If we were a company, that would drive the share price up.'

'Yes,' said Mma Ramotswe, knowing even as she spoke that she sounded rather vague. She had no head for finance, especially when it came to companies and share prices and so on, although she understood the basics and was particularly good at counting. This she had learned from her father, who had been able to count a herd of cattle with astonishing accuracy, even as the animals moved around and mingled with one another. She frowned. Enhanced profit had to come from somewhere. 'But where do these bigger profits come from, Mma?'

Mma Makutsi answered with authority. 'They come from greater turnover, Mma. That is where profits come from: turnover.'

Mma Ramotswe muttered the words *greater turnover*. There was a comforting, mantra-like ring to them, yes, but ... 'Turnover is the same thing as fees?' she asked.

'It is,' said Mma Makutsi. 'Turnover is money going through the books.' She made a curious gesture with her right hand, representing, Mma Ramotswe assumed, the progress of money through the books. It all looked so effortless, but Mma Ramotswe was not convinced.

'More money going through the books, Mma Makutsi, must mean ... ' She hesitated. 'More fees?'

'Yes. In a sense.'

'In a sense?'

'Yes.'

Mma Ramotswe looked down at the business plan. 'So, unless I misunderstand all this, Mma, more fees means more clients, or, I suppose, higher charges to the clients we already have.'

Mma Makutsi stared at her. Her large glasses, thought Mma Ramotswe, reflected the world back at itself. People looked at Mma Makutsi and saw themselves.

'You could say that,' said Mma Makutsi. 'That is one way of putting it.'

Mma Ramotswe's tone was gentle. 'And how are we going to get more clients, Mma?'

Mma Makutsi opened her mouth to answer, but then closed it again. She shifted her head slightly, to look past Mma Ramotswe, through the window behind her.

'There is one arriving right now,' she said.

Mma Ramotswe slipped the business plan into a drawer. The trouble with plans, she thought, was that they tended to be expressions of hope. Everybody, it seemed, felt that they should have a plan, but for most people the plan merely said what they would like to happen rather than what they would actually achieve. Most people did what they wanted to do, whether or not that was what their plan said they should do. So plans were useful only in revealing what people wished for. If you wanted to know what they would actually do, then the only way of finding out was by watching them and seeing what they did. Then you would know what they might do in the future – because most people did what they had always done. That, thought Mma Ramotswe, was well known – in fact, it was one of the best-known things there was.

'We can talk about plans some other time,' said Mma Ramotswe. 'We would not want this client to think that we sit about making plans all the time.'

Mma Makutsi felt rather relieved. She was aware that her business plan was optimistic, but she had found it difficult to write anything that took a bleak view. After all, what did it matter? The important thing was that they were perfectly all right as they were. She had Phuti Radiphuti and her baby and her new house. Mma Ramotswe had Mr J. L. B. Matekoni and her white van and Puso and Motholeli. She had her garden, too, with her *mopipi* tree and the runner beans. And they both had the land about them; the sky that went on for ever, it seemed, and was filled with sun and with the air that they all needed, that the cattle needed, that the animals in the Kalahari needed – there was plenty of that; they had Botswana. So everybody had the things that mattered, when you came to think of it, and if you had that, did you really need a business plan?

Those were the thoughts in Mma Makutsi's mind as she watched the car being parked beside Mma Ramotswe's white van under the acacia tree. Two people got out – two clients, not one: as in the business plan.

*Chapter Two*

# People with Very Long Noses

M ma Makutsi opened the door to their visitors.

'Mr and Mrs ...' she announced, looking at them expectantly.

The man shook his head. 'Not Mr and Mrs,' he corrected. 'Mr and Miss.'

Mma Makutsi was unembarrassed. 'Then Mr and Miss ...?'

The man shook his head again. 'No, Mma. I am Mr and this lady with me is my sister only. We do not have the same name because—'

Mma Makutsi cut him short. 'Because your sister is married? Of course, Rra. That must be the reason.'

The man looked at Mma Ramotswe, who had now risen from her desk to greet them. A look of understanding passed between them – a look that said: we have both had over-zealous assistants – they mean well, of course, but have a lot to learn.

Mma Ramotswe stepped forward. 'I'm Mma Ramotswe,' she said, extending her hand. 'And this lady is my assis—' She remembered barely in time. 'My co-director.'

The words slipped out. Technically, Mma Makutsi had become a partner in the business; had it been a company, she might have been a director, but it had never been incorporated – 'hardly worth doing when the shares would be worth nothing' said Mr J. L. B. Matekoni's accountant, who, as a favour, did the accounts of the agency. Partner, though, had come to mean something else – as Mma Ramotswe had read in a magazine – and she felt a different word was needed. She knew that she could have called her a business partner, but that was cumbersome, almost pernickety, and Mma Makutsi was so much more than a business partner. She was the person who made the tea, who commented on the state of the world as they drank the tea she made, who answered the phone, did the filing, and kept the young mechanics in their place. It was a large role, one for which the term business partner simply seemed inadequate, but which seemed fully worthy of the label *co-director*.

The compliment might well have slipped out unnoticed, but it did not. Mma Makutsi heard it and its effect was electric. She seemed to grow in stature, become a bit taller, and smile a bit more broadly.

The man nodded at the introductions. 'And my name is Sengupta,' he said. 'And my sister . . . ' He gestured to the woman beside him. 'My sister's good name is Chattopadhyay, which was the name of her late husband, my brother-in-law. It is a long name and so people call her Miss Rose, which is easier. That is not her real first name, but it is the one that people use. Just remember: red flower with thorns, and you will not forget her name.'

There was something earnest about his manner that endeared him to Mma Ramotswe. She smiled encouragingly. 'It is a fine name to have.' She had been discreetly studying their visitors and the memory she had been trying to locate had now surfaced. *Sengupta Office Supplies* – she had seen their advertisements in the newspaper. Paperclips, staples, copier paper . . .

'Exactly,' said Mr Sengupta.

Mma Ramotswe looked surprised.

'You mentioned paperclips,' he said.

She had muttered the words without realising, as unintention-ally as she had said *co-director*. It was a worrying prospect: if one started to say what one was thinking, the results could be very embarrassing. She might think, *Oh, there goes Mma Makutsi again – sounding off about the usual things*, and were she to say that, the consequences would be awkward. There would be all sorts of misunderstandings . . . or would they be misunderstand-ings at all? Truth would break out, rather like the sun coming out from behind a cloud, and we would all understand one another perfectly well, because we would know what we thought of each other.

'Paperclips?' said Mma Ramotswe. 'Oh, yes, paperclips. You're the office supplies man, aren't you, Rra?'

Mr Sengupta seemed proud that his business had been recog-nised. 'That is exactly who I am, Mma.' He looked about the office. 'Perhaps you use some of our items?'

Mma Makutsi shook her head. 'We do not,' she said. 'We go to a company out near Broadhurst. They are—'

Mma Ramotswe shot a glance in her assistant's direction. 'I have seen your catalogue, Rra,' she said quickly. 'They are very fine products, I think.'

'There is room for more than one company,' said Mr Sengupta generously. 'Competition in business is a good thing, I believe.'

'It is very important,' said Mma Makutsi.

'But you are the only detective agency in town,' went on Mr

Sengupta. 'Unless there is some other outfit that I am unaware of. Perhaps it is in disguise.' He laughed at his own joke.

'That is very funny, Rra,' said Mma Makutsi. 'They would be very good at disguises but nobody would know they were there.'

Mr Sengupta's response was touched with annoyance. 'That is what I meant,' he said.

Mma Ramotswe judged it was time to take control of the situation. 'Please sit down, Mr Sengupta ... and Miss Rose.' She gestured to the two client chairs before her desk. The chairs had always been in that position – ever since they had moved into the office – although recently Mma Makutsi had shifted them so that they were at least half facing her desk as well. Mma Ramotswe had not approved of this, as she found it awkward talking to people side-on, and had returned them to their original position, facing her directly. But now, as the man and the woman sat down, she realised that there would be further chair issues: one could not have clients sitting with their backs to a co-director.

Mma Makutsi was hovering behind them, and now offered the visitors tea. This offer was gratefully accepted by Miss Rose, who spoke for the first time. 'I am very fond of tea,' she said. 'I drink it all the time.'

'It is very good for the digestion,' said Mr Sengupta.

'And for many other organs,' said Miss Rose. 'It clears the head and the nasal passages.'

'Yes,' said Mma Ramotswe. 'Tea does all of those things. And more, I believe. And yet people still drink coffee ...'

Mr Sengupta started to shake his head. First it went from side to side, over one shoulder and then over the other, but then it started to move backwards and forwards. The signals confused Mma Ramotswe; she knew the Indian habit of moving the head from side to side meant the opposite of what it meant elsewhere and signified approval rather than disagreement, but she was not sure what a combination of movements meant. Perhaps there was something wrong with Mr Sengupta; perhaps his head was loose.

'I am in complete agreement with you, Mma,' he said. 'There is too much coffee being drunk. It is a serious situation.' He paused. 'But that is not the problem that I wanted to talk to you about. I am happy to talk about coffee some other time, but there is another thing that is preying on my mind.'

'Then please tell me, Rra.'

'I shall. But firstly, may I tell you about myself, Mma Ramotswe?'

'And me too,' said Miss Rose.

'Yes, yes, I'll tell them about you, Rosie. But I shall be first because I am the one who is speaking, you see.'

'Do you know India, Mma?'

In the background, the kettle, supervised by Mma Makutsi, began to make sounds of readiness – a faint whistling, like the first stirrings of the wind.

'I'm afraid I don't, Rra. There are many places in this world that I would like to see one day, and India is certainly one of them. It is high on my list.' As she spoke, Mma Ramotswe reflected on the fact that she had never really been anywhere much, apart from a couple of trips over the border into South Africa, and on another occasion north to Bulawayo. That made a total of two foreign countries, but she did not think of Botswana's neighbours as being really very foreign. And as for the list, it was hardly an active one, as she suspected that she would never be able to get away, even if she could afford the fare, and somebody would have to take care of Mr J. L. B. Matekoni and the children. And if Mma Makutsi were left in charge of the No. 1 Ladies' Detective Agency there was always a risk that she would do something that would require sorting out later, co-director or not. Then there was another thing: even if India was on her list, there were other places that were higher up. There was Muncie, Indiana, to which Clovis Andersen, author of her *vade mecum*, *The Principles of Private Detection*, had given her an open invitation before he left Botswana; and then there was London, which she would like to visit in order to see Prince Charles if at all possible, although she was realistic about that and realised that he could well be busy when she was there and unable to fit her in to talk about the things that she had read he liked to talk about. She would like it if they could exchange notes on gardening, and she could tell him about her success with runner beans and her *mopipi* tree, and the difficulties of growing things when the rains were achingly slow to arrive. He would understand all that, she thought, because he had been to Botswana and had gone out into the Kalahari and she could tell that he knew; and she could see that he was a good man.

Mr Sengupta was saying something about Calcutta. 'My family is from Bengal, you see, Mma. Perhaps you know of Kolkata, which they used to call Calcutta. I still call it that because I cannot keep up with all the changes in the world. Change this, change that – who are these people who tell us we must always be changing, Mma Ramotswe?'

Both he and Miss Rose looked at Mma Ramotswe enquiringly, as if the question were not rhetorical, but demanded an answer. Mma Ramotswe was not sure what to say; she agreed with the general sentiment, though. 'They are tiresome people, Rra,' she said. 'You are right about that.'

'But who are they?' repeated Mr Sengupta.

Mma Ramotswe shrugged. 'They are people who write in the newspapers or talk on the radio. They are the people who keep telling us what to think and to say.'

Mr Sengupta leaned forward in his enthusiasm. 'Exactly, Mma!

Exactly! I do not ever remember any election in which I was asked to vote for people for the job – the job of telling others what they can say and what they can't say. Do you remember that election?'

Mma Makutsi had now made the tea and was passing a cup to Miss Rose. 'There was no election like that,' she contributed. 'These are people with very long noses, that is all.'

Mr Sengupta turned to look at her. 'Long noses, Mma?'

'Yes, they have long noses because they poke them into other people's business. That is why they think they can tell us what to say.'

'I tell them to go away,' said Miss Rose. 'I say: go away, you people, just go away.'

This remark was greeted with silence. Then Mr Sengupta continued, 'We should be more prepared to tell people to go away, you know. If more of us stood up and said "go away" we would have less trouble with government people and busybodies of every sort.'

'That would teach them,' said Miss Rose.

'But I must get back to what I was saying,' said Mr Sengupta. 'As I was telling you, my family is from Bengal. My grandfather was a well-known man in Calcutta. He had a street named after him, you know, and he was very well off before he lost all his money in some political dealings with some very rotten fellows. That was a big tragedy for our family, but my father picked himself up and treated it as a challenge. He became a successful man and was able to give each of his four sons enough money to go and start a business somewhere. That is when I came to Botswana – that was thirty years ago. I was twenty-five then, Mma. I was young, but I came and started my office supplies business. It was not easy leaving India and starting up in the middle of Africa, but I did it, Mma. And the moment I arrived in this country I thought: this is a good place. This is a good place because people treat one another well and there is much work to be done. That is what I thought, Mma, and I have not changed my view.'

Mma Makutsi passed Mr Sengupta his cup of tea and he thanked her with one of his difficult-to-interpret movements of the head. 'Then my sister came and joined us with her husband. He worked with me in the business, and started our branch up in Francistown. That did very well until he became ill and subsequently he passed over.' He looked at his sister, who lowered her eyes.

'I am glad that everything went well for you, Rra,' said Mma Ramotswe. 'But I am sorry about your husband, Mma. I am sorry that he is late.'

Miss Rose raised her eyes and acknowledged the expression of sympathy.

'We lead a quiet life,' said Mr Sengupta. 'We are both citizens now – I took citizenship fifteen years ago, and I am very proud of it. My sister took it a bit later, but she is also proud to be a citizen.'

'I am happy to hear that,' said Mma Ramotswe. She was not sure where the story was going. Mr Sengupta had said that he was leading a quiet life, but not so quiet, it seemed, that he had no need to consult the No. 1 Ladies' Detective Agency.

Mr Sengupta suddenly looked grave. 'Then something happened,' he said. 'Something very unexpected.'

They waited. For a full minute he sat in silence before continuing. 'A woman came to our house,' he said. 'She was an Indian person, like us. She walked up to the house. We have a man at the gate. These days people like us have a man at the gate to watch out for people who think they can steal our possessions. They think that just because we are Indian we will have a lot of money and they can come and help themselves to it.'

Mma Ramotswe knew that what he said was true. There were

people who preyed on others: many of them came from outside the country, she believed, but it was not only foreigners who were to blame.

'This woman told the man at the gate that she needed to see me and that she was a friend. He let her in – it was not his fault. These men think that if one Indian person comes asking for another Indian person then she must be a relative or friend. It is natural – I am not blaming him. So this woman came to the door and my sister was the first to speak to her. You tell her, Rosie.'

Miss Rose leaned forward in her chair. 'I had never seen her before in my life, Mma Ramotswe. She was a stranger – a complete stranger.'

'We know most members of the Indian community here in Gaborone,' explained Mr Sengupta. 'You see people at weddings. The big festivals, too – Diwali and so forth. My sister will have met just about every Indian lady in the town – but not this lady, you see, Mma. Not her.'

'So she was a visitor?' asked Mma Ramotswe. 'Or somebody who was working for some firm? South African maybe?'

Mr Sengupta raised a hand. 'No, unfortunately not, Mma. It would have been simple if that had been the case, but it was not. This lady was completely without any connection in Gaborone, or the rest of Botswana, for that matter.'

'It was as if she came from nowhere,' said Miss Rose.

Mr Sengupta laughed. 'Yes, that's exactly it. She is the lady from nowhere, Mma.'

From behind them, Mma Makutsi joined in the conversation. 'She has to come from somewhere. Nobody comes from nowhere. We all come from somewhere.'

Mr Sengupta half turned in his chair to address her. 'Yes, Mma, that is correct. So perhaps I should say of this lady that she *appeared* to come from nowhere.'

'Yes,' said Miss Rose. 'She appeared to come from nowhere. But perhaps that is just where she is from. Nowhere.' She made an airy gesture to demonstrate the curious state of coming from nowhere.

Mr Sengupta's head started to bob about once more. 'We must not get confused. This lady obviously comes from somewhere, but it is not clear where that place is. And what makes this a rather unusual case is that she doesn't seem to know where she comes from.'

'Or her name,' said Miss Rose. 'Can you believe that, Mma? She doesn't know what her name is.'

Mma Ramotswe frowned. Clovis Andersen had said something in his book about a case of his in which somebody suffered from amnesia. This person could not remember what had happened to him when he was found lying by the side of a road. He had been hit by a car, it transpired, and it was only much later he began to remember the sequence of events. 'Was she involved in an accident?' asked Mma Ramotswe. 'Sometimes people cannot remember what happened to them if they have an injury to their head. It is not unknown.'

'No, it is not,' said Mr Sengupta. 'And that was the first thing that I suspected. Obviously I could not send her back out onto the street, could I, Mma?'

'Of course not.' She knew, though, that there were people who would do exactly that in similar circumstances.

'So I got my friend, Dr Moffat, to take a look at her,' Mr Sengupta continued. 'You know him, Mma?'

'Yes, I know him.'

'He said that there was no sign of any head injury and that she seemed to be quite healthy in other respects.'

'Very strange,' said Mma Ramotswe.

'Stranger than strange,' agreed Mr Sengupta. 'So we told her she could stay with us. We couldn't let an Indian lady wander around not knowing who she was – or where she was.'

'Did she really not know where she was?' asked Mma Makutsi. 'Not even that she was in Gaborone?' She shook her head in disbelief. 'You read about these things, but I'm sure they can't be true. How can you forget everything?'

'I assure you, Mma, she had no idea,' said Mr Sengupta. 'I am not a person who is easily fooled, you know. I asked her if she knew that she was in Botswana, and she simply looked at me blankly. Like this.' He affected what he thought would be the look of somebody who had no idea of being in Botswana.

Mma Ramotswe suppressed a smile. 'What did Dr Moffat say about her story?' she asked.

'He said that he thought she was telling the truth. He said that sometimes people claim not to remember things in order to get themselves out of trouble. This lady did not appear to be lying. He said that he thought it was genuine amnesia.'

Mma Ramotswe looked pensive. 'I assume that you want me to find out who this lady is?'

Mr Sengupta sat back in his chair. 'That is why we are here, Mma.'

'But why do you want to find this out, Rra? Is it for you to do that?'

Mr Sengupta sighed. 'There are two reasons for that, Mma Ramotswe. One is that I have taken this lady into my house. And once you have done that, then you cannot walk away, can you?'

'You cannot,' said Mma Makutsi from behind him. 'You cannot walk away.'

'And the second reason,' Mr Sengupta continued. 'The second reason has to do with the immigration people. This lady has no papers – no passport, no driving licence, nothing. I went to see them about getting her permission to stay in the country and they kicked up a very big fuss. They said they cannot receive an application from a person with no name and no address. They said that the most likely thing is that she is from Zimbabwe and that they will have to push her back over the border.'

Mma Makutsi knew what that entailed. 'She will be in trouble,' she said. 'Things are not easy there and she would have to find somebody to look after her.'

'That's quite right,' said Mr Sengupta. 'So I asked them if we could buy some time. I asked, if I engaged somebody to find out who she is, would they delay expelling her? They said that they would – provided the person I got to look into it is suitable.'

'We are very suitable,' said Mma Makutsi. 'We are the only detective agency in Botswana.'

'That is what I said to them,' said Mr Sengupta. 'And you'll be happy to hear, Mma, that they said the No. 1 Ladies' Detective Agency would be perfectly acceptable for this enquiry.' He paused. 'They have given us six months. That is very good, as it gives us a lot of time to sort things out.'

Miss Rose now spoke. 'Will you take on this case, Mma Ramotswe? Will you find out who this poor lady is?'

Mma Ramotswe did not need any time to consider. She could imagine how uncomfortable the woman's situation would be, how confusing and frightening it must be not to know why you are where you are. Of course she would help.

'We shall do this for you,' she said, glancing across the room at Mma Makutsi, who nodded enthusiastically. 'We shall do our best.'

'We cannot guarantee results,' chimed in Mma Makutsi, 'but my co-director and I will do our best, Mr Sengupta.'

*Co-director!* It was as Mma Ramotswe had imagined it would be. There should be a new saying, she thought – after all, somebody had to be the first to coin a saying, no matter how well known and widely used it later became. This one, she thought, could become popular: *Give a secretary a new title, and it sticks.* She smiled at the thought. Life was like that: it revealed just how true all the sayings were. In that respect, at least, there were never any real surprises, no matter how surprising things seemed to be on the surface.

*Chapter Three*

# The Only Purring Baby
# in Botswana

Mma Ramotswe returned home that evening well before Mr J. L. B. Matekoni. He had a meeting of the Mechanical Trades Association and did not get back to Zebra Drive until shortly after seven, by which time she had fed the children and was busy preparing a stew for their own dinner. It was this stew that he smelled as he walked in the back door, took off his work shoes, and went into the kitchen to greet his wife.

'It was a long meeting,' he said. 'But now ... that smell, Mma! That is a very fine stew.' He sniffed at the air. 'It is enough to make me forget all about the meeting.'

'I have had a long day too,' said Mma Ramotswe. 'Some big things happened today – just as I told you they would.'

Mr J. L. B. Matekoni went to the fridge and took out a small bottle of beer. Mma Ramotswe did not drink, but she kept a supply of cold beers for her husband for this sort of occasion.

He sat down at the kitchen table, the opened bottle of beer before him. 'So,' he began, 'this very important day of yours – I'm listening.'

She told him about the visit of Mr Sengupta and his sister.

'I know that person,' he interrupted. 'He is a charitable man: the Lions Club and so on. And I seem to remember Mma Potokwani telling me that he gave her five or six boxes of notebooks and crayons for the children to use.'

'I am not surprised to hear that,' said Mma Ramotswe. 'He has taken in this poor woman who has lost her memory. That is another example of his kindness, it seems.'

She retold the story of the Indian woman and her plight. Mr J. L. B. Matekoni listened intently, and shook his head in disbelief. 'It seems very unlikely, Mma. Surely . . .'

'Dr Moffat said it can happen,' she said.

'Oh, I've heard of it, of course,' said Mr J. L. B. Matekoni, taking a sip of his beer. 'But I've always thought it was one of those things that people talked about but nobody ever came across. Like *tokoloshes* and such things.'

He used the common word for malignant spirits – the sort of thing that people would talk about when they were frightening one another around the campfire. He knew, of course, that there were no such things as *tokoloshes*, but when one was alone at night, on a remote path perhaps, when the sounds of the bush about you were magnified by the darkness, and there were no lights nor moon for comfort, then it was only too easy to believe in the things that you did not believe in. Even the bravest among us would feel a little frightened in such circumstances, and Mr

28

J. L. B. Matekoni knew that most of us are not quite as brave as we would like to be – although sometimes we can surprise ourselves in that regard.

Mma Ramotswe did not want to talk about *tokoloshes*. She finished her account of the Sengupta visit and then went on to tell him about Mma Makutsi's telephone call.

'I knew that there was something going on,' she said. 'After Mr Sengupta and his sister had left, she kept looking at her watch. When she went out to fetch some fat cakes for her lunch, she was keen that I should stay and take a message if there was a phone call. She said she was waiting to hear from her lawyer.'

Mr J. L. B. Matekoni raised an eyebrow. 'Her lawyer? Is she in trouble?'

'No, it was nothing like that. And there was no phone call while she was out. It came an hour or so later.'

'And?'

Mma Ramotswe had been looking forward to breaking the news. 'You won't believe it, Rra.'

Mr J. L. B. Matekoni took another sip of his beer. 'She's going into parliament?'

'No.'

'She's being sent into space?'

Mma Ramotswe laughed, and for a few moments imagined Mma Makutsi in a space suit, her large glasses perched on the outside of her helmet. 'No, she is not going into space, although I am sure she would be good at doing what people who go into space do. Is there filing to be done up there? If there is, then she would do it very well.'

'The papers would float about,' said Mr J. L. B. Matekoni. 'It is not easy to file when there is no gravity. Even Mma Makutsi would find it hard, I think.'

'I have every faith in her,' she said, adding, 'now that she is a full partner.'

Mr J. L. B. Matekoni raised an eyebrow, but said nothing. He had voiced reservations about the over-promotion of Mma Makutsi, but had not pressed his views on Mma Ramotswe – the No. 1 Ladies' Detective Agency was her business, not his. 'Sometimes,' he had said, choosing his words carefully, 'sometimes you have to be cautious about promoting people. Once you promote them you can't really demote them.' He paused. 'It is easier to go up a hill than to come down again.'

Mma Ramotswe had looked puzzled. 'Are you sure of that, Rra? Isn't it easier to come down a hill, because it's downhill? Surely going uphill is more effort.'

Mr J. L. B. Matekoni gave this some thought. 'What I meant to say is that once you cook meat, you can't uncook it. That is what I really meant to say, Mma.'

'And that is true, I think,' said Mma Ramotswe.

'Well,' said Mr J. L. B. Matekoni. 'There you are, then.'

It had not been the most satisfactory of discussions, but even taking his warning into account she had still felt that it was the right thing to do to offer Mma Makutsi a partnership. She remembered their discussion now, though, as she told him about Mma Makutsi's phone call.

'Anyway, Rra, this call of hers came through at last, and it was her lawyer, as she had said it would be. He is a lawyer with a very loud voice . . .'

'That is the best sort of lawyer,' said Mr J. L. B. Matekoni. 'A lawyer who speaks so softly that nobody can hear him is no use.'

'Well, his voice was loud enough for me to hear what he said to her. It came over clearly, even though he was talking at the other end of a telephone line.'

Mr J. L. B. Matekoni looked at her expectantly. 'And, Mma?'

'And he said: "You've got it, Mma." And she shouted, "I've got it? Are you sure I've got it?" And he said, "One hundred per cent sure"—'

'Not ninety-seven per cent?' interrupted Mr J. L. B. Matekoni.

'No, one hundred per cent sure. And all the time I couldn't help listening – I don't like to listen to other people's conversations, but when one of them is in the room with you and the other has a very loud voice ...' She looked at Mr J. L. B. Matekoni for support, and he said, 'Of course, Mma. You could not help overhearing – you need not feel guilty about that.'

Mma Ramotswe continued with her story. 'When she rang off she leaped up from her chair and did a little dance. It was an unusual dance, Rra – not one I have ever seen before – but you could tell that it was the dance of somebody who was very happy about something.'

'About getting this ... this whatever it was she got?'

'A restaurant,' said Mma Ramotswe. 'Mma Makutsi told me after she had finished her dance. She has bought a restaurant. She is going to continue to work in the No. 1 Ladies' Detective Agency, of course, but in her spare time she will be running a restaurant. It will be her extra business.'

Mr J. L. B. Matekoni's eyes opened wide with surprise. 'Ow!' he said.

Mma Ramotswe shrugged. 'I don't know what to think, Rra. I'm not sure if I should be thinking "ow" as well, or whether I should be thinking something else altogether.'

Mr J. L. B. Matekoni started to smile. 'It will be a strange restaurant, Mma, if Mma Makutsi is running it.'

Mma Ramotswe suppressed a grin. He was right, of course, but there were issues of loyalty here. For all her quirks, Mma Makutsi was her colleague and friend; more than that, she was a

woman, and there were still those men who looked with conde-
scension on the business aspirations of women. Mr J. L. B.
Matekoni was not like that, naturally, but Mma Ramotswe felt
that she should not be too quick to call into doubt the business
ambitions of another woman. Even to think 'ow' might be going
too far, and so she did not grin, but instead said, 'I'm sure that
Mma Makutsi knows what's she's doing, Rra. After all, if you get
ninety-seven per cent, then you must have a good head on your
shoulders.'

Mr J. L. B. Matekoni picked up the warning. 'Oh, I'm not
doubting Mma Makutsi's general abilities. She is a very clever
lady, as we all know. It's just that she's a bit ... ' He struggled to
find the word, and Mma Ramotswe immediately felt sorry for
him. Yes, Mma Makutsi was a bit ... a bit ... She, too, found it
difficult to describe exactly what she wanted to say. There were
plenty of people who were a bit ... whatever it was.

'Bossy?' she suggested. 'Is that what you're trying to say, Rra?'

Mr J. L. B. Matekoni frowned. He was not sure if that was
exactly what he meant. Mma Potokwani was bossy – the word
was exactly right for her, but she, of course, had no option but to
be bossy. If you were the matron of an orphan farm, with all those
children running around, then you *had* to be bossy. And presumably any advertisement for that job would have to specify the
need for bossiness. If Mma Potokwani were to retire and a suc-
cessor needed to be found, then the wording of the
advertisement would have to spell things out quite clearly.
*Wanted: an experienced lady for the job of Matron. Only very bossy
ladies need apply.*

He smiled at the thought.

'Something funny, Rra?' asked Mma Ramotswe.

He put out of his mind the picture that had been forming of a
line of bossy ladies queuing up for an interview for Mma

Potokwani's job. There would be a great deal of pushing and shoving and using of elbows, until eventually the bossiest, pushiest lady reached the head of the queue and was straight away appointed.

He returned to the subject of Mma Makutsi's restaurant. 'No, it's not exactly bossiness I'm talking about, Mma. It's more a question of strictness. Yes, maybe that's it.'

Mma Ramotswe nodded. Strictness. That was it. Mma Makutsi could be *strict*.

Mr J. L. B. Matekoni now found the words. 'You will get into trouble if you don't eat everything on your plate, you see. She will be watching through one of those kitchen hatches – you'll just see her spectacles peering out – and she will notice if you do not finish off her food. Then she will come out from the kitchen and ask for your excuse. It will be a very strange restaurant, that one.'

As one might expect, a different conversation took place in the Radiphuti house that evening. Dinner there was always eaten a bit later, as Phuti Radiphuti's day ran on a rather different timetable from everybody else's. Most people were at work by eight, but Phuti had decided some years previously that he would not arrive at the Double Comfort Furniture Store until nine o'clock, and sometimes even half an hour later than that. There were several reasons for this: one was his impatience with the stop-and-start driving that was necessary in the heavier traffic of the rush hour. He had discovered that if you left the house early, you would inevitably get caught up in a long line of cars driven by people who, like you, were eager to make the journey before eight. It was, he thought, rather like trying to get through a door when hundreds of people had exactly the same idea. At least if you were on foot trying to get through a door, people would behave reasonably courteously rather than trample one another or snarl in irritation if anybody were to be too slow, or be indecisive as to whether to turn left or right. How different it was when people were behind the wheel of a car; protected by the metal and glass surrounding them, they showed all sorts of impatience with other drivers, and rarely hesitated to secure some tiny advantage by slipping through a red light or ignoring the unambiguous message of a *stop* or *give way* sign. And this was in Botswana, he thought, where everybody – or at least nearly everybody – was so polite! How much worse was it in other countries not too far away where people drove as if they were being pursued by a swarm of bees; or where they paid no attention to the twists and bends in the road.

The consequences of having such roads were worse, he reminded himself, if you had mountains as well. Botswana at least had flat roads, since there were no real mountains, but it was different in Lesotho, which was not very far away and where all there was, really, was mountain after mountain. As he thought about this he remembered what had happened some years ago to the king of that country, who had been driven to his death off the side of a mountain. Everybody knew that the roads in Lesotho were not in good condition and somebody, surely, should have been more careful with the King in the back seat. Of course you could not tell, thought Phuti. It may not have been the driver's fault, as all sorts of things could happen on a road at night. Cattle strayed onto the tarmac, standing there practically invisible in the darkness until their eyes were suddenly caught in the headlights and it was too late; boulders tumbled down hillsides and came to rest at blind corners; rain washed away whole sections of the road, leaving great gaps into which anybody, even a king, might easily fall. No, you should never blame a driver unless you knew all the facts, and since that poor driver was late, just as the King himself was, you would never know exactly what happened. Some things were accidents, pure and simple, in the same way as had been that incident in which he himself was injured – where the delivery driver did not see him standing there. You should not go around sprinkling blame on other people, thought Phuti Radiphuti.

But it was not simply because of bad driving and traffic jams that Phuti had decided to avoid going into work early – there were good business reasons for his coming into the office slightly later than everybody else. Phuti believed that if there were any problems to be dealt with, they would make themselves known early in the day. Usually these were staff issues, with somebody not coming into work because he or she was ill, or discovering something wrong with some item of furniture, or a difficult letter arriving in the mail that one of his assistants picked up on the way to work. All of these things could very easily be dealt with by one of the three assistant managers, and letting them deal with problems rather than sorting it out himself was not only less stressful for Phuti, but was also a way of encouraging staff. If you were an assistant manager then what you really wanted was the chance to manage, and if the real manager was around you might feel inhibited from managing. By arriving late, he felt, the assistant managers would have an hour or so during which they could manage. Of course there were limits to this approach: if it were left to assistant managers, they would suggest that you arrived late in the afternoon, or even not at all, thus giving them all day to give orders and make decisions, leaving nothing for you to manage or decide yourself.

So it was because of all this that Phuti's day ran rather later than everybody else's. And that meant that Mma Makutsi had more time to attend to the needs of their son, Itumelang Clovis Radiphuti, who was now six months old and not inclined to go to sleep until at least eight in the evening. The three or four hours that Mma Makutsi now spent with him after she returned from work in the late afternoon was, she felt, the most valuable time in her day – and his too. The woman whom they had engaged as nurse to Itumelang was completely trustworthy and had exceeded their expectations in every respect, but Mma Makutsi believed, as did most people, that there was no substitute for the attention of a mother. And Itumelang himself seemed to share this view, as his expression always became one of complete delight when he saw his mother come home at the end of the working day. And when she picked him up and held him to her he would make a strange, gurgling sound – a sound of unconcealed pleasure that Mma Ramotswe, when she witnessed it one day, had described as being like the purring of a cat.

'You can tell that he is happy,' she said to Mma Makutsi. 'Listen. That is the noise that a cat makes when it has been fed and is happy with the world. He is purring, Mma. You have the only purring baby in Botswana.'

'I am very happy that he purrs,' said Mma Makutsi. 'Maybe that means he's a little lion. When he grows up he will be brave and strong – like a lion.'

Mma Ramotswe had laughed, but the comment had triggered a memory that came back to her now, none the less vivid for not having been thought about for years – since childhood, in fact. She closed her eyes for a moment, as if to fix the recollection in her mind before it vanished, as old thoughts can so easily do. For a few moments she was back in Mochudi, still a girl, sitting with her father's cousin, who had helped bring her up, and the cousin had told her a story that she herself must have learned from her grandmother or an aunt or somebody of the generation that still stored all these traditional stories in some corner of their minds.

'A lion,' muttered Mma Ramotswe. 'There was a story about that.'

Mma Makutsi planted a kiss on Itumelang's brow. 'About a boy who was as brave as a lion? Like my Itumelang?'

Mma Ramotswe shook her head. 'I was told it a long time ago by my daddy's cousin. She was the one who helped him when I was a girl.'

Mma Makutsi inclined her head respectfully. She knew about Mma Ramotswe's early years. 'After your mother became late?'

'Yes,' said Mma Ramotswe. 'The cousin was older than my late daddy. She was like a grandmother to me.'

'They are the ones for stories,' said Mma Makutsi. 'They know all those stories about things that happened a long time ago – or did not happen.'

'It doesn't matter if they did not happen,' said Mma Ramotswe. 'There are many stories about things that did not happen.' She paused. 'This one was about a girl who married a lion. She did not know it when she married him, but the young man she had chosen was really a lion. He looked like an ordinary man, but there was something about him . . .'

'It would be the eyes,' said Mma Makutsi, glancing anxiously at Itumelang's eyes to reassure herself. 'You can tell if somebody is really a lion by examining the eyes. Lions have eyes that are a bit yellow, Mma. They are like the colour of grass when there has been no rain for a while. Or sometimes they are the colour of the sand out in the Kalahari, which is also a sort of yellow colour.'

'I think that what makes a lion's eyes different from other eyes is their fierceness,' said Mma Ramotswe. 'There are other animals that have eyes that colour, but they are different. They are not fierce, like a lion's eyes. They do not look at you in the same way – they do not make you wish you were somewhere else.'

Mma Makutsi agreed. 'But what about this girl?' she asked. 'How did she know he was a lion? Was it the eyes, do you think?'

Mma Ramotswe shook her head. 'No, it was not the eyes. She did not say anything about his eyes; in fact, it was her brothers who noticed. It was the girl's brothers.'

'They could tell?'

'Yes, Mma. They noticed that by the way he smelled. If you are a lion, you cannot really disguise the way you smell. You can change the way you look, but not the way you smell.'

Mma Makutsi was thoughtful. 'It is the same with people,' she said. 'You can change your clothes. You can change the look of your hair. Doctors can even change the shape of your nose or ears, but you can never change the way you smell. That will always give you away.'

Mma Ramotswe was used to Mma Makutsi's theories, which were often rather unusual. This one, she thought, was distinctly unlikely, but she did not want to pursue the matter. Mma Makutsi was apt to argue a point tenaciously, and Mma Ramotswe did not want to get involved in a prolonged debate on the way people smelled.

'That may be so, Mma,' she said evenly. 'Or it may not be. But the point here is that the girl's brothers told her they thought her new husband was a lion because he smelled a bit like a lion. And they said there was also something in the way he walked that reminded them of a lion.'

'Lions walk on four legs,' observed Mma Makutsi. 'Was this man walking on four legs? That can be a big giveaway, Mma.'

Mma Ramotswe shook her head. 'He walked normally, on two legs. But there was something in the way he walked that made them suspicious. I do not know what it was, as my cousin did not say anything about that. But you can imagine it, Mma, can't you?

He would have walked with that sort of sway that lions like to use. They sway their hips a bit.'

'I have seen men walk like that,' said Mma Makutsi. 'But I did not think they were lions.'

'So they told the girl, Mma,' continued Mma Ramotswe. 'They said to her: this new husband is really a lion. You will have to get rid of him. And the girl was very upset.'

'It would not be a good thing to discover about your new husband,' said Mma Makutsi. 'I don't know what I would do if I discovered that Phuti was a lion. It would be a very sad thing to find out.'

'I do not think your husband is a lion,' said Mma Ramotswe. 'I see no evidence at all.'

'Thank heavens,' said Mma Makutsi. 'It would be hard for me to go back up to Bobonong and tell my family. They would say: please do not bring your new husband up here, or he might eat our cattle.'

They both laughed. Then Mma Makutsi said, 'I am worried about this young woman, Mma. What did they do?'

'The brothers made a cage,' said Mma Ramotswe. 'This cage was a trap and they put a goat in it. They said, "If our sister's husband is really a lion, then he will smell the goat and he will go into the cage to eat it. Then the trap will close on him and we shall know."'

'And is that what happened?'

'Yes,' said Mma Ramotswe. 'And once he was in the trap, the new husband showed that he really was a lion. He began to roar, and they saw that his teeth were like the teeth of a lion. They saw all this, Mma, and they knew. The girl, of course, was upset, but I think she got over it, once her brothers had chased her husband away.'

'It was best to have discovered it,' said Mma Makutsi. 'I could not live with the uncertainty of not knowing if my husband was a lion. Could you, Mma? Could you live with uncertainty like that?'

Mma Ramotswe could not. 'It is best for a woman to know her husband's weak points right at the beginning. All men have their weak points – although they try to pretend that they do not have any, they are always there. But if you know about them in advance, then you can deal with them. It is the hidden weak points that are the problem.'

They were both silent for a while. Itumelang looked up at his mother, and made his slight gurgling sound. Mma Makutsi was wondering about Phuti's weak points. There was his stammer, of course, and there was also his artificial foot and ankle – the result of that accident with the delivery truck. But although one might think of these as weak points, they were not weaknesses. Weak points were things that had *happened* to him. Weaknesses were character flaws, and Phuti had none of those.

The mention of weak points had Mma Ramotswe thinking about her own husband. Did Mr J. L. B. Matekoni have any weaknesses? He had been a bit indecisive in taking so long over their engagement, but that indecisiveness was probably a result of his simply not being forceful enough, which was a rather attractive quality, she thought. There were more than enough forceful men about, and a man who did not try to force his will on others was a refreshing change. As far as the other common vices went, Mr J. L. B. Matekoni had none of those: he did not drink much – other than the occasional beer – and he was never selfish. He did not gamble, nor did he look at other women, although that did not mean that other women did not look at him; Mma Ramotswe had seen them, and imagined the thoughts going through their heads: *Now there's a nice, gentle-looking man* ... Oh, yes, she could just hear those thoughts, but they did not worry her unduly because she understood how those who did not have the company of a good man, who had been saddled with a bad or indifferent one, with one who never paid them much attention or showed them any affection – she could understand how such women might lay eyes on a man like Mr J. L. B. Matekoni and dream. She did not begrudge such women their dreams. And it was a compliment to Mr J. L. B. Matekoni that women should think such things about him, and usually the women who thought these things did not go on to flirt with him or anything like that. Except sometimes, and in those rare cases Mr J. L. B. Matekoni was always polite and would make a pointed reference to something his wife had said or done, and that was usually enough to put a stop to that. Unless you were somebody like Violet Sephotho, of course; she was shameless and would, if anything, be encouraged if mention were made of a wife. Mma Makutsi had many stories to tell of Violet's husband-stealing activities, including one occasion when she had flirted with a new husband *at his wedding*. Fortunately the new mother-in-law had witnessed this and had managed to seat Violet next to an uncle who was a lay preacher and whose only topic of conversation was the Bible.

'That is a very good way of dealing with somebody like Violet Sephotho,' Mma Makutsi had said, chuckling at the recollection. 'That uncle would have regarded her as a challenge – somebody who clearly needed to be saved, and he would have made a big effort to do so.'

But now Itumelang was asleep and Mma Makutsi was sitting in the kitchen, aware that she would have to start cooking the evening meal, but too excited by the news she had received that day to concentrate on any mundane task. She sat like that for almost twenty minutes, going over in her mind her short, businesslike conversation with the lawyer. Her offer for the lease of the premises had been accepted and, under the power of attorney she had granted him, he had signed it. Nothing remained to be done. For the next five years she was to be the tenant of the commercial premises on Plot 1432 Extension Two, Gaborone; she, Grace Makutsi, daughter of the last Hector Makutsi, of Bobonong – just that and nothing else, but now, all rather suddenly, it seemed, Mrs Radiphuti, mother of Itumelang Radiphuti, and tenant in her own right of commercial premises. It was almost too much to take in, and when Phuti eventually came home she was still thinking of it all with the warm glow that comes from the contemplation of something deeply satisfying, something that one cannot quite believe has happened.

Phuti had been aware that the lawyer would phone that day and he knew immediately. 'Good news?' he said, as he entered the kitchen. 'I think I can tell.'

She nodded, and he stepped forward to embrace her.

'It is all arranged,' she said. 'He has signed the lease for me and I am now the tenant.'

Phuti patted her on the shoulder. 'My Grace,' he said fondly. 'You are a very clever woman. I am proud of you.'

She thought: *It's your money*, but she did not say it. Instead she said, 'I cannot wait, Phuti. He said we can pick up the keys tomorrow.'

'I've spoken to that painter,' said Phuti. 'He says that he is ready to start the moment we buy the paint.'

'Good. And the carpenter?'

'He will be ready to start next week. He says the painter can start as long as he doesn't do the part where the cupboards are going. Then he'll come in and start building all the other things. And the electrician. That Zimbabwean we use at the store says that he will drop everything and come to us the moment we need him.'

Mma Makutsi smiled. She had become aware of Phuti's influence, but had yet to become used to the ease with which he could get tradesmen to dance attendance.

'I think we could open in about a month,' she said.

'As soon as that?'

'Yes. We will need to find a chef and waiters, but that will be easy. There are always people searching for jobs. There are far too many chefs, I think.'

Phuti nodded. He assumed that she knew what she was talking about. He was not sure why there should be such an over-abundance of chefs, but perhaps she was right. 'And a name, Grace? You said that you would think of a suitable name for your restaurant.'

She had already given that some thought, and a name had come into her mind unbidden. It was exactly the right name for her business and she now announced it to Phuti: 'The Handsome Man's De Luxe Café.'

Phuti hesitated. 'For . . . for handsome men?' he asked. He was not a handsome man himself; he knew that.

'Yes,' said Mma Makutsi. Then she laughed. 'Not that other men are discouraged, Rra. All will be welcome.'

'Then why call it the Handsome Man's place? Why not just the De Luxe Café?'

'Because I want it to be a fashionable restaurant, Phuti.' She considered again what she had said about everybody being welcome. That would need some qualification. 'But I do not want any riff-raff coming in and eating there,' she continued. 'I want this to be a big important stop on the circuit.'

Phuti thought of the riff-raff, and found himself feeling sorry for them. Presumably these people – whoever they were – had to eat somewhere, and he did not like the thought of them wandering around, excluded from this . . . this circuit, whatever that was.

'What circuit?' he asked. 'What is this circuit?'

Mma Makutsi made a vaguely circular movement with her hand. 'It is the circuit for fashionable people,' she said. The circular movements became wider. 'It is that circuit.'

'Oh,' said Phuti. And then added, 'I see.'

## Chapter Four

# Electric Dogs and Other Things

The meeting at the Sengupta house had been arranged by Mma Makutsi, who had pointedly insisted on setting it up.

'It will look better,' she said, 'if I telephone to arrange a time to see these people.'

Mma Ramotswe looked up enquiringly. 'But I can do that, Mma. Thank you, anyway.'

Mma Makutsi shook her head. 'No, it would be better if I did it, Mma. If you phone, then they will think that we are the sort of outfit where the bo—' She almost said *boss*, but stopped herself. '. . . where the senior director has to phone herself.'

Mma Ramotswe smiled inwardly. There were two things that had become apparent from this exchange. The first of these was that Mma Makutsi wanted to ensure that she was included in the visit to the Sengupta house, rather than staying behind to keep the office open. The second of these was that even if, as a result of a slip of the tongue on Mma Ramotswe's part, she had now become a co-director, she nonetheless acknowledged that she was the junior co-director, if there could be such a thing. That, at least, was reassuring.

Now, they drew up in front of the Sengupta house. It was an area where the plots were lined with substantial whitewashed walls; the gates set into these walls were generally far from modest – statements of the importance of the people who lived behind them. As they arrived, Mma Ramotswe thought of her own gate on Zebra Drive – a ramshackle affair that had never fully recovered from being hit several years ago by Mr J. L. B. Matekoni's green truck. He had said that he would repair it – and he would certainly be capable of doing that – but somehow it was never done, and the gate languished, tipped at an angle, on its twisted supports. She had raised the subject with him, of course, but that did not seem to make much difference, even when she reminded him that although he was always prepared to respond to Mma Potokwani's request to fix the water borehole pump at the Orphan Farm or attend to her increasingly eccentric minibus, still he could not find the time to repair his own gate. 'I shall do it,' he said. But that, she reflected, was what all husbands promised; every wife, she imagined, had a mental list of things that her husband should do but realistically never would do.

They had been seen, perhaps by a hidden camera, and the gate started to slide open to admit them.

'An electric gate,' said Mma Makutsi.

'You could have one,' said Mma Ramotswe, as she swung the white van onto the driveway. 'Phuti could afford to put electric gates on your new house.'

'We do not need one,' said Mma Makutsi. 'We have two dogs now. They sleep outside in a shed. One is very fat – like a barrel on legs. They bark and bark if somebody comes. That is enough.'

'Perhaps you can get electric dogs now,' said Mma Ramotswe. 'Maybe that will be the new thing.'

Mma Makutsi let out a hoot of laughter. 'Electric dogs . . . '

And then, with a sudden impact, the front wing of the tiny white van hit the edge of the electric gate. The van came to a shuddering stop, as did the gate.

Mma Ramotswe looked at Mma Makutsi. 'I have hit the gate, Mma,' she said.

For a few moments Mma Makutsi said nothing. Then she turned to Mma Ramotswe and put a reassuring hand on her arm. 'The important thing, Mma, is that we are all right.'

'But the gate is not,' said Mma Ramotswe miserably. 'And my van will have a big dent, Mma. I can hardly bear to look.'

'I will look, then,' said Mma Makutsi, opening her door.

She stepped outside and made her way round to the front of the van. Mma Ramotswe watched as Mma Makutsi stooped to inspect the damage. She saw her shake her head and then look up with a grave expression. The large glasses had slipped down her nose as she bent down; she pushed them back into position.

'There is a big dent, Mma,' she said. 'But there is no damage to the lights. They will fix this very easily.'

Mma Ramotswe sighed. Mr J. L. B. Matekoni was understanding, but she knew his views on her van, which he thought should have been retired a long time ago. He would assess the damage and then suggest that rather than fix it he should get her a new van. They had been through that before – on more than one occasion – and she had always resisted the suggestion. Eventually he had taken matters into his own hands and bought her a replacement van, but she had never taken to it and eventually she had got her old van back. She did not want to go through all that again.

'And the gate, Mma?' she asked through the window.

The gate had recoiled a few inches after the impact and seemed now to be hanging slightly askew. Mma Makutsi gave it a tentative push and from somewhere in the vicinity there came the strained, whirring sound of an electric motor engaging. Then it stopped.

'There is still room for us to go through,' Mma Ramotswe called out through the window. 'Get back in and we can park the van. We'll tell them about their gate.'

'Would you like me to speak to them?' asked Mma Makutsi as she got back into the cab.

'No, I can tell them.'

'I meant: would you like me to say that I did it?'

Mma Ramotswe frowned. 'But I did it, Mma. I was the one who was driving.'

'Yes, but it might reflect better on the agency if I said I did. Then they won't think that the person in charge is a lady who goes about hitting gates.'

'But I do,' said Mma Ramotswe. 'I hit a gate up at Mochudi once. And Mr J. L. B Matekoni hit our own gate back at Zebra Drive. We have a bad record when it comes to gates, Mma.'

They both laughed, but Mma Ramotswe had been given something to think about. If proof were needed of the loyalty of Mma Makutsi, and of her concern for the reputation of the business, then it had just been provided and convincingly so. It was loyalty – pure and simple loyalty – and that was something which she could never have learned at the Botswana Secretarial College, but which had to come from somewhere deep down inside.

Having parked the van at the top of the drive, they got out and made their way onto a large shady veranda that ran the length of the front of the house. An elegant cluster of chairs occupied one end of this veranda, and behind them there was a long bar for the serving of food and drinks. The chairs were covered with what looked like zebra skin and there was a distinct air of opulence about the place. Mma Ramotswe and Mma Makutsi exchanged glances.

A door opened and Miss Rose appeared.

'Mma Ramotswe!' she exclaimed. 'And Mma Maputi.'

'Makutsi.' The correction was made in a tone of slight disapproval.

'Of course – I'm sorry, Mma. I should know how annoying it is when people get your name wrong. If you're called Chattopadhyay you know all about that.'

They were still standing on the veranda. As Miss Rose turned to lead them into the house, she stopped and stared down the drive. 'The gate—' she began.

Mma Ramotswe stopped her. 'It is my fault, Mma, I am very sorry indeed. I seem to have hit the gate with my van. I shall pay for it to be fixed.'

Miss Rose turned to face her. 'No, Mma, it cannot be your fault. These electric gates are dangerous. They are always opening and closing according to some strange programme of their own.' She paused. 'And anyway, if it is anybody's fault it is mine. I am the one who operated the switch for the gate to open when I saw your van coming. I must have pushed it the wrong way when you were halfway through.'

Mma Ramotswe held up her hands. 'I'm sure it was not you ...'

'No, it probably was,' said Mma Makutsi.

Mma Ramotswe gasped. 'No, Mma, we must not blame Miss Rose.'

'But she said it was her fault,' said Mma Makutsi.

'Yes, I did,' said Miss Rose, throwing Mma Makutsi a sideways glance. 'But let's not waste our time talking about milk that has already been spilt.'

'Nor crying over it,' said Mma Makutsi. 'You cry over spilt milk, I think.'

'I know that, Mma,' muttered Miss Rose. 'It is a figure of speech, I believe. I know about those things.'

As they were led down a corridor into a large living room at the side of the house, Mma Ramotswe whispered to Mma Makutsi, 'Please try to be tactful, Mma. Have a little tact.'

She could feel Mma Makutsi bristling. 'It was her fault that the gate closed as we were going through, Mma Ramotswe. You heard her. She said it, not me.'

'I know, I know. But the point is, Mma, that she is the *client*. Remember what Clovis Andersen said about the client. You never argue with the client.'

They had reached the end of the corridor and perforce the end, too, of their whispered conversation. The room into which they now went was large and formal, decorated in a somewhat heavy style with a great deal of gilt, fringes and tassels. On the wall there were pictures of idealised landscapes and buildings: Himalayas, Rajasthan, the Taj Mahal by moonlight.

'This is very beautiful,' said Mma Ramotswe.

'Yes,' said Miss Rose. 'It is very fine.' She had become businesslike. 'If you ladies sit down, I'll fetch her.'

'Before you do,' said Mma Ramotswe, 'can you tell me what you call this lady? You said that she could not remember her name.'

Miss Rose smiled. 'We call her Mrs. Just Mrs. That is the best thing. That is what she'll expect you to call her.'

Mma Makutsi opened her mouth to say something, but was silenced by a look from Mma Ramotswe. When Miss Rose left the room, though, she leaned across to Mma Ramotswe and said in a loud whisper, 'But you cannot call somebody Mrs! Mrs is not quite the same as Mma, is it? Mrs needs to be Mrs Something, not just Mrs . . . Mrs Air!'

'Hush,' said Mma Ramotswe. She wanted to tell Mma Makutsi that this was a delicate enquiry – Mrs, after all, had no memory and was presumably in a distressed state – and their questioning would have to be very careful. She searched her own memory for any relevant passage from Clovis Andersen that she could quote to Mma Makutsi, but could think only of the advice he gave not to bully people when questioning them. *The person to whom you are talking will always be readier to help if you are polite and friendly,* he wrote. *Never shine a light in somebody's face. No third degree.* He was right, of course, but she decided that now was not the time to discuss techniques with Mma Makutsi, and anyway, there were footsteps in the corridor outside.

'This is Mrs,' announced Miss Rose.

Mma Ramotswe rose to her feet and shook hands with the woman who had accompanied Miss Rose into the room. She saw a well-dressed Indian woman of about forty, perhaps slightly less, with what Mr J. L. B. Matekoni would have described as a 'pleasing face'. A pleasing face was not necessarily beautiful in the conventional sense – it was, rather, comfortable. It was the sort of face that suggested equanimity.

Mma Ramotswe introduced Mma Makutsi, who also shook hands. Then the four of them sat down around a low table.

'The girl will bring us tea,' said Miss Rose. 'She will not be long. These hot afternoons make me want to drink tea.'

'Tea is the thing,' said Mrs. 'It is always time for tea. Hot afternoons, cold afternoons – it doesn't matter. Tea.'

Mma Ramotswe listened to the voice. It was hard to place the accent – and she felt that she was never very good at that anyway – but the voice did not sound at all out of place. Sometimes when people had recently arrived from India she noticed that they spoke in what struck her as a rather pleasant, slightly musical way. This woman, though, seemed to speak in much the same accent as that of Miss Rose. For a few moments her thoughts wandered. If you lost your memory, why did you not lose your vocabulary, too? Surely words were a memory, just like the things that happened to you? And how would you still remember things like how to turn on a light or boil a kettle? How would you remember that tea is just the thing if you had forgotten everything else?

These thoughts were interrupted by Miss Rose. 'Mrs is happy to answer any questions you have, Mma Ramotswe. That is so, isn't it, Mrs?'

Mrs inclined her head. 'I am very happy that these excellent ladies may be able to help me find out who I am. I shall certainly answer their questions, although . . . ' She left the sentence dangling.

'Although you can remember nothing?' supplied Mma Makutsi.

'Exactly,' said Mrs. 'It is all a blank. There is nothing there. It is as if I had started to live a few days ago, only.'

Mma Ramotswe noticed the use of the word *only*. It was a speech pattern she had noticed in people from India: for some reason they liked the word *only*, just as people from other places had a fondness for certain words or expressions. The South Africans often said yes and no in quick succession – *yes, no* – or they said *hey* a lot at the end of sentences. And the Americans, she had noticed, had a fondness for the word *like*, which was dropped into their pronouncements for no particular reason. It was all extremely odd. But then, she thought, did we all want to speak the same way? No, that would be too dull, like hearing the same song all the time; one song, on and on, day after day.

'When exactly was that?' asked Mma Ramotswe.

'It was about two weeks ago,' said Mrs, looking to Miss Rose for confirmation.

'Yes,' said Miss Rose. 'Two weeks ago today.'

'So you do remember some things,' said Mma Ramotswe.

'I remember what happened recently,' said Mrs. 'I don't remember what happened before I arrived at the house of these kind people.' She nodded towards Miss Rose, who acknowledged the appreciation with a smile.

Mma Makutsi was sitting on the edge of her seat, such was her eagerness to ask a question. 'This is amazing, Mma,' she blurted out. 'You can't even remember your name? What about the names of your mother and father? Can you remember them?'

Mrs frowned. Her expression was one of intense concentration. 'I don't think so. No, I cannot. There is nothing there.'

'Are they still with us or are they late?' asked Mma Makutsi.

'Late,' said Mrs.

There was a silence. Then Mrs spoke again, hurriedly this time. 'Or I imagine they will be late by now.'

'Because you are of such an age that your parents would be likely to be late?' asked Mma Makutsi.

Mrs shrugged. 'I do not know how old I am.'

'Or where you went to school?' pressed Mma Makutsi.

'No, I do not remember that. I think I went to school because, well, I know how to write. But I do not know where this school was.'

Mma Makutsi sat back in her chair. She was staring at Mrs with some intensity now. 'So, what is ninety-five plus two?' she asked.

Mrs seemed momentarily taken aback, but then she answered: 'Ninety-seven.'

Catching the light, Mma Makutsi's glasses flashed out their message. 'So you can do addition. So you were taught that. And what is the capital city of Swaziland?'

Mrs shook her head. 'I do not know where Swaziland is,' she said quietly.

'But you do know where South Africa is? And America – do you know where America is?'

Mrs looked helplessly at Miss Rose, who glanced disapprovingly at Mma Makutsi. 'Please, Mma. This poor lady is embarrassed about what has happened to her memory. We must not confuse her. Please.'

Mma Ramotswe realised that she would have to intervene, but before she could do so Mma Makutsi started to speak again. 'I am not confusing her, Mma. I am trying to help her. Did you know you were in Botswana? Did you know where Botswana was?'

Mrs remained silent and now it was Mma Ramotswe who spoke. 'I think, Mma Makutsi, that Miss Rose is right. We must not upset this poor lady with questions about the capital city of Swaziland.' She paused, looking pointedly in Mma Makutsi's direction. 'I think that there are many people who do not know what the capital city of Swaziland is. I could go out there in the street and ask people and I am sure that many of them would not know.'

Mma Makutsi interrupted her. 'But they would know where America is. They would know that, Mma.'

'That's not the point, Mma Makutsi. The point is that this poor lady has lost some of the things that she knew but remembered some others. It seems to me that the things she has forgotten are the things about herself, while the things that she has remembered are the things that have nothing to do with her. That is perhaps the way this strange condition works.'

'Precisely,' said Miss Rose, glowering at Mma Makutsi. 'The brain is a very complex thing, Mma. If you look at a picture of it you will see all those ridges. It is like a loaf of bread that has come out of the oven very uneven. All those bumps going up and down.'

'I have seen a picture too,' muttered Mma Makutsi.

'Well,' continued Miss Rose, 'those ridges, those bumps, are the different departments of the brain. Different matters are stored in different places. There is one section for facts and another section for feelings. There is probably a special section for love – I do not know, as I am not a brain scientist. But I am sure that there is a bit that makes you fall in love. And out of love, too. I am sure there is also a department for that.'

'And for recipes,' mused Mma Ramotswe. 'Recipes have to go somewhere.'

Miss Rose agreed. 'That would be in the part that deals with facts,' she said. She started to smile. 'You do not find that recipe part in men's brains, I think. Or it is not very big in a man's brain.'

'Nor is the bit for helping around the house,' offered Mrs, grinning nervously.

It was the first time they had seen her smile, and Mma Ramotswe responded warmly. 'Oh, that is very true, Mma. Poor men. No, you are very right about that, Mma.'

The tension that had grown up around the discussion of the capital of Swaziland seemed to dissipate. The maid, a young woman barely out of her teens, brought in a tray and laid it down on the table.

'You have forgotten the sugar,' said Miss Rose crossly. 'Go and fetch it now now.'

The maid scurried out of the room, Mma Ramotswe's eyes following her.

'That girl,' said Miss Rose as she began to pour the tea. 'That girl is always forgetting things.'

'Perhaps it's catching,' said Mma Makutsi with a smirk.

Miss Rose put down the teapot and looked at Mma Ramotswe. 'As long as tactlessness isn't catching, too,' she said. 'That would not be a good thing, would it?'

Mma Ramotswe forced herself to smile. 'Well, here is the tea, then. I am sure that it will be very good. And then I think we shall have to get back to the office. Mma Makutsi and I have correspondence to catch up on – it is always such a chore, but we have to do it.'

The maid returned with the sugar and the tea was served. Mma Ramotswe noticed that Mrs took two spoonfuls and stirred them in vigorously. How did one remember that one took sugar, or were there some things that the body knew? Did those things – and perhaps things of the heart – survive the loss of memory, so that part of you, at least, was still there?

Over tea they talked about other matters. A neighbour's dog had bitten a child and Miss Rose spoke at length about that. Then there was some discussion about the water pipeline to the north and a sale of work that had taken place at Riverwalk. Nothing was said about loss of memory or the identity of Mrs. It was, thought Mma Ramotswe, one of those gatherings where there is a topic that must not be discussed, but which sits sullenly in the corner.

Just as their conversation was winding down, Mr Sengupta appeared in the doorway and came to join them.

'I heard voices,' he said. 'And I thought that I knew who one of them was.' He smiled at Mma Ramotswe, who returned his friendly gesture.

Miss Rose explained that her brother often worked at home. 'He has an office here in the house,' she said. 'He is always working, working, working. Even in the middle of the night you see him in his office – in his pyjamas.'

Mr Sengupta laughed. 'Sometimes I am asleep at my desk. It looks as if I'm working, but I am actually sleeping.'

Miss Rose now stood up. 'We should allow our guests to leave,' she said. 'They will have many other things to do.'

Mrs stood up too. Mr Sengupta glanced in her direction. 'I hope these ladies will be able to help you,' he said. 'They are the best detectives in the country, I believe.'

'I'm sure they are,' said Mrs. 'And I am appreciative of their efforts. If only I could get my memory back ...'

She crossed the room to stand next to Mr Sengupta.

'So, ladies,' said Miss Rose. 'We shall wait for your findings.'

As Miss Rose said this, Mma Ramotswe noticed that Mrs had half turned towards Mr Sengupta and was peering at the left shoulder of the blazer he was wearing. Then she suddenly brushed at the shoulder, as if removing a tiny piece of fluff. He barely took any notice of this, and continued to look at Mma Ramotswe in a slightly bemused way.

As they made their way towards the door, Mma Ramotswe promised to be in touch when further lines of enquiry had been worked out.

'I hope that you will discover something,' said Miss Rose. 'Mrs is very keen to find out who she is so that she can go back to her own home and her own people.'

Mma Ramotswe nodded reassuringly. She had no idea, though, how they could possibly proceed in this case. But she wanted to try, because she had taken to Mrs, and could imagine how terrible it must be to find yourself cast adrift in the world, not knowing who you are or where you are, but aware that there must be people who are missing you and wanting you home.

As they drove back to the office she did not take Mma Makutsi to task. There was no point in that, as there would only be an argument. So she said nothing until Mma Makutsi herself spoke.

'Swaziland,' said Mma Makutsi. 'The capital city is Mbabane, isn't it?'

'I believe it is,' said Mma Ramotswe. But she did not wish to discuss Swaziland, or its capital. What she wanted to talk about was what she had seen.

'Did you notice something, Mma?' she asked. 'When Mrs was standing next to Mr Sengupta back there, she brushed a piece of fluff off the shoulder of his blazer.'

'I did not see that,' said Mma Makutsi. 'And I don't see why that should be important.'

Mma Ramotswe wanted to ask: what does Clovis Andersen say? What does he write about observing the little, apparently unimportant things?

'It might tell us something,' said Mma Ramotswe. 'It might tell us that Mr Sengupta and Mrs know one another quite well.'

'Well, she is staying with them after all,' pointed out Mma Makutsi.

'Yes, I know,' Mma Ramotswe said. 'But don't you think you only take fluff off the shoulders of somebody you have known for some time?'

'No,' said Mma Makutsi. 'I don't think that, Mma.'

## Chapter Five

# Men Often Fail to Take Finer Points

Mma Makutsi's lawyer was a small man, a wearer of horn-rimmed spectacles and a carrier of a neat leather attaché case with the initials KD on the flap: Karabo Disang. She was already standing outside her newly acquired premises when he drove up and parked under one of the several acacia trees that dotted the yard surrounding the building.

'Well, Mma Makutsi,' Karabo Disang said briskly, in his rather loud voice. 'Here you are in front of your new domain.' He waved a hand towards the building. 'The subjects of your lease, as we lawyers call it.'

'I'm very pleased, Rra,' she said. 'It's a very important moment for me.' She looked at him expectantly. 'You have the keys, Rra?'

The lawyer smiled as he flipped open the attaché case. Pulling out a bunch of keys, he dangled them ceremoniously before handing them over to Mma Makutsi. 'I hope I've brought the right ones,' he said dryly. 'My office is full of keys, as I'm sure you will understand.'

The keys bore no label, which offended Mma Makutsi's secretarial soul. One of the first things they had been taught at the Botswana Secretarial College was to attach labels to things. 'Never forget,' said the lecturer, 'that things themselves have no idea what they are. A file cannot tell you what is in it.' This witticism was greeted with laughter. 'So label it, ladies! One little label now can prevent a lot of head-scratching in the future.'

And Mma Makutsi, sitting in the front row and thrilled to be at college at last, had written on the first page of her virginal notebook: *One little label now can prevent a lot of head-scratching in the future.* And here was a lawyer – of all people – failing to label a client's keys.

'It might be an idea to tie a tag to your keys, Rra,' she suggested. 'You know those brown tags with little pieces of string attached to them? You know those ones?'

The lawyer frowned. 'I am too busy for such things, Mma. That is a secretary's work.'

Mma Makutsi stared at him. She reached out, almost reluctantly, to take the proffered keys.

'We lawyers are very busy,' he went on. 'We have to charge our time, you see. And if we sat about tying tags to keys, how could we charge that? You would have to work out whose key was which and then charge for that small amount of time that you spent tying a tag to it. It would be complex, Mma.' He looked at her, as if to ascertain whether his point was understood.

Mma Makutsi's eyes narrowed. 'So secretaries are only for unimportant work? Is that your view, Rra?'

Mr Disang smelled danger. 'Oh no, Mma. I would never say

that. They are very important people. Without my secretary, do you know where I would be, Mma?'

She held him in her gaze. 'Where is that, Rra?'

'Nowhere, Mma,' said Mr Disang, grinning in an ingratiating way. 'She is the one who makes sure that everything runs smoothly. She is vital.' He swallowed. 'In every respect, Mma. In every respect.'

Mma Makutsi gestured to the building and began to walk towards it. 'Should we inspect it, Rra?'

He was relieved to be in less contentious territory. 'That is exactly what we should do, Mma. We should have a quick inspection – so that I can get back to the office and stop charging you.'

She stopped. There was silence apart from the chorus of cicadas. 'You're charging me now, Rra? For this visit? For talking about putting tags on keys?'

Mr Disang gripped his attaché case more tightly. 'Oh no, Mma. That was careless of me. I wasn't thinking, you see. There is no charge for this visit. Not a single *pula*, Mma. Not one.'

'That's very good,' said Mma Makutsi. 'It wouldn't seem right to pay for a conversation about tags and keys and so on. Nor for a quick walk about a building – or subjects, shall I say?' She paused. 'Not after I have paid so much for the drawing up of a lease.'

He was quick to agree. 'Of course not, Mma.'

The building's last use had been as a shop, and when they entered they saw that the previous tenant had left not only the shop fittings but some of the stock as well. The premises had been used by a firm of outfitters for both men and women, and in some of the display cases there was still the occasional blouse or belt. Most of the drawers had been cleared out, but in one there was a tangle of garish ties and three odd socks.

'The tenant should have removed all this rubbish,' said Mr Disang disapprovingly. 'People!'

Mma Makutsi agreed. 'Yes,' she said. 'There are some people who are very sloppy. They just don't care, do they, Rra?'

'They do not,' said Mr Disang vehemently. 'They are useless rubbish, these untidy people. They go about the country making it untidy and expecting other people to clear up behind them.'

In spite of her earlier disapproval, Mma Makutsi found herself warming to Karabo Disang. She had strong views on litter and general sloppiness, and she was pleased to discover that these were shared. Some people, she knew, were unbothered by these matters and merely shrugged their shoulders. These were people for whom it was presumably not an affront that there should be discarded beer bottles and plastic bags lying about on the edge of the road, blown by the wind into small piles, caught on the wire of cattle fences. Well, if they had their way the country would soon be covered with rubbish; so much so, she imagined, that it would disappear altogether. People would say, 'There used to be a Botswana somewhere around here, but we just can't find it now – it seems to have disappeared.' Hah! That would teach those who were unexercised about litter. There should be an anti-litter political party, she decided. It would campaign on a no-litter platform, with a promise that anybody who threw things down on the ground would be forced to spend their weekend clearing up. That would soon stop that. But the party would have to print leaflets to explain its policies to the voters, and everybody knew what one did with political leaflets – one threw them away, and that—

Her train of thought was interrupted by Mr Disang clearing his throat.

'You are hoping to make this place into a restaurant, Mma,' he said. He spoke tentatively – respectfully – as he realised that Mma Makutsi was no ordinary client. One could condescend to ordinary clients, but there was a certain sort of lady to whom one did not condescend, and this was one of them.

'That is my plan, Rra,' said Mma Makutsi rather absently, looking up at the ceiling now. The lights were still there but would have to be replaced, she felt, by something more in keeping with the ambience she had in mind for her restaurant.

'That is very good,' said Mr Disang. 'I am sure that it will be a very popular restaurant.' He paused. 'Of course, if one is running a restaurant one needs somebody to cook. That is very important.'

Mma Makutsi glanced at him. 'Obviously, Rra,' she said. 'If there is nobody to cook, then there will be no food. I don't think there's much point in having a restaurant with nothing on the menu.'

Mr Disang laughed. 'It would be very easy to choose, though. I always find it difficult to make up my mind when I go to a restaurant and I see a whole page of choices. How can you decide in such circumstances? Imagine if you're sitting down for your breakfast and your wife gives you a long list of things you can eat. Imagine that, Mma. What would you do?'

'Or it could be the wife sitting down and the husband giving her the menu,' snapped Mma Makutsi. 'I believe there are some husbands who cook for their wives. I have heard of these people ...' She left the remark unfinished, demonstrating through the look she gave Mr Disang that she certainly did not think he fell into this category.

Mr Disang laughed again, but more nervously now. 'Of course, Mma, of course.' He hesitated. 'But, as I was saying, you will need a cook, I think.'

'They call them chefs,' said Mma Makutsi. 'A cook is any old cook; a chef is much more special.'

'That is very true,' said Mr Disang. 'They are very talented people, these chefs.'

Mma Makutsi started to cross to the other side of the room. Mr Disang followed her.

'I was thinking that I might be able to help you,' he said. 'If you are going to look for a chef, then I think I know one who might be interested in the job. He is a famous chef, I think. He is very good.'

Mma Makutsi looked at her lawyer. She noticed that there were small beads of perspiration on his brow. He must be one of those people who sweat easily, she thought. 'Who is this chef?' she asked.

'I know him quite well,' said Mr Disang. 'He is a person I see from time to time. He is probably the best chef in Botswana – or so I've heard people say.'

Mma Makutsi raised an eyebrow. 'But if he is such a famous chef, then why would he want to come and work for me?' she asked. In business matters she tended to optimism, but she was realistic, too. 'If you're a famous chef, then surely you're very busy cooking at those big hotels. The Sun. The Grand Palm. They are the places where all the famous chefs go.'

Mr Disang seemed unworried by the objection. 'There are chefs who have done all that,' he said dismissively. 'They have worked in all those big places and then they think: I need a new challenge. That is what they think, Mma.'

Mma Makutsi stared at him appraisingly. He noticed, and his confidence seemed to grow visibly. 'I can arrange for you to see him, Mma,' he pressed. 'Think about it: you'll have no need to worry about finding a chef for your new restaurant. All that will be fixed up.'

She hesitated, and sensing her hesitation, he continued: 'You know it makes sense, Mma.'

She gazed out of the window into the yard outside. The previous occupants had left that in a messy state too: there were old barrels, an untidy pile of firewood, the chassis of an ancient car like a skeleton long since stripped of its clothing of flesh. There was much to do: tidying the place up; and then there would be the decoration; and the fitting out of the kitchen. If a chef were to be identified at this stage, then that at least would be one thing less on the list of things to be done.

'You can bring him to see me, Rra?' she asked.

Mr Disang nodded. 'There will be no problem with that. Today, tomorrow – whenever you want to see him, I will bring him for an interview. You will be very pleased with him.'

'What is his name, Rra?'

She noticed that Mr Disang looked away.

'Well, Rra: what is he called?'

Mr Disang cleared his throat. 'He is called Thomas.'

'Thomas what, Rra?'

This was greeted by a long silence. Then Mma Makutsi said, 'Thomas what, Rra? People are not just called Thomas – unless they are in the Bible.'

Mr Disang laughed nervously. 'Oh, that is very funny, Mma. People in the Bible have only one name – that is quite true. They are not called Makutsi or Ramotswe ...'

'Or Disang,' supplied Mma Makutsi.

'No,' said Mr Disang. 'There are no Disangs in the Bible.'

'Well?' asked Mma Makutsi. 'What is his family name, Rra? Thomas what?'

Mr Disang fingered his tie. 'I am not quite sure, Mma. I don't think he uses one.' He suddenly brightened, as if an idea had occurred to him. 'No, that's right. He's one of these people who don't really use a family name any more. I believe they feel that it's old-fashioned.'

Mma Makutsi's eyes widened. 'Old-fashioned? What's old-fashioned about having a family name? Maybe they think it's old-fashioned to have family at all – these people who have no family name. They're everywhere, it seems. Pah!'

Mr Disang had not expected quite so spirited a response. 'Don't blame me, Mma. I always use my family name, as you know, but these chefs are very ... very creative people. They have creative views.'

Mma Makutsi was not convinced. 'I think he may be one of these people with an embarrassing name. You come across them, you know. I came across somebody the other day whose first name was Voetsek. Can you imagine being called that?' *Voetsek* was the word widely used in southern Africa to tell people to go away. It was a very abrupt, dismissive word.

Mr Disang said he thought that was cruel. 'What are parents thinking of when they call a child something like that?'

Mma Makutsi took the view that they were not thinking at all. 'Many people do not think,' she observed. 'They get up in the morning and there is nothing in their heads – nothing. It is a big problem.'

'But we must soldier on,' said Mr Disang. 'Those of us who are always thinking must bear the burden for them.' He sighed. 'Sometimes it is very hard, Mma – very hard.'

'I suppose that's true,' said Mma Makutsi. 'Can you ask this Thomas Nobody to come and see me tomorrow?'

Mr Disang beamed with pleasure. 'I can do that, Mma. And he will cook something for you so that you can see how good he is.'

The offer reassured her. The proof of the pudding is in the eating, she thought. And then she tried to remember where she had come across that saying before; was it something that Clovis Andersen had said in *The Principles of Private Detection*? It certainly had the Andersen ring to it. *All cats are grey in the dark*, he had written in one chapter. *So remember that how much you can see of a situation depends on how much light you can shine upon it.* Well, that was clearly true, just as she felt that the proof of the pudding was in the eating, especially when it came to the appoint-

ment of a chef. She smiled at the thought. She might ask this
Thomas Whoever to make her a pudding at his interview and
then she could test it right there and then and say, *The proof of the
pudding is in the eating*. Of course, the chef might not see the
humour, but then Mma Makutsi felt that men often failed to
grasp these finer points until they were explained to them. That
was not to think less of men, of course – it was simply the way
things were.

## Chapter Six

# I Am Not Rude Any More

Mma Ramotswe had been aware of the fact that something was preying on Mr J. L. B. Matekoni's mind. It was not that anything out of the ordinary had been said: their conversation recently had been much as it usually was – mostly concerned with day-to-day things: the doings of the two foster children, the prospects for the beans in his special vegetable patch, the need to get a decorator to brighten up the paintwork on the veranda, as it was six years since it had last been painted. This was the stuff of ordinary existence; small matters, yes, but the ones that all married couples talked about, and that provided, at least for most people, a sufficient list of conversational topics.

She understood, of course, that spouses could not share absolutely everything. Just as she needed to have time to herself to think about womanly things, so too did Mr J. L. B. Matekoni need to be able to ponder the things that men ponder. She knew that there were women who did not like the idea of their husbands thinking about things without their permission, but she was definitely not such a person. She had known somebody like that – a woman who lived in Mochudi who was married to a rather harassed-looking man. Mma Ramotswe had learned from a mutual friend that this woman made a point of knowing exactly where her husband was at any time, whom he was talking to, and everything that he said and was said to him. She insisted on collecting the mail from their post-box so that she could open any letters addressed to him – and reply on his behalf if needs be. Eventually it had all been too much for him and he had simply run away, not with any real idea as to where he was heading, but running as fast as his oppressed legs would carry him on the road into Gaborone. His wife had pursued him in her car and had eventually brought him down in what appeared to be a very competent rugby tackle, right in front of an astonished group of schoolchildren who were travelling into Gaborone on a school outing.

She had told this story to Mma Makutsi, who had shaken her head and announced that in her view that was no way to run a marriage.

'It is quite understandable for a woman to keep an eye on her husband,' said Mma Makutsi, 'but she should not make him feel that he is a prisoner. Men need to be given air. They need to feel that they are free ...'

'Exactly,' said Mma Ramotswe.

'... even if they are not really free,' continued Mma Makutsi. 'It is called the illusion of freedom.'

Mma Ramotswe was impressed with the term, but thought that she would express it somewhat differently. 'Or kindness to men,' she ventured. 'It is kindness to men not to sit on them too much.'

'That is true,' said Mma Makutsi, suppressing a smile at the thought of Mma Ramotswe sitting on Mr J. L. B. Matekoni. He would find it difficult to breathe, she felt, and the consequences could be serious. It was indeed true that men needed air.

In spite of this recognition of the masculine need for space, Mma Ramotswe felt that in the case of Mr J. L. B. Matekoni it was necessary to be watchful for any signs of moodiness or pre-occupation on his part. Some years earlier, Mr J. L. B. Matekoni had suffered a bout of depression. He had fully recovered, but she had been warned by Dr Moffat to keep an eye out for recurring symptoms. 'If he becomes withdrawn or indecisive,' the doctor had said, 'this could be a warning that the depression is coming back. Be aware.'

So far there had been no such signs, and she had assumed that the pills he had been prescribed had not only dealt with that bout of the illness but also warded off any recurrence. However, as she noticed him sitting in his chair with a fixed, rather worried expression on his face, she wondered whether it was time to make an enquiry. She had waited for her opportunity, which now presented itself, a couple of days after Mma Makutsi had assumed occupation of her restaurant premises.

They had finished their dinner and Mma Ramotswe had settled the children in their rooms for the night. Motholeli was now being given more homework, and was busying herself with that at the new desk they had recently installed in her bedroom. Puso, who had tired himself out in a game of football, had fallen asleep even before Mma Ramotswe had turned out his light. She had tucked him in, smoothed the sheets about him, and then stood for a moment gazing fondly at the young boy's head upon the pillow. She imagined the world of dreams through which he now tumbled – a world of strange and heroic games of football, of bicycles and model cars, of boyish schemes and pranks. She smiled at the thought. We are all sent the dreams we yearn for, she thought; no matter how unhappy or fraught our waking world may be, we are sent dreams in which we can do the things the heart really wants us to do.

Returning to the living room, she found Mr J. L. B. Matekoni sitting with his head in his hands. This was her chance: if one sat with one's head in one's hands, it was tantamount to a declaration that something was wrong.

'Are you worried about something?' she asked. As she spoke, she moved to the side of his chair and laid a hand gently upon his shoulder.

He looked up. For a few moments he said nothing, but then he began to speak. 'I am feeling very sad, Precious. Very sad.'

She caught her breath. He addressed her as Precious only at times of great moment.

'Oh Rra, that is very bad. We can telephone Dr Moffat ...'

'No. No. It is not that sort of sadness.'

She waited for him to continue.

'It is because of something that I have to do.'

She frowned. It was a worrying thing to hear. Was he proposing to ... She hardly dared think it. Did he have some dreadful confession to make? Was he going to tell her that he was having an affair? It was the worst thing that any husband had to do – to tell his wife that he had found somebody else. But Mr J. L. B. Matekoni would never do anything like that; he would never go off with another woman, because he was ... because he was Mr J. L. B. Matekoni – that's why. It was inconceivable.

'What is this thing, Rra?' she asked, her voice barely above a murmur.

71

But he heard. 'It's Charlie.'

She felt a flood of relief. Charlie, the apprentice who had consistently failed his examinations, was always getting into trouble of one sort or another.

She sighed. 'What has Charlie done now? More girl trouble?'

Mr J. L. B. Matekoni shook his head. 'I wish it was, Mma. No, it's more serious than that.'

In Mma Ramotswe's mind that could mean only one thing. 'Police trouble?' she asked.

'No, it's nothing like that,' said Mr J. L. B. Matekoni. 'I'm going to have to lay him off. I'm going to have to fire him.'

Mma Ramotswe sighed again. She was aware that Charlie's work was often unsatisfactory; that he was rough and impatient with engines and that he sometimes broke parts by forcing them. If Mr J. L. B. Matekoni had simply run out of patience with the young mechanic, then she would not be unduly surprised. 'What has he done now?'

'He has done nothing,' said Mr J. L. B. Matekoni. 'But I cannot keep him on. There is less work than there used to be and I have to make a choice. Fanwell has got his qualification now and he is a far better worker than Charlie. One of them has to go, and it must be Charlie.' He shook his head sadly. 'It has to be.'

She felt an immediate rush of sympathy for her husband. Mr J. L. B. Matekoni was a soft-hearted man, and she knew how painful it was for him to have to get rid of the young man whom he had trained and nurtured. Charlie was not easy – everybody knew that – but he was essentially a good young man. His obsession with girls and fashionable clothes was no worse in him, she thought, than in so many other young men, and he would surely grow out of it in the fullness of time. She had read somewhere that some young men did not really mature until they were in their late twenties; she had been surprised by this, but she had decided that it was probably true. She could think of several young men who had been her contemporaries who had not settled down until then, or even later in some cases. Charlie was probably one of those, and would become a respectable, settled citizen in due course, escorting his children to school and doing the sort of round-the-house tasks that husbands were now expected to do.

She squeezed Mr J. L. B. Matekoni's shoulder. 'Are you sure, Rra? Are you sure there's no alternative?'

'I have been thinking and thinking,' he said. 'But I cannot come up with any alternative. I have had a letter from the bank manager. He said that I have exceeded my overdraft limit again this month and he will freeze my account if I do it one more time.' He paused, and looked up at her. She could see his anguish. 'How am I going to pay anybody if the account is frozen? I won't be able to pay Fanwell. I won't be able to pay the petrol people for the petrol and oil. I won't be able to pay the insurance premium and that means that if Fanwell's hurt in an accident at work we could be sued and they could take the house. I cannot risk that, Mma; I just can't.'

She knew he was right: there was no alternative. 'When are you going to do it?' she asked.

'Tomorrow,' he said. 'I shall tell him tomorrow morning. I will give him one week's wages, which is all I can afford. He's entitled to more, but I'll ask him to give me time to pay those. He will get half at the end of this month and the other half next month.'

She said nothing because she felt that there was nothing she could say. Charlie, for all his faults, had been part of their life for many years. He would never get another job as a mechanic because he did not have the formal piece of paper he needed. This meant he would have to do something quite different, but in a world in which jobs were few and far between for young men without any qualifications, it was difficult to see what he could do.

'He'll have difficulty finding something else,' she said. 'It would have been different if he had finished his apprenticeship.'

'I know,' said Mr J. L. B. Matekoni. 'But what else can I do?'

'You can do nothing else, Rra,' said Mma Ramotswe. 'This is one of those cases where being a boss is not easy.'

'It is never easy,' said Mr J. L. B. Matekoni. 'People don't realise it, but it is never easy being a boss, no matter how well things are going.'

And so it proved. The following morning, Mma Ramotswe decided not to close the door between the office of the No. 1 Ladies' Detective Agency and the workshop of Tlokweng Road Speedy Motors. This was unusual, as the door was normally kept firmly closed to keep out mechanical noises emanating from the garage.

'I shall close the door, Mma,' said Mma Makutsi, glancing up from the statement of expenses she was preparing. 'We do not want all that banging and clattering to distract us.'

Mma Ramotswe raised a hand. 'No, Mma. Please don't.'

Mma Makutsi frowned. 'But the noise, Mma Ramotswe. Bang, bang, clatter, clatter, and so on. How can anybody work with that going on? And if somebody telephones us, what will they think? They'll hear all that going on and they'll wonder what sort of office we have. It could be bad for business.'

Mma Ramotswe shook her head. 'I want to hear what happens out there,' she said. 'Mr J. L. B. Matekoni may have a crisis on his hands and we may need to help.'

Mma Makutsi was intrigued. 'There's something going on?'

Mma Ramotswe rose from her chair and crossed the room to stand beside her colleague. She bent down and whispered into Mma Makutsi's ear. 'Mr J. L. B. Matekoni has to fire Charlie this morning. He cannot keep him. He cannot pay him.'

There was a sharp intake of breath from Mma Makutsi. She and Charlie had had a tempestuous relationship over the years, but she would never have wished this on the young man. She thought that he was silly, but then most young men were silly to a greater or lesser extent, and Charlie would grow up – eventually. She started to say something to Mma Ramotswe, but at that moment they were aware that there was silence next door; the banging and the clattering had suddenly stopped.

'I think he may be talking to him now,' whispered Mma Ramotswe.

The silence was broken by the sound of voices, low at first, but gradually rising. And then, quite suddenly, there was a shout – a wail, rather. Mma Makutsi gasped. She had heard a wail like that before, when she had been obliged to break some bad news to a cousin – news of the loss of the cousin's father in a road accident up near Francistown. There had been that same, heartfelt scream; that raw cry of pain which cut and cut, and could not be assuaged by the balm of human comfort.

'It's done,' muttered Mma Ramotswe.

And then the door was flung wider and Charlie came into the room, an adjustable spanner in his hand. He stood there for a moment before dropping the spanner on the floor. It hit the concrete with a sharp, clanging sound.

'You cannot let this happen, Mma Ramotswe,' Charlie shouted. 'Please, Mma. Please don't let him fire me.'

Charlie looked imploringly first at Mma Ramotswe, and then at Mma Makutsi.

'Mma Makutsi,' he began, the words pouring out in an anguished torrent, 'I'm sorry. I promise you, Mma, I promise. I will do my best now. That's all over, all that nonsense. Over. I am not rude any more – that was another person speaking, not me, Mma – not me. I will try to take the exams again. Please tell the boss I've changed, he will have no trouble now. No trouble. I'll work all the time. Six o'clock in the morning, first thing, I'll be here and then . . . ' He faltered. He was choking on his words, and now they were replaced by sobs.

Mma Makutsi looked across the room at Mma Ramotswe. 'Mma . . . ' she began.

'No,' sobbed Charlie. 'It is true. I am different now. There's a new Charlie, and he's begging you to speak to the boss. Tell him I'm different now. He'll believe you. If you say it, then he'll believe it.'

Mma Ramotswe could not sit still. Everything within her went out to Charlie; she could not sit and watch a grown man cry as he now was crying; no woman could. But as she stood up and tried to put an arm around the distraught young man, he evaded her embrace and fell to the floor. For a few moments he was motionless, and Mma Ramotswe feared that he might have hit his head on the concrete and knocked himself out; but then he writhed, and began to scrape at the floor with his fingernails as if to dig himself in.

'Don't do that, Charlie,' shouted Mma Makutsi. 'You'll break your nails.'

Charlie's eyes had been shut, but now he opened them and stared at his hands. The interruption to his agonised display was the signal for Mma Makutsi to get up from her desk and cross to the young man's side. 'Here,' she said, reaching down to pull him to his feet. 'Take my hand.'

Charlie complied somewhat sheepishly and was soon stand-

ing at Mma Makutsi's side. He brushed at the dust on his overalls.

'Now you can sit down and get your breath back,' said Mma
Makutsi. 'Then we can talk about the future calmly.'

'There is no future,' muttered Charlie. 'I'm finished.'

Mma Makutsi led him to her chair. He hesitated; he had once
been found sitting in her chair while she was out of the office, and
there had been a terrible row: grease from his overalls, she had said,
would ruin the upholstery. But now that was not mentioned: it was
not a time for concern about grease and the stains that grease
brought. 'You sit down right there,' said Mma Makutsi. 'I'll make
you a mug of tea.'

This was another first.

Charlie sunk his head in misery. 'I have to go home now,' he
muttered. 'There's nothing for me to do here.'

Mma Makutsi shook her head. 'Losing your job is not the
end,' she said. 'They taught us that at Botswana Secretarial
College. Losing your job is a challenge. That's what they said. It's
a challenge to go and get something better.'

Charlie said nothing.

'Mma Makutsi's right,' said Mma Ramotswe gently. 'There is
always something else. It may take a little time, but somebody
who wants to work will always find something.'

'Such as?' grunted Charlie.

'There are jobs in the paper,' said Mma Makutsi brightly.
'There are jobs at the labour exchange. There are always people
looking for intelligent young men like you.'

Charlie looked up. 'But you said I was stupid – remember?'

Mma Makutsi drew back. 'When did I say that?' she snapped.
'When did I call you stupid?'

Charlie shrugged. 'Many times, Mma. All the time, in fact.' He
paused. 'Three days ago, for instance. You said I was stupid when

I asked you whether Itumelang was talking yet. Remember? You told me that babies of six months cannot talk and then you laughed and called me stupid.'

Mma Makutsi made light of the accusation. 'But I was only joking, Charlie. Don't be so stu—' She stopped herself, but not in time.

'There,' said Charlie. 'You see. You still think I'm stupid.'

Mma Ramotswe decided that it was time to intervene. 'I don't think there's much point in talking like this,' she said. 'Sometimes people say things they don't really mean. It's the way they talk, Charlie, surely you should know that by now.'

'And you too, Mma Ramotswe,' said Charlie. 'You think I'm stupid, too.'

'I do not, Charlie,' said Mma Ramotswe. 'You're not stupid. You have a very good brain in your head – if only you'd use it ...'

'There you go,' said Charlie. 'You think I've got no brain.'

'I didn't say that,' protested Mma Ramotswe. 'All I said was, I wish you'd *use* your brain. That's all.'

'Yes,' said Mma Makutsi. 'We're on your side, Charlie. So is Mr J. L. B. Matekoni.'

'Then why did he fire me?' asked Charlie. 'If he's on my side, why did he get rid of me?'

'There's no money,' said Mma Ramotswe. 'A business can't keep people on if there's not enough money coming in. It's hard, but that's the way it is.'

Charlie listened in silence. He had not touched the tea that Mma Makutsi had made him, and Mma Ramotswe reminded him of it. 'Don't let your tea get cold, Charlie. You should drink it. It will make you feel better.'

Charlie looked down at the mug that Mma Makutsi had placed on the table beside him. For a moment or two he did nothing, but then, quite suddenly, he swept the mug off the table with a sharp sideways motion of his arm. The tea sprayed out, some of it splashing his overalls.

Mma Makutsi shrieked.

'I don't need tea if I'm going to die,' muttered Charlie as he rose to his feet and began to leave the room.

Mma Ramotswe caught her breath. 'Charlie!'

'I'm going to die,' repeated Charlie. 'Soon soon. You'll see.'

*Chapter Seven*

# Pilates with Cake

Mma Potokwani, matron of the Orphan Farm, and substitute mother, over the years, to almost eight hundred children, each of whose young life had had such a bad beginning, took most things in her stride. Mr J. L. B. Matekoni had once remarked that she was the only woman in Botswana who could be struck by lightning and make the lightning blow a fuse. 'And I wouldn't want to be the lion who tried to eat her,' he had added. 'That lion would learn a lesson, I think.' An exaggeration, of course, but Mma Potokwani had certainly never let the world put obstacles in her path. She had survived the intrusions of bureaucrats, and the indifference and selfishness of those who, having made their money, refused to share it. She had begged and borrowed and scraped in order to provide for the orphans in her care, and prided herself on the fact that none of them, none at all, had gone out into the world without knowing that they were loved and that there was at least one person who wanted them to make something of their lives – one person who believed in them.

'Maybe I can't give them everything they need,' she once said to Mma Ramotswe, 'but at least they know that I have tried.'

And Mma Ramotswe, who was well aware of the heroic efforts that Mma Potokwani made, had replied, 'They know that, Mma. They definitely know that.'

As did many others. Everybody now was aware of the scheme that Mma Potokwani had cooked up with Mr Taylor at Maru-a-Pula School to give orphans what amounted to the best education available in Botswana. The children chosen for that scheme had done every bit as well as the pupils who came from backgrounds of comfort and privilege, and had gone on to train for jobs that would otherwise have been way beyond their wildest dreams. A child who had nothing, who had been passed from pillar to post among struggling relatives, or who had not even had such relatives and had been completely abandoned because there was no grandmother to shoulder the burden – something that went against every fibre of Botswana traditions – such a child might find himself or herself training as a scientist, a doctor, an agronomist. And in the audience at such a graduation would be sitting Mma Potokwani in pride of place, in a sense – even if she were not physically there.

It was mainly for this determination that Mma Ramotswe admired her friend. But it was also for her wisdom, which had shown itself time and time again. It was this wisdom that had helped her so much during Mr J. L. B. Matekoni's illness or at those times when Mma Makutsi had been unsettled or demanding. It was this wisdom that had helped her in cases where she had found herself pursuing a line of enquiry that seemed to be getting nowhere; a question from Mma Potokwani, perhaps on the surface somewhat opaque, had turned her in a direction that had ultimately proved fruitful.

That afternoon, with the painful memory of Charlie's outburst still fresh in her mind, she left the office early in order to go out to the Orphan Farm. She liked the drive, which took her along dusty back roads that twisted this way and that around people's houses and yards, past small islands of scrubland that had survived encroachment and were now claimed by itinerant herds of cattle. The cattle picked their way through thorn and acacia scrub, making a living somehow, prized by somebody for whom they represented the hard-earned savings of a lifetime. She sometimes slowed down to look at these cattle and judge the state they were in. Her late father had always done this; he could not drive past cattle without stopping and commenting on how well or how badly they were doing. He might say something about the cattle's ancestors, if he recognised some handed-down characteristic that only a cattle man would know about: a way of holding the head; unusual markings; a special shape to the hump of a Brahmin bull. These meant nothing to those who did not know cattle, but were there to be read by those who did.

Now, as she made her way out to see Mma Potokwani, she stopped the van for a few moments to gaze at a cow that was standing under an acacia tree chewing the cud, her calf at her side. She imagined that her father was in the van beside her, and she could hear his voice as clearly as if he had been there. The cow was thin, he said, but would put on weight when the rains came and there was grass again, rather than only hardened earth; and after that her calf would grow as it should and the owner would be content. And then he said something about the place where the rain-bearing clouds came from, and she did not hear it properly because the voices of late people were hard to make out sometimes and there were many of them wanting to talk to us, and the sound became like the sound of a swarm of bees, or the chatter of birds in the high branches of a *mopani* tree; not like words at all, but reminders nonetheless of how we shared the world with people who were no longer with us, but were in that other Botswana that cannot be seen, to which each of us would go in due course, when our time came, as it surely would.

She left the cow and calf; they would be there, she imagined, in exactly the same place when she came back; there was no reason for them to move, just as there was often no reason for any of us to move, if we only thought about it. We could stand under trees, too, and look about us, and think about things. Not only *could* we do that, she thought, but we *should*. It was called meditation – she knew that – but she did not consider that we needed a special word for standing under a tree and thinking. People had been doing that well before meditation was invented. There were many things, she reflected, which we had been doing as long as anybody could remember and which had suddenly been taken up by fashionable enthusiasts and given an unnecessary new name. Mma Ramotswe had been invited to a Pilates class in a local church hall; it would be of great benefit to her, she had been told. But when she had gone to the class and seen what Pilates was, she had realised that she did not need to pay fifty pula a session to do the things that she had been doing for years anyway: lifting and pushing and stretching your muscles was nothing new; she did all of these things when she worked in her garden, and Mr J. L. B. Matekoni did Pilates, too, when he fiddled about under cars or struggled to mend a bit of old machinery at the Orphan Farm. In his case he was doing what might be called Pilates with Cake, as Mma Potokwani unashamedly bribed him to undertake the repairs for which she would otherwise have to pay.

Mma Ramotswe was now only minutes away from the gate

that marked the entrance to the Orphan Farm. The farmlands were protected by a cattle grid that clattered in protest as she drove over it. And then there was the painted sign that said: *Please remember that children live here – drive carefully.* She had often thought that she might erect such a sign on Zebra Drive, warning drivers that people lived there and asking them to drive with consideration. But drivers would pay no attention, she feared, because they always seemed to be in such a hurry. There was no real reason to be in a hurry, when one came to think about it; important people, she had noticed, did not walk fast, but seemed to amble, and if they were not in a hurry when they had all those things to do and to worry about, then why should the rest of us imagine that we needed to be in any sort of rush?

She drew up beside the tree under which she always parked when she came to see Mma Potokwani, and sounded her horn, as she always did to notify the matron of her arrival. This worked, and Mma Potokwani's window was flung open and a hand emerged, beckoning her in.

By the time Mma Ramotswe had reached the veranda of Mma Potokwani's office, the matron had appeared at the doorway to welcome her. 'So, Mma Ramotswe, you always come at a convenient time. As it happens, I have just put on the kettle and I baked a cake this very morning.'

'You know my weakness,' said Mma Ramotswe. 'You know that I cannot resist your fruit cake.'

'And your husband is as bad,' said Mma Potokwani with a smile. 'Mr J. L. B. Matekoni will fix anything if you offer him a piece of fruit cake. My husband can no longer be bribed with such offers. I cannot make him do things any more.'

Mma Ramotswe laughed. 'It is a very bad situation when we can no longer get our husbands to do what we want them to do.' She paused, and became serious. 'Of course there are also those times when they do something that you don't want them to do. Those times are also difficult.'

Mma Potokwani knew immediately that this was what Mma Ramotswe had come to talk about. Her friend did not always visit her for a specific reason, but when she did, it did not take Mma Potokwani long to work out what it was.

'So,' began Mma Potokwani. She stared at Mma Ramotswe with astute eyes. 'So Mr J. L. B. Matekoni has done something – am I right, Mma?'

Mma Ramotswe did not beat about the bush. 'He's fired Charlie.'

This was unexpected news for Mma Potokwani. The two apprentices had been at the garage for so long now that it was difficult to imagine how it would be without them.

'Charlie's the good-looking one. Isn't he?' she asked. 'The one who's always getting into trouble.'

'That's him,' said Mma Ramotswe. 'The other one is Fanwell. He's completed his apprenticeship exams now and so he's a sort of assistant mechanic – something like that. Charlie never wrote his exams, He's still an apprentice – or was, should I say.'

Mma Potokwani looked thoughtful. 'He's fired him for a good reason, I suppose? These days you can't get rid of people just like that, you know. There is one of the cooks I'd dearly love to replace – a very lazy woman – but I know that if I tried to do that there would be letters from lawyers, and a tribunal, and money to pay and so on. Everybody would say: that Mma Potokwani goes round firing people left, right and centre. You know how people are, Mma.'

Mma Ramotswe explained why Charlie had to go. 'I don't think that Mr J. L. B. Matekoni was looking for an excuse,' she said. 'The garage has not been making much money recently and there hasn't been enough work. I think that this really is the case.'

Mma Potokwani shook her head sadly. 'We had to do the same thing last year,' she said. 'We had one too many men working on the farm. We couldn't sell enough produce to justify his salary. I was very unhappy about it, but we had no choice, I'm afraid.'

'Charlie took it very badly,' said Mma Ramotswe. 'He burst into tears and then ...'

'Yes, Mma?'

'Then he said something about dying.'

Mma Potokwani sat back in her chair. 'Ah,' she said. 'They do that.'

'Who does it?'

'Teenagers. They often say things like that.'

'It made me very anxious,' said Mma Ramotswe.

'But they rarely do anything about it,' went on Mma Potokwani.

'Charlie isn't really a teenager,' pointed out Mma Ramotswe.

'Not technically, Mma, but men can be teenagers until well into their twenties. I have read all about that.' She paused. 'And seen it, too.'

'Well, he is very sad,' said Mma Ramotswe. 'So sad that I want to do something for him.'

Mma Potokwani now reached forward to cut the cake that her secretary had placed on a large plate on her desk. She cut two slices – a large one for herself, and a slightly larger piece for Mma Ramotswe.

'You do not have to give me the biggest piece,' said Mma Ramotswe.

'But I do,' said Mma Potokwani. 'I have to give a good-sized piece of cake to a woman who is my guest. That is the rule.'

Mma Ramotswe toyed with the cake on her plate. Mma Potokwani noticed this and it told her that Mma Ramotswe was really troubled. 'I'm going to give him a job,' she blurted out.

Mma Potokwani's eyes opened wide with surprise. 'Charlie? Employ Charlie?'

Mma Ramotswe nodded. 'There will always be some small piece of work to do in the agency.'

Mma Potokwani was incredulous. 'For clients? But what will they think when they see you've put a young man like that on to their case?'

Mma Ramotswe shrugged. 'He will be in the background.'

Mma Potokwani answered her own question. 'I can tell you what they'll think, Mma. They'll say to themselves: we could get somebody like him just by going into some bar and picking the first young man we see. That's what they'll say, Mma Ramotswe. And then your business will become a joke.'

'But—'

Mma Potokwani ignored her friend's attempt to defend herself. 'I think you're making a big mistake, Mma. Your own business barely makes any profit – you've told me that yourself. What if it has another mouth to feed? You'll go bankrupt, Mma. You and Mr J. L. B. Matekoni, and then where will you be?'

Mma Ramotswe said nothing for a few moments, and Mma Potokwani might well have concluded that her point had been taken to heart. But then she came up with her plan. 'I know that we have very little money in my business account,' she said. She paused. Somewhere outside, a go-away bird uttered its plaintive cry. 'But you are forgetting, Mma, that I have many cattle.'

It was now Mma Potokwani's turn to lapse into silence. This was dangerous territory; in Botswana, cattle mattered above all things: one did not talk lightly about disposing of a herd one had inherited, and even if Mma Ramotswe had sold a number of cows in order to set up her business, those that had been sold had soon been replaced by calves. Now, with good management and prudence, her herd was considerably larger than it had been. That did not mean, though, that cattle should be sold for so risky a venture as employing Charlie; nobody would see the merits in that.

Mma Ramotswe decided to anticipate Mma Potokwani's objections. She knew these would come – and would be forcibly expressed unless she dealt with them in advance. 'I know you disapprove,' she said. 'And I understand why.'

Mma Potokwani struggled with conflicting views. Mma Ramotswe was her friend and could not be allowed to do anything unwise without at least being warned in advance. On the other hand, her cattle were her affair and if she chose to use them to help somebody – even Charlie – then she should be allowed to do that. She closed her eyes. 'They are your cattle, Mma. They are not mine. So you should do what you think is the right thing.'

Mma Ramotswe was staring at her friend. 'I wondered . . . ' she began.

'Yes, Mma?'

'I wondered whether you might like to buy some of my cattle,' said Mma Ramotswe. 'Maybe five.'

The offer was met with a frown. 'Me, Mma?'

'You have some cattle, don't you?'

'Yes,' said Mma Potokwani hesitantly. 'I do not have many. But there are some that my brother gave me.'

'You could expand your herd,' said Mma Ramotswe. 'But only temporarily.'

'Temporarily? I don't think I understand, Mma.'

She explained her plan. 'I would sell you these cows, and then, later on, I would buy them back. Two of them will have had calves by then. You keep the calves and I pay you back the money you paid for the cows in the first place.'

Mma Potokwani looked puzzled. 'But why, Mma? This sounds like . . . almost like a loan.'

'You could call it that.'

Mma Potokwani pressed for an explanation.

'There isn't enough money in the business to pay Charlie,' said Mma Ramotswe. 'And I think we have to do something for him.' She paused. 'Of course, you may not have the money to do this ...'

She knew that this was unlikely. Mma Potokwani may not have been wealthy, but Mma Ramotswe knew that in the background there was a rural store of which she owned a half share, inherited from her mother. Those stores were profitable.

'I do have a little spare cash,' said Mma Potokwani. 'And the way you put it, I can't really lose, can I?'

'I do not think so, Mma.'

'But I will not take both calves,' went on Mma Potokwani. 'That would not be the right thing to do. You are my friend, Mma Ramotswe.'

'And you are mine, Mma.'

'Yes, and that is the reason why I cannot take both calves. I shall take one to pay for the grazing. You will get the other one back, with all the others – after you have paid me back the money, of course.'

'Of course. You will get the money. And if I do not have it, then you keep the cattle.'

They shook hands on the arrangement and Mma Ramotswe prepared herself to leave.

'You know, Mma,' said Mma Potokwani as they walked back to the tiny white van. 'There are two ways of looking at our problems in this life. One is with our head ...' And here she tapped her forehead. 'And the other is with our heart.' Her hand went to her bosom.

'I know that,' said Mma Ramotswe. 'And I know that I am making this decision with my heart. I know it is the wrong thing to do.'

'No,' said Mma Potokwani. 'It is never the wrong thing to do.

Never.' She reached out and stopped her friend. 'You know something, Mma Ramotswe? Every decision I've made in this job – every single one – has been made with the heart rather than with the head.'

Mma Ramotswe smiled, and touched the matron's hand gently. 'I think I knew that, Mma,' she said.

She went round to Charlie's house that evening. The young man lived with an uncle and the uncle's girlfriend in a two-room house in Naledi, the shabbiest part of town. The local council had done its best to provide basic services for the people of this straggling suburb: there was some lighting on the streets and stand pipes had been set up to give everyone water, but some of the houses were barely better than shanties, with tin roofs patched up here and there with tarpaulin or bits of salvaged timber. The uncle's house was one of the better ones, being constructed of unpainted breeze blocks, but it was a world away from Mma Ramotswe's home on Zebra Drive, and even further away from the spanking new establishment built by Mma Makutsi and Phuti Radiphuti.

Charlie shared the room at the back with two male cousins, slightly younger than he was, and a ten-year-old boy who was the son, by another man, of the uncle's girlfriend. The room was just big enough for the two narrow beds and two sleeping mats, but when the sleeping mats were unrolled there was no space left to negotiate one's way round the room. Clothing was hung on four pegs knocked into the wall and what few belongings the young men and the boy possessed were stored on a rough-timber shelf that ran the length of the room. There was one window, high up at the back, which afforded a small amount of natural light, and additional lighting was provided by a single naked bulb dangling from the ceiling. From the cable that she saw coming into the house and then leading off into a bush, Mma Ramotswe could tell when she arrived that the electricity supply was stolen. This happened: people found the wires that the electricity board tried to bury and cut their way into the supply with crudely rigged arrangements. This theft of electricity had its dangers, and occasionally people were electrocuted or badly burned in the process; houses could be destroyed, too, by amateur wiring unequal to the load imposed on it.

When Mma Ramotswe announced her presence with the usual *Ko, ko!*, the uncle and his girlfriend were sitting in the front room, along with Charlie's two cousins. She had met the uncle before – he worked in the supermarket patronised by Mma Ramotswe – but she had not met his girlfriend. Now he introduced her and the two cousins; the polite enquiries that form dictated were made – *You are keeping well, Rra? Yes, and you, Mma?* There were no surprises in the answers such questions elicited – there never were – but these conversations still had to take place: it was not what was said that counted, but the fact that it was said.

'I am looking for Charlie,' said Mma Ramotswe.

The uncle smiled. 'He is not far away, Mma.' He made a movement of his head towards the second room. 'But then in another sense he is far away.'

The girlfriend laughed. 'Drowned his sorrows,' she said. 'He lost his job today.'

'I know that,' said Mma Ramotswe. 'And I am sorry. That's why I've come to see him.'

The girlfriend smirked. 'To tell him you're sorry for what your husband has done? There are many women who have to say sorry about what men have done.'

The uncle clearly did not approve of this tone. You were not rude to visitors in Botswana; he would tell her that later, in private. 'I'm sorry, Mma,' he said, rising to his feet and making towards the connecting door that led to the other room. 'Charlie has drunk too much beer. Look for yourself.'

He pushed the door open to reveal the pitiful surroundings of the second room. The woman's young son was on his sleeping mat, naked but for a pair of briefs, his skinny arms folded back to make a pillow for his head. On the larger of the two narrow beds lay Charlie, fully clothed, but with his shirt half opened. The air was fetid with exhaled beer fumes.

The uncle closed the door again. 'You see, Mma? I don't think you'd get much sense out of him until tomorrow morning.'

Mma Ramotswe lowered her eyes. 'I'm sorry, Rra. He has been very upset.'

'Yes,' said the uncle. 'Charlie doesn't normally drink much. Today was unusual.'

Mma Ramotswe nodded. 'I'm not blaming him. It is a hard thing for a young man to lose his job. Charlie is a good young man – at heart.'

'Yes,' said the uncle, hesitating slightly. 'At heart.'

Mma Ramotswe reached into her handbag. 'May I leave him a note, Rra?'

'Of course.'

'He can read it in the morning, when he can think straight again.'

The uncle laughed. 'His head may be a bit sore then, but I'm sure he will understand it.'

Mma Ramotswe tore a page out of the notebook she always carried with her. She accepted the uncle's invitation to sit down at the table and she began to write.

*Dear Charlie, I am sorry that you were sound asleep when I came to see you. I am sorry, too, that you have been so upset by what happened at the garage. I do not want to see you without a job and so I am making a special position for you at the agency. You will be an apprentice detective – if that is what you wish. You will be paid the same wage that Mr J. L. B. Matekoni paid you. The job will be for eight months, and then we shall see.*

She looked down at what she had written. There was something that needed to be added.

*There is one condition, Charlie, and it is an important one. You will be working with me and with Mma Makutsi. That means that you will have to be polite to Mma Makutsi, and you must not be rude to her, as you sometimes have been. She is now your boss – along with me, of course – and that means that you must do as she says, with no backchat. I am sure you will be able to agree to this as I have always thought that you were a sensible young man, even if not everybody has agreed with me about that.* And she thought: Mma Makutsi, first and foremost, but naturally she did not write that down.

She stopped, and then signed her name: *Mma Ramotswe.* She read through the letter once again, pausing over the final sentence. What she had written was undoubtedly true, but there were situations, she felt, in which it was perhaps best not to tell the whole truth. This, she decided, was one of those, and so she crossed out the final words about the views of others. She hoped that her crossing-out was sufficient to obscure what she had written, but the thought occurred to her that it would not be too hard to work out what words lay beneath – and if Charlie were to be a detective, even for eight months, then he should be able to do that without much difficulty.

## Chapter Eight

# Where Fashionable People Go

Two things of note happened the next day. Both of these developments involved Mma Makutsi, and one was positive, while the other was negative. The positive thing concerned the Handsome Man's De Luxe Café; the negative involved a disagreement between Mma Ramotswe and Mma Makutsi. It was not the first disagreement they had had, but it was certainly one of the most serious, and although Mma Ramotswe disliked confrontations of any sort, this dispute turned on something that would have had to be settled sooner or later. As the late Obed Ramotswe had said, in one of his observations that so neatly encapsulated some truth about the world, 'When you don't talk about something, then something will talk about itself for you.' When, as a girl, she had first heard him say this, Mma Ramotswe had had no idea of what he meant; at the time, it seemed to her

that this was one of those nonsensical things that people sometimes said because they liked the sound of the words, even if they
had no inkling what the words meant.

Mma Makutsi did not get into the agency before half past twelve
that day – in time to take her lunch break, which started fifteen
minutes after her arrival. Her day had begun much earlier than
that, though, with a series of meetings at the premises of the
Handsome Man's De Luxe Café. There was still very little furniture
there – no more than the table and four chairs Phuti had delivered
from the Double Comfort Furniture Store – but this was enough
to allow Mma Makutsi to conduct both her important meetings of
the day, the first of which was with the builder who was to fit
the new kitchen and decorate the whole building according to the
scheme that Mma Makutsi had alighted upon. This involved
the liberal use of greens and browns – the greens representing the
trees of Botswana and the browns the colour of the Kalahari. 'This
will make people feel at home,' she said. 'It will be very calming.'

The builder nodded, but did not pay much attention to issues
of decoration. 'The painter will do whatever you ask him,' he
said. 'He will not argue with you, Mma.'

'I should hope not,' said Mma Makutsi. 'You don't argue with
the people who are paying you, do you?'

The builder looked at her guardedly. 'Not in general,' he said.
'But there are some cases, Mma, where people ask you to do
things that simply aren't possible. If you did what they asked you,
the building would fall down.'

'I'm not asking you to do anything like that, Rra.'

The builder glanced at the plan that Mma Makutsi had
sketched out on a piece of paper. 'There's one thing, Mma,' he
said hesitantly. 'If we lay things out like this, there will be no wall
between the kitchen and the dining area. I'm concerned about
that, Mma – just a little concerned.'

Mma Makutsi looked down at her sketch. 'That is so, Rra. And there is a reason for that.'

The builder raised an eyebrow. 'Really, Mma?'

'Yes. I have read all about this in a South African magazine. It had pictures of very important restaurants down in Cape Town. These are restaurants where very fashionable people go. There are many fashionable people who go to Cape Town, you know.'

'I've heard that,' said the builder.

'They go to drink wine and show off their clothes,' said Mma Makutsi.

The builder shook his head in wonderment at the ways of the world. 'There is no end to what people will do,' he said. 'They are always thinking of new things to get up to.'

'Yes,' said Mma Makutsi forcefully. 'They are.' She paused. 'Of course I'm not expecting to get the same people here who go to those places in Cape Town. They are very busy going out for meals and to fashion shows and such things. They will not have time to come up to Botswana.'

'No,' agreed the builder. 'They are all down there.'

'But we have our own fashionable people,' continued Mma Makutsi. 'They are here too.'

The builder frowned. He was not sure that he had met them, but he did not move in such circles, and it was possible that they were there. Certainly there were enough Mercedes-Benzes in town to cope with the transport needs of fashionable people. 'They will come to your restaurant, Mma – I'm sure of it. All those people – they'll be there.'

Mma Makutsi spoke in the tone of one explaining something extremely obvious. 'And that is why I do not want to have a wall to hide the kitchen,' she said. 'These people are very interested in food. They like to watch what is going on in the kitchen. They can see the chef working. They like that sort of thing.'

'Oh,' said the builder. 'So they like to see what the chef is putting into the pot? Is that it, Mma?'

Mma Makutsi smiled. Builders were practical people, she thought; they were not the sort to have a great deal of imagination. Which was just as well, she decided, as they were concerned with the construction of pillars and walls and one did not want too many imaginative questions if one were erecting pillars and walls. 'I do not think they will be paying too much attention to that, Rra,' she said. 'It will help to create *atmosphere* if people can see the chef and his helpers in the kitchen.' She dwelt for a moment on what she had said; yes, atmosphere was what people wanted when they went out for a meal. 'It's all about creating a buzz, Rra.'

The builder stared at her. 'A buzz?'

'Yes.'

'A noise, Mma? The noise that a power saw makes?'

Mma Makutsi laughed. 'Not that sort of buzz, Rra – a feeling that something is about to happen, or is even already happening.'

'What will be happening?' said the builder, puzzled.

Mma Makutsi closed her eyes briefly. Really, it was impossible to discuss anything with a man like this. The problem was that he was uneducated, or not educated enough, and she, with her ninety-seven per cent from the Botswana Secretarial College was just ... well, there was no point in thinking about all of that. Some people understood, and some people did not. It was not the fault of those who did not understand; they could not help their limitations, but it could be very frustrating for those who had the benefit of great understanding to try to explain things to them.

'Let's not think about it any more, Rra,' she said finally, pointing at her sketch. 'This is what I want.'

'You're the customer,' said the builder. 'But before we get a draftsman to do the drawings, I'm going to have to run this past an engineer, Mma. They can tell whether something will stand up or fall down.' He looked at her earnestly; none of the buildings he had built had fallen down – not one – and he did not want that to happen now. 'The problem with having no walls is that the roof can fall down. And if there are people eating in your restaurant at the time, they will find the roof coming down on their heads. They will not like that, Mma, however much atmosphere there is. In fact, I think that sort of thing can definitely spoil the atmosphere.' He jabbed at the air for emphasis. 'This is not an idle warning, Mma. This is very serious.'

Mma Makutsi nodded. 'You ask an engineer, Rra. He will tell us.'

The builder left, and Mma Makutsi watched his truck trundle down the short driveway in front of the restaurant. She was pleased with the result of their meeting; in her mind's eye she could see how her restaurant would look, and she liked what she saw. She was pleased, too, by the builder's assurance that the work would be completed in the extraordinarily short time of two weeks – as he would have several crews working on the project at the same time. The most substantial work would be the removal of the current partition wall between what would become the dining area and what would become the new kitchen; that, he said, would take a week to do, but could be done at the same time that the electrician was rewiring and putting in the new lighting. Once all that was done, and the kitchen units installed, it would be a question of completing a bit of plastering and painting. 'Nothing much,' said the builder. 'And then, Mma, all will be ready for these hungry people who will be coming in the door.'

She was thinking about this when the chef arrived for his interview. Two weeks was impossible – anybody with any experience of builders knew that – but even if she multiplied the estimate by two, the premises would still be ready much earlier than she had anticipated. And if she were looking for an omen for the success of the new business, then surely that would be a positive one; just as it was a good omen, she felt, that the chef recommended by her lawyer should arrive, as he did, ten minutes early.

'I am called Thomas,' he announced as he greeted her. 'I think you're expecting me, Mma.'

She took his proffered hand and shook it.

'I am Mma Makutsi,' she said. 'I am the . . .' She hesitated; she was the owner and should not be embarrassed to say it. 'I am the managing director, Rra.'

If only they could hear her up in Bobonong. If only her late aunt, the one who had said all along that she would make something of herself; the same aunt who had sold one of her only three cattle to help with the fees at the Botswana Secretarial College; that aunt, if only she could have heard her now, how proud would she have been, how loudly would she have issued the ululations that expressed joy in Botswana.

She looked at the chef, a large-framed man with a reassuring paunch – a thin chef, Mma Makutsi reflected, would hardly inspire confidence. She immediately liked what she saw; she liked his broad features and the moustache he had cultivated on his lip; she liked the good humour that seemed to sparkle in his eyes. There was nothing shifty about this chef – quite the opposite, in fact. This was a chef with whom one could settle down for a good meal or a party – an open, cheerful chef who obviously liked his food and wanted others to do so too.

'I have heard all about you from my . . . from the lawyer,' said Thomas. 'He has told me all about your plans, Mma. He says that he is pretty sure that you will make this one of the best restaurants in Botswana.'

'*The* best restaurant,' said Mma Makutsi.

Thomas laughed. 'Yes, I am sure that is what he meant to say.'

Mma Makutsi indicated that they should sit down at the table. She had heard him say 'my' and then correct himself. My what? she wondered. My friend? Or had he been about to say 'my lawyer' and had stopped himself because he did not want her to know that he had had some brush with the law. Suddenly she reinstated the guard that any prospective employer must have when assessing whether somebody was right for a job.

'You know this lawyer well, Rra? Is he a close friend?' she asked as they took their seats.

The chef shook his head. 'He is not, Mma – more of an acquaintance. I would like to be able to say that I am a close friend of an important lawyer like that, but I am not. I am a very ordinary person, Mma – a nothing person, you might say.'

'Nobody is a nothing,' said Mma Makutsi. She thought of Bobonong, and of the people up there. There were some who might say that they were nothing, that she herself was a nothing Makutsi.

'I do not mean to say that I am nothing,' he said. 'You're right, Mma. Nobody is a nothing. What I meant to say is that I am not an important lawyer like he is. That is what I meant.'

'Being a chef is important, is it not?' asked Makutsi.

'Of course, Mma. Of course it is. A chef can make people very happy.' He paused. 'And that is what I like to do. I like to make sure that everybody who eats in any restaurant I work in goes out very full – and very happy.'

Mma Makutsi nodded. 'That is a good way to look at it,' she said. 'But tell me, Rra, where were you making all these people happy before now?'

The chef beamed as he replied, as if the memory of his customers' happiness still filled him with warmth. 'In many places, Mma. In many kitchens.'

'Such as?'

He shrugged. 'I have cooked in the Sun Hotel. I have cooked in the lodges up in the Okavango. That is where I was last. Up near Maun.'

'Which lodge, Rra?'

He waved a hand in the air. 'There were many. Sometimes they needed a chef in this one, and then next week they needed a chef in that one. You could never tell. I was a sort of flying chef, Mma. You've heard of the flying doctors in Australia?' He smiled, and for a moment Mma Makutsi thought he winked at her. She did not approve of that: she was a married woman, she was Mrs Phuti Radiphuti no less, and she had no time for these men who went around winking at women, whether or not they were married. Yet she could not be sure that he had winked, and even if he had it had been very much a passing wink, indistinguishable from an involuntary twitch.

'Well,' he went on, 'I was a flying chef. They have these small planes, you see, that fly people into the safari lodges. Well, I went on those.'

She looked at him. He was not giving her the details she felt she should have, but it was difficult not to warm to this good-spirited man. She could check up, of course: she could write to Mma Ramotswe's relative up there and ask her to make enquiries; it would be easy enough to do that, but somehow she felt that this was not what she wanted. It would be easy enough, she thought, to find out whether a chef was any good. And yet part of her was unwilling to seek out information that might force her to turn him away. Even if it transpired that he was not the chef he claimed to be – that he was no more than a lowly assistant chef – or even an assistant to an assistant – that did not mean that he might not benefit from a chance to be in charge of his own kitchen. She knew what it was like to be at the bottom of the heap, as she had been there herself in those days when she had been searching for a job and all the available positions went to glamorous, fifty-per-cent girls from the Botswana Secretarial College – girls like Violet Sephotho, of all people, who had breezed into job after job on the strength of her looks and her shameless, coquettish flirting. The sheer injustice of this still rankled, and had made Mma Makutsi a firm believer in giving everybody a chance, which is what she would do with this man. She had intended to get him to cook a meal – as a test – as she had discussed with Mr Disang, but now she made up her mind. She would not have time to find another chef. No, she would take him untried, although he could still be invited to cook a meal for her and Phuti, as a taster of things to come.

'Would you mind cooking a meal for me and my husband?' she asked.

He did not hesitate. 'I will do that, Mma. You tell me what you want and—'

She interrupted him. 'Of course I will provide all the ingredients. All you'll have to do is cook.'

He beamed with pleasure. 'No, I'll do the whole thing myself. You leave everything to me.'

From his lack of hesitation, from the smile that he gave her, from his confident *That's what I do best* she made up her mind. She now had a restaurant, a builder and a chef.

And it was with a decided spring in her step that Mma Makutsi arrived at the office, eager to tell Mma Ramotswe about the progress she had made that morning.

'I have been very busy already, Mma,' she said, as she opened the door that led from the premises of Tlokweng Road Speedy Motors into the headquarters of the No. 1 Ladies' Detective

Agency. 'Busy as a guinea fowl ...' It was an unusual metaphor, but one that Mma Makutsi used from time to time, and Mma Ramotswe knew exactly what she meant.

She stopped; she had seen Charlie. For a few moments she stared at him before recovering her composure. 'Charlie,' she began, 'I thought that ...'

Mma Ramotswe cleared her throat. 'Charlie is no longer working in the garage.'

'That's what I thought,' said Mma Makutsi.

'And so he's working here instead.'

Mma Makutsi looked uncomprehending. 'Fixing cars in *here*?'

Charlie's face broke into a smile. 'Not fixing cars, Mma. You couldn't fix cars in here with all your papers, all this stuff ... No, I'm a detective now.'

He looked to Mma Ramotswe for confirmation. She swallowed hard. 'I've given Charlie a job,' she said quickly. 'You know how busy we've been.'

Mma Makutsi's mouth opened. She stared at Charlie and then transferred her gaze to Mma Ramotswe. 'But we haven't been busy,' she said. 'In fact, things have been rather quiet. You said so yourself, Mma, the other day. You said—'

Mma Ramotswe interrupted her. 'That's not the point, Mma,' she said. 'You have to expand to get bigger. *You* said that, you know.'

'I did not, Mma,' Mma Makutsi protested. 'It makes no sense to say that you have to expand to get bigger. You expand *because* you're getting bigger. You bring in new staff when you start to get bigger. That's how it works, Mma.' She paused before addressing Charlie. 'Sorry, Charlie, I know it's hard for you to lose your job, but I don't think Mma Ramotswe has worked all this out.' There was another pause. 'Maybe you could go to the post office for me. You can do that at least.'

Charlie was disgruntled. 'I am not an office boy.'

'If you don't mind,' said Mma Makutsi, more firmly now. 'These letters must be posted. They are ready to go.' She reached into the tray on her desk, picking up three large envelopes and handing them to Charlie. The young man looked at Mma Ramotswe, who nodded her assent.

Once Charlie had left, Mma Makutsi strode across the room to switch on the kettle on top of the filing cabinet. 'This is a very big surprise for me, Mma,' she said. 'I am very shocked.'

Mma Ramotswe sighed. 'I'm sorry, Mma. Sometimes we have to act quickly. I was worried about Charlie. He was very upset. He went out and drank too much.'

Mma Makutsi listened impatiently. 'Young men often drink too much, Mma,' she snapped. 'It goes with being a young man. That is what they are like.'

'And you heard what he said about not wanting to live.'

Mma Makutsi shook her head. 'They are always saying that. Young people lie in bed in the mornings because they are too lazy to get up. Then they say that they don't want to go on living. Then they get up and go to parties. That is how they behave, Mma.'

Mma Ramotswe pursed her lips. 'I decided to give him a job,' she said. 'It was a decision I took. I shall be paying him out of my own account.' She wondered whether to tell Mma Makutsi about the arrangement with Mma Potokwani, but deemed any mention of that would be inflammatory. Mma Potokwani and Mma Makutsi had never got on particularly well, and to bring the matron into this conversation would not help.

Mma Makutsi tapped the kettle. This was a bad sign: Mma Ramotswe had seen her tap the kettle before, and on each occasion it had preceded an uncomfortable flare-up.

'I don't think it's a good idea,' Mma Makutsi began, 'to take people on when there is nothing for them to do. I know that sometimes we might feel that we should give some unfortunate person a job – if they don't have one. I know that, Mma. But if we did that all the time, then where would we be? There are many people who do not have a job. I am sorry for these people, Mma, but if we went out and said to them, "If you have no job then come quickly and we'll give you one," then we would be crushed in the rush, Mma. There would be very big crowds of people, all of them wanting a job, and there would be no room for us after a while.' She shook her head in apparent disbelief. 'There is a lot of suffering in the world, Mma, but we cannot put an end to all of it.'

After she had finished speaking there was silence. Mma Ramotswe stared down at her desk. A shaft of midday sun was shining in upon it; there were tiny specks of dust floating in the light. 'I haven't given a job to the whole world,' she muttered. 'I have simply helped a young man who is . . . who is one of us.'

'You should have asked me,' said Mma Makutsi. 'What is the point of my being co-managing director if I am not consulted on something as important as staffing? What is the point, Mma?'

Mma Ramotswe looked up in surprise. Co-managing director? 'I do not think we used those titles, Mma,' she said mildly. 'I have made you a partner in the business – that is true – but I think that I am still the managing partner.'

Mma Makutsi tapped the kettle again. 'Managing partner? We have never discussed that, Mma. I do not remember ever talking about managing partners.' Her fingernails drummed on the kettle. 'I do not remember seeing any signs around here saying *Managing Partner*. Maybe I have not been looking in the right place.'

Mma Ramotswe took a deep breath. She sensed that this was the moment when something important needed to be established. 'Mma Makutsi,' she began, 'I am the person who started this business. It is therefore my business. I am grateful to you for all that you do for the business and very happy to have you as a partner in it. But I am the one who has the final say in all matters. I shall always consult you—'

'But you did not,' interjected Mma Makutsi. 'You did not ask me whether we should take Charlie on. You just did it.'

'That was an emergency decision. Sometimes I shall have to decide things without asking you. That is the way it is: it simply is. That is it, Mma.'

The kettle had now boiled, and Mma Makutsi busied herself with pouring the water into the teapot. Mma Ramotswe watched her. 'You know something, Mma Makutsi?' she said quietly. 'When I took you on right at the beginning, I did so even though I could not really afford it.'

Mma Makutsi replaced the kettle in its cradle; she said nothing.

'I did it because I could not turn you away,' continued Mma Ramotswe. 'I could have said that there was no work – and there really was not much, Mma. But I did not want to do that – and I am grateful that I did not.'

The silence continued.

'So,' concluded Mma Ramotswe, 'that is why I have done what I have done with Charlie. And I did it because it is my business when all is said and done. You are my partner in that business, but every business has junior partners and senior partners. That is just the way it is, Mma. I am the senior partner because I am older than you. I am also the founder of the business.'

Mma Makutsi poured out the tea. Her anger, quite visible before, now seemed to have evaporated. 'Don't think I am ungrateful, Mma – I am not.'

'I know that,' said Mma Ramotswe.

'And I know that you are the senior partner. I know that, Mma.'

'Good. I thought you knew it, Mma. Now you have told me and I don't think we need to talk about that matter again.'

Mma Makutsi passed Mma Ramotswe her cup of tea. 'What is Charlie going to do?'

Mma Ramotswe smiled with relief; disagreements with Mma Makutsi tended to end as abruptly as they started.

'We shall use him on the Sengupta case,' she said. 'I have had an idea.'

# Chapter Nine

# Botswana Was a Good Place

It was rare for Mma Ramotswe to be without any idea of how to proceed, but it did happen, and this was one such occasion. Her philosophy of detection had always been simple; moulded, in part, by the sage and level-headed advice of Clovis Andersen – whom she and Mma Makutsi now considered a friend – and in part by common sense. To that mixture might have been added a pinch of the old Botswana morality, which could be used to good effect when appealing for help; if people were sheltering others, or were reluctant to talk, the invocation of the old Botswana morality could be just the thing to shift the log-jam. *You have to help, Rra, because that is what is expected of you. What would your father/grandfather/great-grandfather have said if they saw you staying silent while some worthless person got away with his bad behaviour ... ?*

That sort of appeal, made directly and in all sincerity, could work wonders, as it had in the case of the hotel manager who had frightened his staff into concealing his wrongful removal of guests' lost property. That had been a difficult case until one of the maids, shamed by the reference to the old Botswana morality, blurted out the manager's secret. She revealed that guests were always leaving their watches and earrings and such things in the bathroom of their rooms, and then phoning, in panic, from the airport or from their homes to enquire as to whether their property had been found. It had usually been dutifully handed in by the maids, but the hotel staff were instructed to deny it. This they did, although they knew full well that the missing items would soon appear on the shelves of the manager's own second-hand goods store near the bus station.

With the maid's statement in hand, Mma Ramotswe had confronted the manager, whose response had been to run away immediately, leaving his own property behind. This was an odd collection – a radio, a couple of pens, and a rather smart briefcase made out of zebra skin – but all of this had been handed over to the maid who had ended the manager's lucrative scheme.

'I hear that he has left the country,' said Mma Ramotswe. 'And so he will not be needing these things.' She paused. 'I suppose he has gone off to be bad somewhere else.'

'There are many places for bad men,' said the maid, shaking her head.

Mma Ramotswe had thought about this. *There are many places for bad men* . . . yes, the maid was right; there were many such places. But there were also good places, and if we tried hard enough we could make more of these good places, or make the places that were already good a bit larger. Botswana was a good place – it always had been – and Mma Ramotswe knew that she would fight to keep it that way. She would fight against the people who wanted to make it exactly the same as everywhere else – which meant to make it as corrupt as the rest of the world. No, she would not allow that – or, rather, she would do her utmost to prevent it happening. There was not all that much that one person could do; it was not possible for one woman to hold back the tide of greed and self-centredness that seemed to be sweeping across the world, but she would do whatever lay within her powers to do. And Mma Makutsi, she knew, felt the same and would do whatever she could – which was a bit more now that she was married to Mr Phuti Radiphuti and had the Radiphuti name and means to help her in their crusade.

Grace Radiphuti! That was the most extraordinary development, Mma Ramotswe reflected. That a person from Bobonong – a person with very little in this life – could come down to Gaborone, take the Botswana Secretarial College by storm, climb up the ranks of a business (even if the business only had one employee) and then, to top it all, marry into a furniture-selling and cattle-owning family; that was surely a miracle that defied all those who said that it was impossible to make something of one's life if one started poor. *Nonsense!* she thought. One might start with nothing and end up with everything, if one had the right attitude and was prepared to work hard. It was also true, of course, that one might start off with nothing and end up with nothing; or start off with very little and end up with even less; but these were not possibilities that one should dwell on before one started. There was no point in thinking of the bottom when one wanted to get to the top.

In the case of the dishonest hotel manager Mma Ramotswe had been able to deal with the issue quickly and conclusively, but now, in the Sengupta case, she simply had no idea where to begin. There was no point in interviewing Mrs again because it seemed that she had nothing to say. And even if they imagined that she might throw some light on her situation, Mma Ramotswe was under the impression that Miss Rose did not want her guest troubled by the sort of insistent questioning that would be required to uncover it. And if she could not do that, then she wondered where on earth she could possibly start.

It was something that Clovis Andersen had said, and it came back to her rather suddenly, triggering the rush of excitement that can accompany the solution to a tricky problem. Clovis Andersen had written that in cases where there did not appear to be any obvious way forward, the best thing to do was to follow the principal suspect. *If you have no leads,* he wrote, *watch your most likely suspect and that person will lead you to the leads.* Of course this was not a case in which there was a suspect as such, but there was no doubt that Mrs was the principal object of interest in this case. If they watched her, it was possible she might do something that could give them a clue as to who she was. This was not to suggest that she was concealing anything; it was perfectly possible that what she did would be the result of things in the back of her mind, memories that she did not know she had but which might cause her to act in a particular way. She had heard that people could go back to places they had forgotten they knew; that there was something deep in their memory that drew them back. Could this be the same with this poor woman who had lost her memory?

It would be difficult for Mma Ramotswe or Mma Makutsi to follow Mrs, as she had met them both, and would think it a bit odd if she saw Mma Ramotswe sitting in her tiny white van outside the Sengupta gates.

'Hello, Mma,' she might say. 'What are you doing parked here?'

And Mma Ramotswe would have to affect surprise and answer:

'Oh, I see that I am in front of Mr Sengupta's house – so I am! I had just parked to have a bit of a rest after a long drive – you know how it is, Mma.'

To which Mrs might say, 'But wouldn't it be better to drive back to your own house, Mma Ramotswe? It is not far away, after all, and then you could get out of your van and go and have a rest on your comfortable bed.'

It would be difficult to argue with that, and Mma Ramotswe would have to say, 'You know, Mma, that's a sensible suggestion. I shall do that immediately.'

Of course it would be a bit different if Mma Makutsi were to be seen watching the Sengupta house. That would lead to an entirely different meeting, thought Mma Ramotswe.

'So, Mma, you are sitting outside our house.'

'And what of it, Mma?' she would reply. 'Is this not a free country? Is this not a place in which people may sit exactly where they please? Perhaps I am old-fashioned – perhaps it is no longer the case that we can sit where we like on a public road; perhaps we now have to ask permission from the people who live in houses nearby and say, "Do you mind if we sit in the public road? Do you mind if we park near your house?" Perhaps the sky is no longer the property of all of us, but has been sold by the government to this person and that person and we have to ask for permission to sit beneath particular bits of sky.'

No, it would not be possible for either of them to watch Mrs – that would have to be done by somebody whom she had never seen before and would not notice. If she and Mma Makutsi had an assistant, then she could be sent to shadow Mrs ... or *he* could ... There was Charlie – of course there was Charlie. Nobody noticed a young man – unless, naturally, you were a young woman (before you grew out of noticing young men, which, in the case of some people, took rather a long time). For most of us, thought Mma

Ramotswe, young men were just . . . young men, and one did not pay particular attention to the question of who these young men you saw about the place were. It would never occur to Mrs that the young man sitting in a van on the other side of the road was anything but a young man sitting in a van.

When Charlie came back to the office, Mma Ramotswe called him over to her desk and gave him his instructions.

'We have a very delicate job for you, Charlie,' she said. 'It is a bit of important detective work.'

Charlie beamed with pleasure. 'That is what I am now, Mma. I am a detective. At your service.'

Mma Ramotswe could see Mma Makutsi looking disapproving. She hoped that there would not be an intervention from that quarter, but there was.

'Oh, so you're a detective already,' said Mma Makutsi. 'That's quick.'

Charlie sniggered. 'I'm a quick learner, Mma.'

Mma Makutsi shook her head. 'A quick learner? I don't think so, Charlie. No, you are an apprentice detective, Charlie – just as you were an apprentice mechanic.' She paused. 'I hope that you will not be an apprentice all your life – I really hope that. It would be awful if you ended up as an apprentice old man. Hah! That would be very odd.'

Mma Ramotswe gave Mma Makutsi a look that was halfway between a warning and an imprecation. 'Please,' she said. 'We are all working together now. Charlie has to learn somewhere, and this is where he will start.'

'That's fine by me,' said Mma Makutsi. 'All I'm saying is that he is an apprentice detective. You cannot be a detective on the first day – just like that. That is not the way it works, Mma.'

Charlie looked at Mma Ramotswe anxiously. 'I don't mind,

Mma. If she wants me to be an apprentice detective, then I am happy to be that.'

'Very well,' said Mma Ramotswe. 'If everybody's happy, then I am happy too. Now I can tell you what I want you to do.' She paused. 'There is this woman, you see.'

Charlie grinned. 'I know about women, Mma Ramotswe. I am the man for this job: the number one expert in women.'

Mma Makutsi's glasses, catching the light, sent a threatening signal across the room. Mma Ramotswe closed her eyes; she did not like the bickering that sometimes took place between Mma Makutsi and Charlie. At heart they were fond of one another, but the problem was that they were too similar, at least in their tendency to make remarks that they must have known would stir people up. Charlie did it with his bright and breezy comments; Mma Makutsi did it with her sensitivity to insult – one only had to mention Bobonong in anything but tones of hushed admiration and she would accuse you of being indifferent to the people of Bobonong, or of implying that Bobonong was a backwater. And the same thing applied to any mention of the Botswana Secretarial College. There had been a very awkward incident recently when a client had made a reference to a niece of his who had failed to get into the university and had been forced to enrol in the Botswana Secretarial College. 'Still,' he had said, with an air of philosophical acceptance, 'half a loaf is always better than no bread at all, I suppose.' That had brought a predictable outburst from Mma Makutsi, and Mma Ramotswe had been worried that the client would simply rise to his feet and walk out of the office. He did not, as it happened, but meekly accepted the tirade directed against him and apologised profusely for the slight. Some men, thought Mma Ramotswe, become supine when faced with a strong woman.

No, Charlie and Mma Makutsi were two peas in a pod. What

did people say? Put two cats in a box and they will fight? It was probably true, as so many of these popular sayings were.

Now she made an effort to smile at Charlie. 'I am sure that you know a lot about women, Charlie, but now is not the time to talk about what you know—'

'Or what you don't know,' interjected Mma Makutsi, adding, 'And that will be quite a lot, I think.'

Mma Ramotswe made an effort to reassert control of the conversation. 'If you are to be a detective, Charlie, it is important to listen.'

'I am listening,' said Charlie. 'That is what I am doing – I am sitting here and listening to you.'

'Good. Well, there is a very unfortunate woman who does not know who she is.'

Charlie frowned. 'Then her friends can tell her. If I didn't know who I was, you would be able to say to me "You are Charlie". That is all you would need to say, and then I would know.'

'It's not that simple,' said Mma Ramotswe. 'This woman has lost her memory.'

Charlie made a sympathetic sound.

'Yes,' went on Mma Ramotswe. 'It is very sad for her, because she is in trouble with the immigration authorities. If she does not find out who she is, then they will send her out of the country.'

'You want me to find out who she is?' asked Charlie, rubbing his hands together with the air of one who cannot wait to get down to work. 'That will be no problem.'

'Oh, really?' interjected Mma Makutsi. 'So how would you find out, Charlie?'

Charlie appeared to think for a moment. 'I would put her photograph on a notice and stick it on a pole somewhere. The notice would say: *Who is this woman? Big prizes for identification. Contact the No. 1 Ladies' Detective Agency if you have the answer.*

Mma Ramotswe was about to dismiss Charlie's idea out of hand, but stopped herself. Actually, it was a perfectly reasonable idea, and could draw a response from somebody. But then it occurred to her that her clients had asked for discreet enquiries, and this would be anything but that.

'I don't think we can do that, Charlie,' she said. 'No, what I would like you to do is to follow her. See where she goes. Then give us a report.'

Charlie's eyes lit up. 'Follow her, Mma? In a car chase?'

'There will be no need to chase her,' said Mma Ramotswe. 'This lady will not be running away from you – in fact, she mustn't know that you are there.'

Charlie nodded enthusiastically. 'I can do that. I have seen that sort of thing at the cinema.'

'Be discreet,' said Mma Ramotswe. 'You can borrow my van. Park it in a place that is not too obvious, and wait to see who leaves the house she is staying in. Then follow her and see where she goes.'

'What if she goes inside?' asked Charlie. 'What if she goes to somebody's house? Can I creep up and look through the window?'

'No, you may not,' said Mma Ramotswe. 'What you should do is find out who lives in the house. Ask somebody. People know who lives where.'

'Then?'

'Then come back here and tell us.' Mma Ramotswe paused. 'Do you think you can do that, Charlie?'

Charlie made an expansive gesture. 'No problem,' he said.

Mma Ramotswe exchanged glances with Mma Makutsi. She could tell that Mma Makutsi was doubtful, but now that she had taken Charlie on in the agency, she had to put him to some use. And this, she thought, was not an unduly complicated thing to do. Following somebody, she had read in *The Principles of Private Detection*, was the first thing a detective should learn to do. *If you can follow somebody without being spotted,* wrote Clovis Andersen, *then you are on your way to achieving what every private investigator wants above all else: invisibility.*

She looked at Charlie. Invisibility: she would have to have a word with him about the fancy sunglasses he had put on for his new job; and the white trousers and red shirt as well. But not quite yet, she thought. Progress in learning a job was made through encouragement, not censure. Charlie would get plenty of censure, she suspected, from Mma Makutsi, and so she should take charge of the encouragement side of things.

'I am sure that you will do this very well, Charlie,' she said. 'You are a quick learner.'

'Yes,' said Charlie. 'I know that, Mma.'

That evening, Mma Makutsi said to Phuti Radiphuti: 'There's something bad going to happen, Phuti. You know the feeling? You realise that something bad is going to happen but there's nothing you can do to stop it.'

'A bit like when you're being stalked by a lion and you know he's going to pounce, but you can't do anything about it. If you start to run, it only makes it worse: a lion will always chase you when you start to run.' He shuddered. 'I hate that feeling.'

'But have you ever been stalked by a lion, Phuti?'

'Never, thank heavens. But I can imagine what it's like.' He paused. 'Anyway, what is this bad thing, Grace?'

'It's Charlie.'

Phuti Radiphuti knew Charlie. He sighed. 'This is nothing new.'

'But it is,' said Mma Makutsi. 'Mma Ramotswe has taken him on because Mr J. L. B. Matekoni couldn't employ him any more.

And now that he's with us in the office, I can see some bad developments looming.' She shook her head. 'She's put him to work on a very sensitive case and there's going to be big trouble.'

Phuti Radiphuti gazed out of the window into the African night. 'I hope not,' he said.

'So do I,' said Mma Makutsi. 'But I'm afraid it's going to happen. Charlie is going to get himself – and the agency – into big, big trouble. Definite. Guaranteed. One hundred per cent guaranteed.'

'Oh,' said Phuti.

'Yes,' said Mma Makutsi.

'But I thought that Mma Ramotswe was usually right.'

Mma Makutsi shook her head. 'She is usually right – except when she is wrong. Her problem is that she is too kind. You have to be careful about being too kind in this life, Phuti.'

'That is probably true ... and yet ... '

'And yet nothing. If you are too kind, then there are people waiting round every corner ready to take advantage of you. You can be kind to some people, yes, but you cannot be kind to everybody. If you are kind to everybody, then you end up being kind to nobody.'

Phuti Radiphuti was confused. 'I'm not sure that I understand,' he muttered.

Mma Makutsi explained. 'What I meant to say is this: Mma Ramotswe has given Charlie a job out of kindness. Charlie is hopeless, Phuti, everybody knows that – probably even his mother. They probably said to his mother: *Throw this one away, Mma – he is no good and will be trouble.* And she refused, which is what mothers often do, because that is what mothers are like with their boys – they do not see how bad their sons are. They are ready to see the faults in their daughters – oh yes, they see those clearly enough – but when it comes to their sons they will not see the faults.'

Phuti looked thoughtful. 'Will you see Itumelang's faults?' he asked.

Mma Makutsi fixed him with a discouraging stare. 'What faults?' she asked.

*Chapter Ten*

# Cool Jules Is on the Case

Charlie had spent his end of service payment from Mr J. L. B. Matekoni on the purchase of new sunglasses, a blue jacket, a red shirt, and a pair of tight-fitting jeans that had not one, but two designer labels displayed on the pockets. One of these labels said *Town Man* and the other said *Cool Jules*. He liked both of these, but had a slight preference for Cool Jules, which he thought more accurately reflected his overall image. In such a pair of jeans, he felt, might anything be possible.

To have clothes like this *and* to be an 'auxiliary detective' – which was the title he had decided on for himself, having rejected, on reflection, Mma Makutsi's belittling title of 'apprentice detective' – to be so attired and so employed was surely greater good fortune than any young man could realistically wish for. He thought of the greasy overalls that he had exchanged for this new outfit – how had he put up with those for so long? And how had he tolerated being told to do this and that all the time: fix that ignition, Charlie; change that rear tyre, Charlie; check the suspension on this car, Charlie. It had been the same thing day after day. Where was the pleasure in spending one's time under a car, with oil dripping onto your face and the curious dusty smell of the underside of a vehicle strong in your nostrils? And all for what? For a pay packet that left very little for any purchases or entertainment after you had paid your rent and given money to your uncle's girlfriend for the food of which your little cousins ate more than their fair share? It was true that Mma Ramotswe was proposing to pay him what he had received for his work in the garage, but at least there was the prospect of advancement in this job: being an auxiliary detective was just the beginning, and his likely success in the role would almost certainly lead to some more senior, better-paid post – or even to his own business. There was an idea: the No. 1 Men's Detective Agency – that would be a name to conjure with! That would be the place where all the important investigations would be brought, because every-body knew, thought Charlie, that you could not entrust a really serious investigation to a firm made up of women, even to one led by such a kind and generous woman as Mma Ramotswe.

Of course he could invite Mma Ramotswe to join him if her agency went under as a result of the success of the No. 1 Men's Detective Agency – he would certainly be magnanimous in that respect, although if Mma Makutsi came too she would have to content herself with the role of secretary. For a moment he imagined himself asking Mma Makutsi to take dictation; she would sit there while he strolled about the room dictating important letters to clients. *I refer to yours of the twelfth inst* ... That is how one should begin an official letter. And then he would say, 'Am I going too fast, Mma? Perhaps you need to brush up your shorthand

skills – you might have got ninety-seven per cent in the final examinations of the Botswana Secretarial College, but that was a long
time ago, Mma, and nothing stands still in this world ...' Hah!
That would teach Mma Makutsi to push him around and belittle
him with those comments of hers. But at the end of the day he
would be kind. He would say to her that, although he could easily
get a younger and more glamorous secretary, he would still keep
her on for old times' sake, so to speak. She would appreciate that.

Of course, fashionable clothes of the sort he was wearing
deserved a better vehicle than Mma Ramotswe's white van that
she was lending him for the task of watching the Sengupta house.
Even an auxiliary detective deserved something better than that,
with its compromised suspension – on the driver's side – and bat-
tered appearance. But it was better than nothing, and it would
not do to have to carry out such an assignment on a bicycle.

'I do not need the van while I am here in the office,' Mma
Ramotswe had said, 'as long as it is back by four-thirty every
afternoon.'

'But what if I am in the middle of a car chase, Mma?' complained Charlie. 'A detective cannot suddenly look at his watch
and say, "Oh, it's time for me to get back home," and then turn
round. He cannot do that, Mma.'

'There will be no car chases, Charlie,' said Mma Ramotswe.
'There will be no need for a car chase.'

'But if she is going somewhere – slowly – just before four-
thirty ...'

Mma Ramotswe sighed. 'Every rule has its exceptions, Charlie.
In that case I shall know that you are busy and I shall not expect
you back at the normal time. If I need to get home, I shall ask
Mma Makutsi to take me in that Radiphuti car that comes to col-
lect her. Or Fanwell can drive me back in Mr J. L. B. Matekoni's
truck.'

'Fanwell is a bad driver,' said Charlie. 'He has never been able to tell left from right.'

Mma Ramotswe remembered a conversation. 'Mr J. L. B. Matekoni says that he has become much better. He said that some people take a little time to mature as drivers. Maybe Fanwell is one of those people.'

'And some people cannot drive at all,' Charlie countered, looking across the room towards Mma Makutsi behind her desk.

Mma Makutsi appeared to ignore the comment, but then, without raising her eyes from the document she was perusing, she said, 'Some people do not *need* to drive, of course. When the Lord made people, he did not make cars for them, I believe. He made them legs. Some people know that and use their legs so that they won't fall off.' She paused. 'Some people appear not to know that. They are the ones who will end up having no legs.'

Mma Ramotswe reached for the keys of the van and handed them to Charlie. 'Never mind all that, Charlie. Never mind about Fanwell and his problem with left and right. You have a job to do, so go and do it. Watch carefully. Be patient. Rome was not built in a day.'

Charlie was puzzled. 'What is this about Rome? That is the Pope's place – what about it, Mma?'

Mma Makutsi looked up. 'She said that it was not built in a day, Charlie,' she repeated. 'It is an expression that people use.'

'I have never heard it,' said Charlie.

'Well, it's all about taking time to do things,' explained Mma Ramotswe. 'So don't rush this. Don't give yourself away on the first day. Park far enough away so that they do not see you, or, if they see you, they think *There is a young man waiting for his girlfriend* – something like that.'

'I shall be very discreet, Mma. Very.' He looked down at his feet, and then added under his breath: 'What does discreet actually mean, Mma?'

'It means not doing things that will get you noticed,' said Mma Ramotswe.

'Or dressing loudly,' offered Mma Makutsi.

Charlie nodded. 'I shall be very discreet, Mma. I promise.'

Mma Ramotswe smiled at him. 'Then good luck, Charlie.'

After he had left the room, Mma Makutsi sat back in her chair and rolled her eyes upwards. 'Well, I would hardly call that discreet. Those glasses. Those jeans. That is not discreet, Mma.'

'He is a young man,' said Mma Ramotswe. 'Young men are like that, Mma. You know that.'

'Yes, but this is a young man wanting to be a detective.'

Mma Ramotswe sighed. 'We all have to start somewhere, Mma. Even you. You must remember your first case? You must remember how worried you were that you were doing the right thing? And you must remember all the mistakes you made – just as I do, Mma.'

Mma Makutsi bit her lip. 'Possibly,' she said.

'Well, there you are, Mma. That is Charlie, too. We all have to be Charlie at some time in our lives.'

Mma Makutsi looked thoughtful. 'Do you think this woman will stay in the house? Do you think Charlie will see her go out?'

Mma Ramotswe shrugged. 'I am not sure, Mma. No, maybe I am. Surely she will go out because nobody likes to stay in the house for days on end. She will go out, Mma, and Charlie will see her.'

Mma Makutsi considered this. 'What do you think is really going on, Mma?'

Mma Ramotswe reached for her pencil and began to play with it, passing it from one hand to the other. It was something that she did when she was thinking very hard, and Mma Makutsi, recognising the sign, waited attentively for the answer.

'I have been thinking about this case a lot recently,' she said. 'I am changing my mind.' She spoke hesitantly, but then appeared to become more convinced. 'I think that she is lying, Mma. I think that Miss Rose is lying, too, and Mr Sengupta. I fear they are all telling lies.'

'But why?' asked Mma Makutsi.

'Because they are trying to conceal the truth about Mrs.'

'But why?'

Mma Ramotswe hesitated once again. 'I think that Mrs is their sister. They want her to live with them, but perhaps she has not received a residence permit. You know how difficult it can be. They say: not everyone can come to Botswana, don't they? It is hard for people. Of course she knows who she is.'

Mma Makutsi was not so sure. 'How do you know that, Mma?'

'Do you remember what I said about her brushing fluff off Mr Sengupta's shoulder? Remember what I said, Mma Makutsi?'

'You said that they knew one another well.'

'Yes. I think they may know one another very well. I think Mrs may be their sister. They want her to live with them but there is something that makes it impossible for her to apply for a residence permit here.'

'Why should there be anything like that, Mma? And what exactly would it be?'

Mma Ramotswe had no idea – yet. 'That's what we have to find out,' she said.

'And how will we do that, Mma?' asked Mma Makutsi.

'That's what we have to find out,' said Mma Ramotswe. 'There are some occasions on which you have to find out how to find out. That is well known, Mma.'

It is *not* well known, thought Mma Makutsi, but decided not to press the point. There were times that points should not be pressed – and that, everyone agreed, *was* well known.

Charlie drove the tiny white van past the university, past the Sun Hotel, and then turned across the traffic into the street where Mr Sengupta lived. It was a long street and almost all of the houses were surrounded by walls high enough to prevent anything but a glimpse of their roofs and, in the case of those houses with two storeys, a sight of the first-floor windows. The road itself was a bit broader than many around it, and vegetation had grown up along the edges: thorn bushes, high tufts of grass, acacia trees. Among this growth were the paths that were always there in Africa, following some inexpressible logic of their own, winding this way and that, sometimes seeming to go nowhere at all. You rarely saw people on these paths, yet they were always well trodden, flattened into hard earth and dust, small hand-made features that took no notice of the more formal constructions around them: the tarred roads, the bridges, the car parks.

Charlie slowed as he passed the large gates of the Sengupta house, and then continued to the end of the street: as this was a cul-de-sac there was a turning circle, and Charlie stopped there briefly before proceeding back down the road. He had seen his spot – a place at the side of the road, backed by a plot of land that had yet to be built upon. This plot was to all intents and purposes thick bush: acacias had seeded themselves in profusion and those vicious arresting thorns, the *wag-'n-bietjie*, the wait-a-bit thorn, the *mokgalo*, famous for its ability to latch onto the clothing – or flesh – of the incautious passer-by, had taken firm root. At the edge of this plot there was a place for the van to be parked, shaded by the canopy of a large jacaranda, concealed from most of the houses and from the road itself, and yet affording a view both of the Sengupta gate and, because of slightly increased elevation, of part of the garden beyond the gate.

It was the ideal spot to begin the task of surveillance and Charlie quickly settled down to it, lowering the rather shaky-looking sun visor in front of the driver's seat. On the other side of the visor was a mirror, fixed there by Mr J. L. B. Matekoni after Mma Ramotswe had complained that the makers of vans seemed to forget that many drivers were ladies and might have need of such a mirror. Removing his sunglasses, he glanced at his reflection and said to himself: very smart, very smart. Then he straightened his jeans so that the fabric was pulled tight across his thigh muscles, and finally, replaced his sunglasses. *I am on duty, watching,* he thought. *They may come out at any moment and I will be ready to see where they go.*

An hour went past, during which nothing happened. Charlie had begun his watch at nine, and now, at ten, the sun was climbing steadily in the sky. The screech of cicadas, the accompaniment to any stretch of Botswana bush no matter how small, intensified as the day heated up. So familiar was this sound that few people noticed it, but Charlie did now as he sat in the small cab of the van, the sound filling the air with the density, it seemed to him, of a buzz saw – a ceaseless drone, rising in pitch and then descending before picking up again.

At the end of the first hour, he saw a figure emerge from the side of the house. It was a woman, who stood still for a moment before glancing over her shoulder and going back into the house. He did not have time to work out whether it was Mrs; Mma Ramotswe and Mma Makutsi had provided him with a fairly detailed description of her and it was easy, they said, to distinguish her from Miss Rose, as Miss Rose was tall and Mrs was below average height. 'And another thing,' Mma Makutsi had said. 'Miss Rose wears Indian clothes – those saris – while Mrs wears ordinary clothes.'

'Or she did when we saw her,' pointed out Mma Ramotswe.

Mma Makutsi paused, and then said, 'That's true.'

Mma Ramotswe wondered whether she should quote the relevant section of *The Principles of Private Detection* to Mma Makutsi, but decided against it. She recollected that Clovis Andersen had written: *Before describing people by what they are wearing, remember that they can always change their clothes.* That was true, and yet she felt that there were people who could be described very well by reference to their clothes *because they never wore anything different.* So if Mr J. L. B. Matekoni were ever to go missing – and some husbands did – she could give a good description to the police. *A man of reliable appearance wearing khaki trousers and khaki shirt, possibly with a khaki overall on top, and oil-stained suede desert boots.* That would be accurate because that was how he always looked. And if for any reason he changed his clothes before going missing, he could be described as *A man who looks as if he should be wearing khaki trousers and khaki shirt . . .*

Then there was Mma Makutsi. She at least had a number of different outfits, but there were always her shoes. Again, there were many pairs now, but they all had a certain look to them and, if mentioned alongside her characteristic round glasses, would provide a perfectly adequate description. *A lady in large round glasses (very large) and brightly coloured shoes, often with bows.* That would point very well to Mma Makutsi, and one need not even mention her slightly troublesome complexion or her general air of having come from Bobonong. It was difficult to put one's finger on the Bobonong factor, but it could always be spotted if one were attuned to such things. Nor would one have to mention that the shoes had a tendency to speak – a very unusual attribute, and one that defied rational explanation, but nonetheless one that set Mma Makutsi apart from most people; from everybody, in fact.

But now the woman, whoever she was, had returned inside and Charlie, sitting in the increasingly hot and stuffy cab, was beginning to feel uncomfortable. He opened the door, hoping to cool the cab that way, but found that this simply let the sun beat directly down on his Cool Jules jeans, making his legs unpleasantly warm.

He got out of the van altogether and made for the shade of a nearby tree. At the foot of this tree was a stone, and Charlie sat down on that, stretching out his legs before him. From his seated position he could no longer see into the Sengupta garden but he still had a good view of the gate, and he watched that from his new position.

The street was quiet, and because it led nowhere, only the occasional car passed by. Nobody took any notice of the young man under the tree or of his half-concealed van – why would they? Botswana was a country where people could still sit under a tree and look up at the sky if they so wished, or watch cattle as they moved slowly across the veld, or even just close their eyes and look at nothing because they had seen everything there was to see on their local patch of earth and did not need to see anything more. And even if the young man was dressed a bit loudly, that did not matter, as people could dress loudly if they wanted to, and it was no business of others to pass comment on what they were wearing.

An elderly man came past, and he paused and studied Charlie for a full minute or two before he spoke. 'Are you well, young man?'

'I am very well, Rra. And you are well too?'

'Oh, I am well. I used to be more well than I am now, but I am still well. And we should always remember that there are some people who are not well. We must remember them.'

Charlie nodded. 'Yes, Rra, we must remember them. I do not forget them, I can tell you.'

'Good.'

There was a silence. Then the man spoke again. 'Where is your village, Rra?'

Charlie pointed over towards the east. 'I come from that side. It is not a big place and I never go there any more. My father is late, and so I live with my uncle here in Gaborone.'

The man lowered his eyes. 'I am sorry that your father is late. There are many people who are late these days.' He paused. 'But then, we all become late when it is time for us to go. Do I know your uncle?'

Charlie shrugged. 'It's possible, Rra. He is working at that supermarket, that Pick and Pay. He works with the vegetables there.'

The man knew the place. 'I have been inside, but I did not buy anything.'

'That is a pity, Rra. It has very good food, that place . . .'

They looked at one another. It seemed to Charlie that the man wanted to tell him something but could not find the words. What was it? That he was lonely? That the world he knew had somehow been lost. Old people could be like that, Charlie thought, but there was nothing he could do to bring their world back; they shouldn't look at him and hope.

The old man suddenly seemed to remember something. 'I must go now,' he said. 'I shall be late getting to the house of my son.'

'Then you must go,' said Charlie. 'Go well, father.'

Now he was alone again under this hot sun and with the sweat beginning to make his Cool Jules outfit damp and rumpled. He was no longer sure whether he really wanted to train as a detective now that he saw how mundane the work was. Anybody, he said to himself, could sit in a car and wait for somebody to come out of a house; anybody could follow another car and note where it stopped and who got out of it. There was no special expertise in that – indeed there was far less skill involved than in changing the oil filter on a car. And to think that Mma Makutsi sat there and put on airs and graces about how complicated her work was and how you needed to have ninety-seven per cent, or whatever it was, to do it. Nonsense! You could do this sort of work even if you didn't have your school certificate – a twelve-year-old could do it. And you didn't need to be smartly dressed either. It was all very well putting on your best clothes, your Cool Jules jeans and the like, but nobody saw you and anybody who did would be indifferent to what you wore. It was all a waste of time – a complete waste of time, and he would hand in his notice if it continued like this . . . No, he would not do that. He had to live. He had to pay rent for his room – or his bit of a room. And that was another thing: how could you be taken seriously as a detective if you had to share a room with your cousins, including one who was a small boy who sometimes had nightmares and woke you up with his crying? How could a detective entertain the ladies that detectives needed to entertain if you had a small boy in the room who would want to cuddle up with the lady in question and thereby prevent the detective from having the discussions that he needed to have? It was all very upsetting, and all the more so because Charlie saw no way out. He would never get anywhere as a detective with those ladies sitting on all the available work.

He suddenly became aware that in the distance somebody was walking down the road towards him, and almost at the same time realised that this was a woman. It was the walk: Charlie was an expert in the way women walked – or so he believed.

He waited. As the figure came closer, he realised that not only was she indeed a woman, but she was a young woman – and smartly dressed.

He took his sunglasses out of his pocket and put them on. He adjusted the crease of his Cool Jules trousers so that it ran straight down the middle of the leg. When the young woman drew level with him, he cleared his throat. She had been studiously avoiding looking at him, but now she could hardly ignore him.

'Going anywhere special, honey?'

She gave him a scornful glance. 'I am not your honey.'

He laughed. 'Just an expression. I didn't know your name, you see. Honey is friendly.'

He could see that she was scrutinising him, as if weighing something up.

'My name is Charles,' he said. 'They call me Charlie.'

She allowed herself a flicker of a smile. 'Hello, Mr Charlie.'

'Not Mr Charlie – just Charlie. And you ... your name?'

She hesitated, but only for a moment. 'I am Alice.'

He gave a soft whistle of admiration. 'That is *very* nice. Alice ... Alice. That is a really good name.'

They regarded one another. He could tell that she was interested in him – and who wouldn't be, he thought, with the Cool Jules look?

'Alice who?' he asked.

'Alice Bombwe.'

He let out another low whistle. 'That's some name!'

She looked at her watch. 'I'm glad you like it.'

'Alice, can I help you to get where you want to go? If you're going to see your husband ... '

'There is no husband,' she snapped. 'I am going shopping.'

Charlie smiled. 'Shopping? I am a big expert in shopping. Let me take you.'

She hesitated once more, but again not for long. She named a collection of stores near Kgale Hill. 'Could you drive me there?'

'Alice, I could take you wherever you wanted to go. Johannesburg, even. You name it – I can go there.'

They moved towards the van. Alice opened the door and lowered herself into the passenger seat. From behind his dark glasses, Charlie inspected his new friend. She was about his age – perhaps slightly younger. The perfume she was wearing was quite strong, even after she had been walking out in the sun. He breathed it in – he knew that scent. It was called Miss Glamour, or something like that; he had seen it being promoted outside one of the clothes shops and he and his friends had laughingly insisted that a sample be dabbed on their wrists.

'You're wearing Miss Glamour,' he said. 'That is very good.'

She did not conceal her surprise. 'Ow! How can you tell that?'

Charlie affected a careless sophistication. 'That is what I am trained to do. You see . . . I shouldn't really tell you this, but I'm a detective – a private investigator.'

Her expression was one of complete admiration. 'A detective!'

'Yes. I'm on a case at the moment, actually. Surveillance, you know.'

Her eyes widened. 'Surveillance?'

'That means watching somebody. An international criminal.'

Her eyes widened even further. 'There are international criminals right here in Gaborone?'

'You better believe it, doll,' said Charlie. 'You want to watch with me? We can go to the shops a bit later.'

She nodded enthusiastically.

'You keep your head down,' he said. 'If things get tough, just do as I say, okay?'

'Okay.'

'I use this van for cover. Nobody pays attention to it, you see. If I drove my Mercedes they'd look at me.'

Alice was impressed. 'A sort of disguise, I suppose.'

'Exactly,' said Charlie. 'A disguise. You see, one of the things you learn when you're a detective—' He broke off. The gate of the Sengupta house, operated by remote control, was beginning to slide open. A car was nosing out of the driveway – a green Mercedes-Benz. There was a woman at the wheel, and another woman beside her in the passenger seat. It could only be Miss Rose and Mrs.

'Something's happening,' he said to Alice.

She gave a muffled gasp. 'It's them?'

'Yes,' said Charlie. 'We're going to start following. Hold on tight, okay?'

Swinging out onto the road, he began to follow the other car, his heart thumping within him at the thought of what he was doing. Those women in the office had said no car chases – well, what was this? This was a car chase, and he was participating in it! He adjusted his sunglasses and took a quick glance at Alice. It was clear that she was impressed.

'We just drive normally,' he said. 'We never draw attention to ourselves – never. You see these guys in the movies driving like they are crazy but that would alert the suspect. Easy does it – that's what we pros say.'

But the car carrying the two women had accelerated rapidly, and Charlie was obliged to speed up to ensure that he kept them in sight. The van's engine strained as it was pushed to its limits and an alarming rattle developed somewhere under the floor.

'They're going to get away,' said Alice. 'We're going to lose them.'

'No chance,' said Charlie. 'You haven't seen anything yet, let me tell you.'

At the end of the road, the other car slowed, but did not stop altogether. Charlie slowed down too, and then followed his quarry into its left turn. After a few hundred yards the car turned again, into another long residential road of whitewashed garden walls and high gates. He was aware of the fact that the brake lights of the car ahead were signalling another slowing down, this time before a driveway. He accelerated to keep up and did not see the large black car suddenly appear from a side road.

'Watch out!' shouted Alice.

He swerved and applied the brakes as hard as he could. The van jolted and came to a halt, but not before it had been dealt a glancing blow by the car. Now both vehicles were stationary.

'We've crashed,' said Alice.

Charlie sat quite still as he struggled to reconstruct in his mind what had happened. The other car seemed to have come from nowhere; he should have stopped – wasn't there a stop sign there? He turned his head to look. Yes, there was a sign: the other driver was in the wrong. *Not my fault*, he thought. *Not my fault*.

The other driver had opened his door and was coming towards the van. Charlie took a deep breath and got out of the cab. He looked at the man, trying to judge whether he was angry. People could become violent in such circumstances, even if they had caused the accident; he had seen it happen before.

There was no question of that here, though. The other driver looked at Charlie anxiously. 'Are you all right?' he asked.

Charlie nodded, but said nothing.

'I'm very sorry,' said the man. 'I know I should have stopped. I wasn't thinking.'

Charlie took a deep breath as he felt his anxiety evaporate. 'That's okay, Rra,' he said. 'I don't think the van is damaged very much. Just this dent here. Oh, and that dent over there, but that is a historical dent, that is not a new dent. And your car . . . ' He peered over the man's shoulder to take in the damage: it was negligible.

The man bent down to examine the side of the van. 'This is quite a dent,' he said. 'I'll get my insurance.'

He turned round and went back to his car. A few moments later he came back with a blue plastic document. As he opened the folder, he looked towards Alice. 'Is the young lady all right?' he asked.

'She's fine,' said Charlie.

'I'm sorry about your van,' said the man.

In his euphoria over the fact that he was not being blamed for anything, Charlie spoke freely. 'Actually, it isn't mine,' he said. 'It belongs to my boss, Mma Ramotswe.'

He knew the moment he spoke that he had said something he should not have. The man looked up sharply. 'Mma Ramotswe? The detective lady?'

Charlie swallowed. It was too late to retract. 'Yes,' he said. 'That is her.'

'I know her,' said the man, straightening up. He extended a hand towards Charlie. 'My name is Sengupta.'

Charlie froze. 'You are Mr Sengupta?'

'That's what I said. And your name, Rra?'

'I'm Charlie. I work for Mma Ramotswe.'

Mr Sengupta nodded. 'If you let me know what the cost of fixing that dent is, I'll pay Mma Ramotswe directly. I can claim it back from my insurance later – if it's above my excess.' He paused. 'Sometimes it's cheaper not to get the insurance people involved at all – bunch of crooks.'

'I shall let you know,' said Charlie. He was on dangerous ground. What if Mr Sengupta told Mma Ramotswe that there had been a young woman in the van with him at the time of the accident? He might let this information slip casually, and then she would think that he had been picking up girls rather than carrying out his task of surveillance. And then Mma Makutsi would add her contribution, and he would have his knuckles rapped in front of everybody, Cool Jules or not. He could hardly keep the incident from Mma Ramotswe – the dent was too obvious for that – but he would have to try to handle the matter himself as much as possible without bringing Mma Ramotswe and Mr Sengupta together. It was so unfair! Everything was unfair, he felt – everything, without exception.

Mr Sengupta gave him his telephone number and the name of his insurance company, just in case. 'We can sort this out,' he said. 'And I am sorry, you know. These stop signs – it's so easy to forget about them.'

'Of course it is,' said Charlie, and tried to smile. Stop signs were unfair as well.

They returned to their respective vehicles.

'It was his fault, wasn't it?' said Alice as he got into the driver's seat.

'Yes,' said Charlie. 'All his fault.'

He looked down the road. Miss Rose's car had disappeared, and he was not sure through which gate it had entered. Somewhere down on the right, he thought; about halfway, or not quite halfway. Well, there was nothing he could do about that now.

Alice was looking at her watch. 'I think we should go,' she said. 'I have to get to the shops.'

Charlie sighed. 'All right,' he said. 'I'll take you.'

'Pity about the international criminals,' said Alice. Her tone was that of one who did not believe in international criminals.

Charlie did not reply, but concentrated on starting the van.

'Let's not hang about,' said Alice. 'I've got a lot to do.'

She was beginning to irritate him, and she irritated him more as they drove back past the Sun Hotel.

'I was offered a job there once,' she said. 'But I didn't take it. I don't want to be stuck in this place for ever. I want to go to Johannesburg – that's where people move to who are really going to make a go of it.'

The implication was clear: a private detective who remained in Gaborone was obviously one who was not going to make the grade. The international criminals in Gaborone were small beer indeed compared with international criminals elsewhere.

Charlie fumed. He was doing her a favour and she seemed to be entirely unimpressed, and ungrateful. Who did she think she was?

He was thinking these thoughts as he drew up at the red lights at an intersection. Delayed shock from the accident was now having its effect, and he felt himself shaking. He breathed in deeply and for a moment closed his eyes. That helped to calm him down, but when he opened them and the lights turned green, he saw, stopped on the other side of the intersection, a familiar truck. It was Mr J. L. B. Matekoni – and he had seen him.

Charlie pretended not to notice the truck as he pulled away from the intersection, but out of the corner of his eye he saw Mr J. L. B. Matekoni wave, and he saw the look of surprise on his face.

*Chapter Eleven*

# Ninety-eight Per Cent

Phuti Radiphuti had expressed reservations about the speed with which the various tradesmen claimed they would be able to prepare the premises of the Handsome Man's De Luxe Café.

'You have to watch these people,' he said. 'They always claim they can do the work in a very short time, but that's just to get you to give them the job.' He shook his head sadly, in contemplation of the ways of the building trade. 'So you accept their quote and then you discover that they have another four or five jobs on the go – all of them urgent.'

Mma Makutsi had had similar misgivings herself, and Phuti was an experienced businessman who knew about these things. But when it came to the start date for the works on her café, the tradesmen were there at seven in the morning, their various vans loaded with all the supplies they needed. Work had started by eight, and that evening when she visited the site with Phuti, they were both astonished at the speed with which the transformation was being effected.

'These men are amazing,' Phuti conceded. 'Maybe it is your manner, Grace. Maybe they take you seriously.'

Mma Makutsi smiled modestly. 'I told them that I'd be taking a close interest in the work,' she said. 'They know that.'

Phuti touched her arm playfully. 'You know how to deal with men,' he said.

She laughed. 'That is something I have had to teach myself,' she said. 'Perhaps they should introduce a new subject at the Botswana Secretarial College on how to cope with men and their ways – in the office, of course. "How to deal with a difficult boss", perhaps. Or "How to explain things so that a man can understand them".'

Phuti smiled at that. 'That is very funny,' he said.

Mma Makutsi took off her glasses and polished them. Then, replacing them, she said quite evenly, 'No, it is not meant to be funny. There are many things that men have difficulty in understanding, Phuti. I could make a long list of them.'

Phuti gestured towards the works. 'Well, it is almost ready. It will not be long now.'

The foreman came to talk to them, and the subject of men and their limitations was dropped. Then Phuti went off with one of the electricians to inspect the new power points that were being installed in the kitchen area. Mma Makutsi wandered over to a window, where a man in blue overalls was busy applying putty to the seating of a pane of glass. They greeted one another before Mma Makutsi leaned forward to examine his handiwork. 'I could not do that, Rra,' she said. 'I would not be as neat as you.'

The man smiled. 'I am a glazier,' he said. 'That is what I do. And when you do something for long enough, you learn how to do it without making a mess.'

She asked him how long he had been putting glass into windows.

'I have been doing this for twenty years.'

'That is a long time, Rra.'

'Yes, it is. And I have only broken ten panes of glass in that time.'

He spoke with pride, and Mma Makutsi made sure to show her admiration. The man beamed with pleasure.

'It is good to like your work,' she said. 'I can tell that you are happy in what you do.'

The man applied a final squeeze of putty and then smoothed it elegantly with his knife. 'Yes, I think that it must be sad to have to do something you hate. That is what I say to my children. Choose something that you like to do. Do not be a bus driver if you do not like driving. Do not be a nurse if you can't stand the sight of blood. Do not be a person who fixes roofs if you get dizzy when you climb a ladder.'

'That is called vertigo,' said Mma Makutsi.

'Vertigo,' said the man. 'I should not like to have that disease.'

She asked after his children.

'I have seven,' he said. 'And one who is late, who did not live long – only a few days. But all the others are healthy.'

'I have one son,' said Mma Makutsi. 'He is called Itumelang.'

The man stood up from his work and laid down his putty-knife. 'That is the name of one of my sons. He is the second born. The first born is a girl called Tebogo. She is nineteen now and is at a special college.'

Mma Makutsi smiled encouragingly. 'What college is that, Rra?'

The man took a cloth out of his pocket and wiped his hands. 'She is at that college at the moment, but I'm afraid that we may not be able to keep her there.'

'Oh?'

'Yes, with seven children there are always many things to pay for. My wife used to work, but now she has hurt her shoulder and she cannot do the work that she did. She worked for one of the hotels, and they have said that if she cannot carry the laundry in and out of the room with her bad shoulder, then she cannot stay. So she has no job now.'

Mma Makutsi made a sympathetic noise with the tip of her tongue and her teeth. 'And what is this college, Rra? What is your daughter studying?'

The glazier sighed. 'She was doing something very useful. It is the Botswana Secretarial College.'

This answer was greeted with silence. The man looked at Mma Makutsi, and saw himself reflected in her large round glasses.

Now she muttered the name, lingering on each word, as if to savour its power. 'The Botswana Secretarial College.'

'Yes, Mma. It is a good college, I think.'

Mma Makutsi recovered. 'Oh, it is a very good college indeed, Rra,' she said forcefully. 'That is one of the finest colleges in the country. I was there, you know. I was at that college. I was there, at that very college.'

'Ah,' said the man. 'Then you are a secretary yourself, Mma.'

'No; I was at one time, but I am no longer a secretary. Now I am a partner in a detective agency – the No. 1 Ladies' Detective Agency.' She pointed out of the window. 'You may know it – it is on the Tlokweng Road.'

The man nodded. 'I have seen the sign, Mma. That is the place that they say is run by that large lady.'

'Traditionally built,' corrected Mma Makutsi. 'That is Mma Ramotswe. She is a traditionally built lady.'

'Of course. Traditionally built.' He looked at her admiringly. 'So that is where you work. You are the first detective I have met, you know that? The very first. I have met bank people and people in the diamond trade – people like that, but never a detective, Mma. Never once.'

She made a self-deprecatory gesture. 'Your daughter,' she said. 'Your Tebogo – you cannot find the money for her fees?'

The man lowered his eyes. 'There are nine mouths, Mma, if you count mine. Seven children, one mother and one father – nine altogether.'

'But this is her big chance.'

He looked miserable. 'That is so. But then we cannot always take the chances we get. That is a hard lesson that children have to learn. Sometimes there is just no money.'

Yes, thought Mma Makutsi, it is a hard lesson. She remembered when she had been at school up in Bobonong and there had been a trip to Gaborone arranged by the pupils. The parents had been required to find the money for their children's bus fare, and even if it was not very much, there were some who could not afford it. She had been one of those who could not go, and they had watched their classmates – the fortunate ones – pile into the bus and wave as they left; not cruelly, not to crow over their good fortune in being on the bus, but simply to wave goodbye, as children will do, without realising the disappointment of others.

'How much does she need, Rra? Can she not work part-time? There are jobs, surely.'

The man sighed. 'She is already doing that. She has a job at the hospital – in the kitchen. She works there for three hours every evening. It is very hard for her, because she has her college work during the day and then the hospital.'

'So how much does she need?'

'About three thousand pula.'

Mma Makutsi frowned. 'That is not all that much.'

The man made a gesture of helplessness with his hands. 'When you only have a handful of pula left over each month, if that, then three thousand pula seems like a lot.'

Mma Makutsi knew, and she remembered how she had not even had a few hundred pula to spend each month, but still less; how sometimes she had had nothing at all left by the time payday arrived, and the last few days of the month had been days of scratching about for the few scraps left in the kitchen, of drinking tea without milk or sugar (and reusing the teabags), of walking rather than catching the minibus to work. She realised she should not have said that three thousand pula was not much; for many, it was a great deal of money. It was easy to forget things like that once your circumstances were more comfortable, as hers now were.

She made up her mind. 'Excuse me for a moment, Rra. I'll come back. I need to talk to my husband over there.'

'I will finish this window,' said the man. 'I have to scrape the putty back a bit – just a little bit. Then the painter can paint everything.'

While the glazier applied himself, Mma Makutsi crossed the room and drew Phuti aside.

'Is everything all right, Grace? Are the windows—'

She cut him short. 'Yes, everything is fine. The glazier is doing a good job.'

He looked at her expectantly. 'So there are no problems?'

'Not with the windows,' she said.

'And everything else is going very well,' said Phuti. 'I was talk-ing to that carpenter and he said that—'

Again she headed him off. 'The glazier was telling me about his family. He has seven children, that man.'

Phuti shrugged. 'There are many big families. There is some-body in the store who says he has fifteen children.' He made a face. 'Fifteen.'

Mma Makutsi glanced across the room. The glazier was still bent over his work. 'He has a daughter at the Botswana Secretarial College.'

'Ah,' said Phuti. 'You must have been pleased to hear that – and he must be a proud man.'

'Yes, he is proud of her. But now she has to leave.'

Phuti frowned. 'She is being expelled?'

'No, she is not being expelled.' As she spoke, Mma Makutsi tried to remember whether she had ever heard of anybody being expelled from the Botswana Secretarial College. She could not think of anybody to whom this had happened, although if she were to be asked to make a list of those who *deserved* such a fate, there was one name that led the rest: Violet Sephotho. Now there had been a thoroughly worthy candidate for expulsion, with her constant talking in class, her sniggering, her ostentatious painting of her nails while the lecturer in accountancy – a mousy man with little self-confidence – tried to explain the principles of double-entry book-keeping. Violet Sephotho had sat there and applied nail polish to show that she was somehow above such matters as double-entry book-keeping. How dare she! And who was the one person – the only one – who declined to contribute to the birth-day cake they arranged for their shorthand tutor, by far the most popular member of staff? Violet Sephotho again, who said that she had better things to spend her money on than cakes for the staff. Mma Makutsi remembered her words, her very words:

'They are all too fat anyway. They take our fees and spend it on fat cakes and things like that.' It was such a calumny, but nobody had sprung to the defence of the lecturers apart from Mma Makutsi herself. She had protested that Violet had no evidence for such an accusation, only to be laughed at by Violet with the taunt, 'And what do you know? What does anybody from Bobonong know about these things? You haven't even been to Johannesburg.'

It was a cutting remark, all the more wounding because it was true. Mma Makutsi had never been to Johannesburg, and it was true, too, that there were people from Bobonong who were not all that well informed about the wider world. They knew about Bobonong, of course, and, to an extent, about Francistown, but many of them did not know about much else. Yet the difference between them and the likes of Violet Sephotho was that they, unlike her, were prepared to apply themselves if given the chance. The road from Bobonong to Gaborone was a long and a hard one, but those who were able to take it, took it in a spirit of humility and willingness to learn. That was the difference.

She brought herself back to where she was, speaking to Phuti. 'No, there is no question of expulsion. It is all about money, Rra.'

For a moment he said nothing, but then he made a *tsk* sound. 'Money, yes, it is often about money.'

'Three thousand pula,' said Mma Makutsi. 'That's all. Three thousand pula.'

'That's not very much.'

She seized the cue. 'That's exactly what I thought, Phuti. Three thousand is nothing – but when you're poor and there are so many other children ... ' She paused. She could see that he sympathised; some men would not, but Phuti would – she knew that. 'We could help her, Rra.'

'Give her the money?'

'It could be a loan. She could pay us back when she gets a job.'

Phuti looked uncomfortable. 'But we can't go round lending money to everybody who needs it. Word would get out. We'd have people lining up outside the door – you know what it's like in this country: people love to borrow money.'

Mma Makutsi lowered her voice. 'Phuti, we are very lucky. We have that house and Itumelang and we have so many other things. That poor girl has one thing in her life: her chance at the Botswana Secretarial College. We can afford to lend her father the money.'

She looked at him intensely. He had never refused her anything, and she realised that he would not refuse her now.

'Give it to her,' he said suddenly. 'Interest free. Give it to her.'

She wanted to make sure that she understood. 'You mean, she doesn't need to pay any interest at all?'

'Yes, that is what I mean. She pays us back when she can.'

She glanced over towards the glazier. He seemed to have finished what he had been doing and was now standing back to admire his handiwork. 'May I tell him now?' she asked.

'Yes, you tell him, Grace.'

She crossed the room to speak to the man. He stood quite still as she spoke, and then, without any warning, threw his hands in the air and uttered a roar of delight. The sound echoed in the unfurnished room, and the other workers turned round to see what was happening.

'I cannot believe this, Mma,' stuttered the glazier. 'I cannot believe that anybody would do this. Oh, I am a happy, happy man, Mma.'

Mma Makutsi felt herself on the verge of tears. And why should I not cry? she thought. Why should I not cry at this man's happiness?

She controlled herself. 'Well, we are happy too, Rra,' she said. 'You should thank my husband now – it is his money really.'

'And the college will be pleased, too,' the man continued. 'She has been doing so well that they will be pleased she is staying.'

Mma Makutsi was interested. 'Doing well, Rra? In all her subjects? Shorthand too?'

'All of them,' he said. 'In her last examination she got a very, very high mark, Mma. The college was very pleased.'

Mma Makutsi hesitated. 'A high mark, Rra? What was that?'

'It was ninety-eight per cent, Mma.'

Mma Makutsi opened her mouth to speak, but then closed it. The man stared at her: he could not understand why she should look dismayed. Did she realise how high that mark was, or did she imagine that people should get one hundred per cent?

'Ninety-eight per cent is a very high mark, Mma. It is almost impossible to get.'

Mma Makutsi made a supreme effort. 'I am pleased to hear that, Rra. That is very good.'

It was bound to happen, she thought. Some day there would be somebody who would get ninety-eight per cent; there was a certain poetic inevitability to it. And people could not hope that their records would last for ever; that was not what records were. They were made to be beaten by the next generation; they were made to be bettered. And for existing record-holders there was no dishonour in that process – none whatsoever.

'She must be very good at being a secretary, Rra,' she said.

'You are kind to say that, Mma. She is.' He mused for a moment. 'Ninety-eight per cent, Mma! Would you believe it?'

'I do,' she said. 'You see, I ...' But she did not go any further. There were things that were best left unsaid, and this, she realised, was one of them.

As the man crossed the room to speak to Phuti, Mma Makutsi

walked to the window he had been working on and looked out. It was while she was standing there that she heard a chirpy, rather squeaky voice from below. She glared down at her shoes.

*Ninety-eight per cent, Boss! How about that? Beats ninety-seven per cent, we think! Okay, only by one per cent, but one per cent is all you need, Boss!*

# Chapter Twelve

# I Did Not Come About a Cat

When Charlie returned to the office he found that neither Mma Ramotswe nor Mma Makutsi was there. Mma Ramotswe had left early as there was a parents' meeting at the school at which they were to receive a report on Puso's progress, and Mma Makutsi had gone off to meet Phuti at her restaurant. There was a note from Mma Ramotswe on the door of the agency, though, that gave him his instructions. *I have taken a taxi home. Leave my van in the garage when Fanwell shuts up for the day. You stay here until five o'clock and answer the phone. Write any messages down on the pad on my desk. There is milk for tea – if you want it – in the garage fridge and half a fat cake. God bless. PR.*

He was touched by the fact that she had left him milk for his tea and half a fat cake. He was touched, too, by the *God bless,* because he could not remember when anybody had last said that to him. She wanted God to look after him – that was what it amounted to. Mma Ramotswe cared about him. And what had he done for her? He had dented her van and lost – or as good as lost – the people he was meant to be following. He had also used the van for a purpose he knew she would not approve of – taking a glamorous, but annoying, young woman to the shops. And he had been seen by Mr J. L. B. Matekoni.

He had mentally prepared his report. He would tell her about the accident, of course, and he would tell her that the other driver had accepted full responsibility. He would try not to mention that it was Mr Sengupta, but would do so if asked. He would say nothing about Alice, as there was no point incurring wrath unnecessarily – and he hoped that Mr J. L. B. Matekoni would say nothing either. As for the surveillance – well, he had seen more or less where the other car had disappeared to and he was sure he would be able to find the house if required. He would be positive about that, as he wanted this job. He wanted to be a success as a detective, and the thought of facing Mma Makutsi's derision if he confessed to failing at his very first test was too much. He would do better next time, but for the moment the report would have to be as positive as possible.

The following morning, Charlie was in the office when Mma Makutsi, who was first to arrive, came in the door.

'Well, well,' she said benignly. 'Nice and early today, Charlie. And very smart-looking too, if I may say so.'

Charlie smiled. 'I like to get in early,' he said. 'Then I am ready for work.'

'Very wise,' said Mma Makutsi, placing her handbag on the shelf it always occupied. 'Phuti says that too. And Itumelang, for that matter. He likes to have his breakfast at five.'

'Hah!' said Charlie. 'That's what babies are like.'

Mma Makutsi threw him a sideways glance. 'You have experience, Charlie? You know about babies?'

'There are babies everywhere you turn, Mma. Everybody has a baby these days.'

Mma Makutsi made a non-committal sound. Then she said, 'What happened yesterday? Anything?'

'I have a report to make,' said Charlie, somewhat officiously.

Mma Makutsi nodded. 'We'll wait for Mma Ramotswe. It's her case, you see. In this business, there is one person in charge of each case, understand? That is the way it works.'

Charlie nodded. 'I know that, Mma. It is the same in the garage business. One mechanic, one car.'

A few minutes later, Mma Ramotswe arrived with Mr J. L. B. Matekoni. Charlie glanced at his former employer, and for a moment their eyes met. Neither said anything. *He understands,* thought Charlie. *He knows, but he understands. He will not tell Mma Ramotswe about seeing me driving a girl around. He is a man, like me. We will not betray one another.* Mma Makutsi put on the kettle, and Charlie, having volunteered to wash the mugs, retreated to the sink they shared with the garage. This was in a corridor that ran between the two parts of the building, and it meant that for a few moments he was out of earshot.

'He says he has a report,' announced Mma Makutsi.

'That's good,' said Mma Ramotswe. 'We can hear all about it over our tea.'

Mma Makutsi looked doubtful. 'Heaven knows what he saw. Frankly I can't imagine him noticing very much. You know how dozy these boys are.'

Mma Ramotswe raised a finger to her lips. 'Shh! We must give him a chance, Mma.'

Charlie came back into the room and a few minutes later tea was served.

'Right, Charlie,' said Mma Ramotswe. 'Tell us what happened.'

'There is one little problem I must deal with first,' he said. 'There is a small dent in the van.'

Mma Makutsi gasped, but Mma Ramotswe remained calm. 'What happened, Charlie?'

'A man did not stop at a stop sign. He came right out. I was able to take prompt evasive action ...' He paused for the effect of this to be absorbed. 'But unfortunately we made contact with one another.'

'Made contact,' snorted Mma Makutsi. 'Crashed.'

Charlie ignored her. 'The other driver admits it was his fault. He has given me his insurance details and telephone number. We can get it repaired at his expense – it will not be a big job.'

'Where is it?' asked Mma Ramotswe. 'Where is my van?'

'It's round the back,' said Charlie. 'I left it in the garage as you told me to, and this morning I put it round the back.'

'I'd like to see it,' said Mma Ramotswe.

Charlie led her to the van, followed by Mma Makutsi.

'You see,' he said, pointing to the dent made by Mr Sengupta's car. 'It is not a big thing at all. They will fix it at the panel beaters. I can speak to them – we know them well. They'll give us a special price. They can also fix that dent there, that historical dent.'

Mma Ramotswe reached forward to touch the damaged metal. She had suspected that Charlie was probably minimising the damage, but she realised now that it was not extensive. She had caused many such dents herself on various occasions, some of them quite recent.

'Well,' she said, 'it's not too bad.'

Mma Makutsi stepped forward and peered at the damage. 'It doesn't look very good to me.' She turned to Charlie. 'What speed were you doing?'

Charlie sniffed. 'I've told you: the other car didn't stop when he should have. It's not my fault. I wasn't going fast.'

Mma Ramotswe said hurriedly, 'It's all right. These things happen. Speak to those people about fixing it.'

Charlie glanced defiantly at Mma Makutsi, who simply shrugged. In normal circumstances, he would have engaged in the argument she seemed determined to have, but he did not want to prolong the discussion in case anybody asked who the other driver was.

They returned to the office, where Mma Ramotswe invited him to sit in the client's chair and give his report on the surveillance.

Charlie took a deep breath as he began his account. 'I proceeded to the house of Mr Sengupta,' he began.

'Proceeded!' exclaimed Mma Makutsi.

Charlie faltered. 'That's what people say . . . '

'Of course they do, Charlie,' said Mma Ramotswe. 'We know what you mean.'

'You went,' said Mma Makutsi. 'You mean to say that you went.'

Charlie resumed his report, now pointedly addressing it only to Mma Ramotswe. 'I went to the house, Mma Ramotswe. I found a good place to park the van – there is some scrubland, you see, and I was able to park under a tree. It gave me a good view of the house. I sat there for a long time. There was nothing happening in the house. Then a lady came out and stood in the sun for a while. She was breathing, I think. Then she went back in.'

There was a snort from Mma Makutsi. 'She was breathing? Are you sure?'

Mma Ramotswe came to Charlie's defence. 'I think that Charlie meant she was taking the air.' She paused. 'Carry on, Charlie.'

'Then maybe half an hour later, maybe a bit more, the gate opened. A green Mercedes came out, driven by that lady, Miss Rose – the one you told me about. There was another lady in the car with her. I think that must have been the lady you called Mrs.'

Mma Ramotswe urged him on. 'And?'

'I got into the van and followed them. I did not get too close, and I do not think they saw me.'

'Where did they go?' asked Mma Makutsi.

'I was getting to that,' said Charlie peevishly. 'I am trying to tell this story, but I cannot tell it if I am interrupted all the time.'

Mma Ramotswe sighed. 'Carry on, Charlie, we're listening.'

Charlie drew in his breath. 'They went round the corner, Mma. Then they went to a street that was not very far away. They drove into a driveway there and the gate closed. That is when the accident happened and I had to return.'

He stopped. He looked down at his hands. Mma Makutsi looked at Mma Ramotswe, who looked at Charlie. In the garage next door, they heard Fanwell shout something to Mr J. L. B. Matekoni; there was the sound of a car engine being fired, sputtering and then dying. Then silence.

Mma Ramotswe fiddled with her pencil. She had a pad open in front of her, but she had not noted anything down.

Mma Makutsi broke the silence. 'Whose house was it?' she asked.

Charlie shrugged. 'How can I tell?'

'You ask,' said Mma Makutsi. 'You ask somebody. People know. There are no secrets in this town, Charlie.'

Charlie spoke defensively. 'I didn't have time to find anybody. I looked but there was nobody.'

Mma Makutsi was about to say something, but Mma Ramotswe stopped her. 'Never mind, Charlie,' she said. 'At least you saw the house. Now you can take me there and we shall see what we can find out.'

Charlie's reaction was not what Mma Ramotswe had expected. 'I don't want to put you to any trouble,' he said quickly.

Mma Ramotswe assured him that it would not be any trouble. 'Mma Makutsi can look after the office while we go there,' she said. 'We can make enquiries as to who lives in the house. We can easily do that.'

Charlie glanced about him nervously. 'I think we should wait,' he muttered. 'I should do more observation.'

'Yes, you can certainly do that,' said Mma Ramotswe. 'But there's no need to wait to find out about the house. We can do that right now.' She rose from her seat, and Charlie also stood up, albeit reluctantly.

Mma Makutsi busied herself with some task at her desk. 'I hope you find something out,' she said. 'It's always more difficult later on, you know. That's why I always follow through with my enquiries, even if it means I'll be late home as a result . . . ' She left the censure unfinished, indifferent to Charlie's hostile stare.

'Come along now, Charlie,' said Mma Ramotswe breezily. 'No time like the present.'

'No,' said Mma Makutsi. 'Indeed not.'

Mma Ramotswe tried to make conversation with Charlie as they drove in the tiny white van, but her every effort seemed to be met only with silence, or, at best, with monosyllabic replies. Eventually, when they stopped at a red light, she turned to him and said, 'There's something wrong, isn't there, Charlie?'

Charlie hesitated, and for a moment it seemed as if he was going to reply, but then the traffic light changed to green and the moment was lost.

Mma Ramotswe sighed. 'You know you can talk to me,

Charlie – you know that, don't you?'

He nodded. 'I know that, Mma.'

'And you know that however much trouble you're in,' she continued, 'I won't shake my finger at you and refuse to hear you out. You know that, too?'

'I know that, too, Mma.'

'Very well. Now, we're almost there. When we arrive, you show me which way they went.'

Charlie muttered something that she did not catch.

'What was that, Charlie?'

He raised his voice. He sounded peevish now. 'I said that I don't think there's much point. Maybe they just went there for tea or something like that. That won't give us any information we don't know.'

Mma Ramotswe shook her head. 'But that's where you're wrong, Charlie. In a case like this, where there is no information to begin with, every little fact, no matter how irrelevant it seems, may tell us something important.'

They had reached the Senguptas' road and rather than turning into it, Mma Ramotswe drove down the adjacent road that Charlie now pointed out to her. Then at the corner, after a further turn, he told her to stop. 'It is along there,' he said. 'It is that house there.' Under his breath he added, 'I think.' Mma Ramotswe did not hear.

They drove towards the gate Charlie had pointed out. They could see that the garden behind it was large as there were several clumps of trees, including a palm tree, rising above the top of the surrounding high wall. Along the top of this wall was a double row of electrified wire. Mma Ramotswe made a clicking sound with her tongue. 'Security,' she said. 'Why are all these people so keen on security?'

'Burglars,' said Charlie.

Mma Ramotswe chuckled. 'But if you put up an electric fence, then every burglar in town is going to say, "That's the house we need to break into – that one with the electric fence. That means there are some very expensive things inside. They will be very well worth stealing."'

She peered again at the wall. 'I think I know what to do. I shall go and speak to them.'

'You can't, Mma,' Charlie said with concern. 'You can't do that. You don't know who they are.'

Mma Ramotswe smiled at him. 'Since when have you had to know people to speak to them? This is Botswana, Charlie, and you don't have to know people before you speak to them.'

'But what are you going to say, Mma?'

'I will say that I am looking for my friend who lives near here.'

Charlie thought for a moment. He appeared uncomfortable. 'And then when they say they do not know your friend – what then?'

Mma Ramotswe was amused by Charlie's embarrassment. That was a problem of the young, she thought: they were very conservative underneath it all; they were reluctant to stand out in any way.

'We'll see how things go,' she said, her finger poised above the bell set into the wall. 'It will be simple, Charlie.'

She pressed the bell, and almost immediately the electric gate began to open, revealing the paved driveway of the house beyond. Charlie said nervously, 'These people are very rich, Mma.'

'Yes, there are some rich people around,' said Mma Ramotswe. 'But they are just like us, remember. They have two arms and two legs, same as us.' She paused. 'I have never seen a rich person with four arms, Charlie, or two heads. Have you?'

He did not reply.

A woman had appeared on the veranda and was beckoning

them to join her. 'Up here, Mma,' she shouted. 'Come up here.'

They walked up the driveway. As they did so, Charlie glanced through the open garage door to the side of the house. 'Look,' he whispered. 'That must be the only Porsche in Botswana. Look, Mma Ramotswe!'

'It is just a car, like any other car,' she replied. 'Rich cars don't have more than four wheels, do they? And do they have two steering wheels? I don't think so. They are exactly the same as poor cars, Charlie.'

The woman standing on the veranda now greeted them properly, according to custom, and Mma Ramotswe replied in the same way.

The woman looked her up and down. She did not invite her in, but addressed her from where she stood.

'Have you much experience, Mma?' she asked.

Mma Ramotswe hesitated. 'Quite a bit, Mma.'

'That's good. And you're in a job at the moment?'

Mma Ramotswe understood. Glancing at Charlie, she saw that he, too, had realised what was happening. 'I am working,' she said.

'Can you cook?' asked the woman.

Mma Ramotswe nodded. 'I have been working for Mr Sengupta. Perhaps you know him, Mma.'

The woman frowned. 'Sengupta? Sengupta? Who is this Sengupta?'

'He lives a few streets away, Mma. He is an Indian person, and there is his sister, who is called Miss Rose. Do you know her, Mma?'

The woman made an impatient gesture with her hand. 'Why are you asking me? I have no idea who these people are. It is not for you to ask me questions, you know.' She looked at Charlie. 'And this young man is your son, I take it. There will not be enough

159

room for him, I'm afraid. There is just one room for the maid.'

Mma Ramotswe shifted her weight from one leg to another. She had had enough. 'You are a rude lady,' she said.

The woman took a moment to react. Then she shouted angrily, 'What did you say, Mma? What did you say to me?'

'I said that you are rude, Mma. And I have not come about a job. You must have been expecting somebody else. I am a detective, if you must know who I am.'

This had an extraordinary effect. The bombastic, arrogant manner disappeared, to be replaced by an air of apprehension. 'You . . . '

'Yes,' said Mma Ramotswe. 'I am a detective. But now, Mma, I think I have found out enough.'

The woman reached out to steady herself on one of the veranda pillars. 'We have nothing to hide here.' Her voice faltered. 'It is all above board. All of it.' She looked about her wildly before continuing, 'My husband has a very good lawyer, you know. He will be here soon.'

Mma Ramotswe could have enjoyed herself, but she did not. She turned to Charlie and gestured towards the still-open gate. 'I think we should go, Charlie,' she said.

They returned to the van. 'I don't think that was the house,' said Mma Ramotswe.

Charlie giggled. 'Did you see how she changed? Like that! One minute as bossy as Mma Potokwani herself – sorry, Mma, I know Mma Potokwani is your friend – the next like a naughty child caught doing something wrong.'

'I suspect they have done something wrong,' said Mma Ramotswe. 'Many rich people have something to hide, I think. Not all of them, of course – but many.'

Mma Ramotswe asked Charlie whether it was the gate next door that Miss Rose had driven through. He looked down the road. It was because of the accident that he found it hard to remember; everything had happened at once. He tried to reconstruct the sequence of events in his mind. He had turned and had not gone far; the green Mercedes-Benz must have been about three quarters of the way along this road, and that meant that if it wasn't this gate it must have been the gate next door, or the one after that. He scratched his head.

'I think that maybe it's the one after that, Mma. I think that might be it.'

Mma Ramotswe started the engine 'Well, there is only one way to find out,' she said. 'Let's go there.'

She drove the van a few hundred yards further along the road and then parked in the shade of a conveniently placed acacia tree.

'Here we are,' she said. 'We can try this place.'

Charlie became anxious again. 'But we can't just go in, Mma. What will you say?'

Mma Ramotswe looked at him teasingly. 'I shall try something different. I shall ask them whether they have seen a cat.'

'But you haven't got a cat, Mma Ramotswe.'

Mma Ramotswe was enjoying herself. 'Well, they don't know that, do they?'

'You cannot lie,' said Charlie. 'You told me that yourself. You keep saying it: don't lie.'

'But I will not lie,' Mma Ramotswe assured him. 'I shall say, "Have you seen a stray cat?" They will probably think that I am searching for my own cat, but the question I am actually asking them is quite different. I shall be asking them if they have seen a stray cat.'

'But that's ridiculous, Mma.'

'I don't think so. It's worked before. You'd be surprised at the number of people who are very happy to start talking to you once you mention a cat – or a dog, for that matter. Off they go, and before you know it, you've learned all about them – who they are, what sort of dog or cat they themselves have, what they think of their neighbours' dogs, and so on.'

Charlie was unconvinced. 'You can't do that, Mma! You can't go in like that and ask those silly questions . . . '

'You can stay in the van if you like, Charlie, but I think it would be better if you came in with me. Part of your training, you see.'

Charlie trailed behind her as she walked up to the gate. Once again, there was an intercom bell. As she pressed this, a blue light came on above the button. After a few seconds, a woman's voice, tinny and crackly, sounded through the small loudspeaker. 'Yes. What is it?'

'It is me,' said Mma Ramotswe, winking at Charlie as she spoke.

The voice came back immediately. 'Me? Who is this *me*?'

'I've come about a cat.'

The voice sounded puzzled. 'About your hat?'

'A cat,' repeated Mma Ramotswe. 'May I come in, please, Mma. It is hot standing here, and I am thirsty.'

It was a direct plea for something that Mma Ramotswe knew could not be ignored in any Botswana household. To say to somebody that you were thirsty was to appeal to a most basic rule of the old Botswana morality: you could never refuse to give drinking water to another. This came from a time when water was even more precious than it is now; from a time before there were pipes and public water supplies; from a time when, out in the Kalahari, the desert people husbanded their water in buried vessels – calabashes tucked away under the sand. These could be retrieved and broached to yield their life-saving supplies. But if you took a sip, then you had to be prepared to let others take a sip, too. You simply had to. And in villages, where there were wells, people similarly had to allow a stranger to quench his thirst, for that was the morality of a people who had always lived in a dry place, on the very edge of a great waterless expanse.

The woman at the other end pressed a switch that cut off communication, and within a few seconds they heard the whirring of the electric motor controlling the gate.

'We are invited in,' said Mma Ramotswe. 'You see, Charlie.'

The open gate revealed a surprisingly lush garden – a sign that the property had a good borehole. The house was markedly less opulent than the one they had just visited, being an older bungalow-style building, but it was clearly kept in good repair. A woman had emerged from the front door of the house and was coming down the drive to meet them.

Once again Mma Ramotswe offered the usual polite greetings. These were reciprocated, although while she enquired after Mma Ramotswe's health, the woman was looking suspiciously at Charlie.

'This is my assistant,' said Mma Ramotswe. 'He works with me.'

The woman nodded but kept her eyes on Charlie, as if assessing him.

'May we come in, Mma?' said Mma Ramotswe. 'It is very hot.'

'Yes, yes,' said the woman. 'You may come in, Mma. I shall give you some water.'

'You are kind,' said Mma Ramotswe.

As they approached the house, they heard the electric gate closing behind them.

'You have a fine garden,' said Mma Ramotswe conversationally. 'You must be proud of it.'

'Yes,' said the woman. 'I set out this garden. My late husband was not interested in it.'

'I am sorry to hear that your husband is late,' said Mma

Ramotswe. 'When did he become late, Mma?'

'Two years ago,' said the woman, briskly. 'He had a hole in his heart. He lived with it and then one day it became bigger and he became late. The Lord called him.'

They had reached the front door, and the woman gestured to Mma Ramotswe to go inside. She glanced at Charlie, and then whispered to Mma Ramotswe. 'Would you mind if your assistant stayed outside, Mma? He will be comfortable on the veranda here.'

'Of course not,' said Mma Ramotswe. 'Charlie, will you stay out here, please?'

Charlie said nothing, but made his way to the far end of the veranda, where he sat down on a chair. Mma Ramotswe accompanied her hostess inside.

As soon as they were through the door, the woman turned to Mma Ramotswe and gripped her upper arm. 'Why have you brought that . . . that young man?' she hissed. 'Did they not tell you that we do not allow men here? Did you not know that, Mma?'

Mma Ramotswe thought quickly. 'No,' she said. 'I knew nothing about it.'

This answer seemed to irritate the woman. 'That makes me very cross, Mma. We tell them and we tell them, and then some inexperienced person goes and spoils everything. We have to be confidential – we have to.'

'I'm sorry, Mma,' said Mma Ramotswe. 'I won't do it again.'

The woman seemed mollified. 'I should give you my name, Mma. I am called Maria. That is not my Setswana name – obviously – but I have always been called that. My mother was a Catholic, you see. I am not, because my late husband was Anglican. He was a sidesman at our church, you know. And the treasurer, too.'

Mma Ramotswe inclined her head in recognition of the late husband's achievements. And she felt a flush of shame – she had gained entrance to this woman's house on false pretences. They were harmless false pretences, of course, and they had been made purely in the interests of a distressed client, but they were false pretences nonetheless. And she could tell that the woman to whom she was speaking was a good woman, and should not be deceived in any way.

What would her own father say – the late Obed Ramotswe, who would never have spoken anything but the truth, in any circumstances? What would he say, she asked herself, if he could see his own daughter going into the house of another with some ridiculous story about a stray cat? She put the thought out of her mind, but mentally she made her apology to him, in the same way, and same spirit, as she had apologised to him when she was a young woman and had deceived him once about seeing Note Mokoti. He had asked her whether she was seeing anybody and she had said that she was not – but she was: she was seeing Note Mokoti, trumpeter and fatal attraction to any woman who got close to him. That had been a lie – there was no other way of describing it. She had lied to her father. And later, when her marriage to Note had come to its disastrous end, she had tried to tell him that she had deceived him and the words had stuck in her throat and she had become silent. He had taken her hand and told her that it did not matter what had happened; that he understood. He had accepted an apology that had not even been made.

Of course, that was the sort of thing we all did when we were young. You cannot judge somebody of eighteen by the standards of somebody of thirty, even less by the standards of somebody who was forty. And those things that we did when we were young were not so important, really, provided that we stopped doing them as we grew older and saw them for what they were. Which was what worried her now: she had no excuse for deceiving this woman. Her job as a private detective in itself gave no justification. She was a woman first and foremost, a citizen of this fine country, the wife of a respected mechanic, and, perhaps most importantly of all, the daughter of that great man, the late Obed Ramotswe. Those were all things that outweighed the requirements of her unusual and sometimes rather demanding job. They outweighed them. They just did.

She looked at Maria. 'I need to tell you something, Mma,' she began. 'I did not come about a cat.'

The woman did not seem surprised. 'Of course you didn't, Mma. I didn't think that you did.'

This took Mma Ramotswe by surprise. 'Oh . . . ' she said.

The woman held out her hand. 'You are safe here, Mma. I shall not tell anybody you have come. You can trust me.'

This was a strange thing to say, thought Mma Ramotswe. But everything about this encounter so far was strange. What did Maria mean by saying that she was safe? Safe from whom?

'You see,' Maria went on, 'this is a house of trust. Any woman who comes here must be able to trust anybody she meets under this roof. I insist on that, Mma. It is the basis of what we do.'

Mma Ramotswe was beginning to understand. 'I see,' she said.

'Yes,' said Maria. 'We get women here who are at the end of their tethers, Mma. They will have suffered so much from people whom they once trusted, and that trust has been abused. That is why they come to us, and we never turn anybody away. Never.'

It was clear now. And it confirmed that this was the right house. Mrs had come here because she was in danger. It all made sense. 'I see,' said Mma Ramotswe.

Maria started to lead her towards the kitchen, but continued to talk. 'But almost everybody who comes here starts off without telling me the whole truth. There is often a reason for that. They are so used to having to cover up, to having to say all sorts of things to the men who are tormenting them that they carry on with it. It takes time for them to be able to speak without fear – and that is when the truth will start to come out.'

'I have not—' began Mma Ramotswe.

Maria interrupted her. 'No, of course you haven't. All in good time. But you might tell me one thing: why did you come, Mma? Who was it?'

'There is an Indian woman,' said Mma Ramotswe. 'She came to see you yesterday with her friend, Miss Rose. I have been asked—'

Maria brightened. 'Ah, Lakshmi. She said that she knew another woman who was suffering too, and that she would pass on our details. So she has sent you.'

Mma Ramotswe frowned. The work that Maria did was good work, and she did not want to mislead her. 'I do not really know her, Mma.'

Maria was brisk. 'But she said to me that she told you every-thing. She said that she told you about what happened with her husband.'

'She . . .' began Mma Ramotswe.

Maria brushed the interjection aside. 'I thought that the two of you were close friends, but maybe she is closer to you than you are to her. That can happen, you know, Mma. Women who are desperate for somebody to talk to can seize on people they don't really know all that well. They can become dependent very quickly. Maybe that is what happened when you met her.'

They had reached the kitchen, and Maria now poured Mma Ramotswe a glass of water. 'There,' she said. 'That will make you less thirsty.' She paused. Mma Ramotswe, now actually thirsty, drained the glass.

'Lakshmi told me about your husband, Mma. I was very sorry

to hear about it. I said to her that you should even consider going to your brother. You have to be careful about getting other male members of the family involved, as it can lead to trouble, but since your brother—'

Mma Ramotswe put down the glass. The misunderstanding had gone on quite long enough.

'Excuse me, Mma,' she said firmly. 'She was not talking about me. There is nothing wrong with my husband. He is a good man. And I have not come here because—'

Again, Maria did not let her finish. 'Mma,' she said, holding up a hand, 'Mma, we understand. You are being loyal, because women are loyal – in the face of everything, they are loyal.'

Mma Ramotswe found that she had to laugh. She tried to stop herself, but she failed. Maria looked at her severely.

'This is no laughing matter, Mma.'

No, of course not; and suddenly she was back in school, in Mochudi, on a hot afternoon. She was sitting in the classroom with the summer sun like a hammer on the tin roof and the bolts that kept the sheets of tin in place cracking loudly as the heat made them move; she was sitting at her desk with a schoolbook open in front of her, *The History of Botswana*, and she noticed the name of the publisher: *Published by Longman*, and the question occurred to her: who is this Longman? She imagined him – a tall man, much taller than those around him, carrying copies of *The History of Botswana* under his arm – and the thought made her begin to giggle. At first the giggles were controlled and barely audible, but then they welled up within her and began to attract attention. *There is nothing funny*, the teacher had snapped, glaring at her from the front of the classroom, and of course that only made it worse, for when somebody says that there is nothing funny, it only makes everything seem even funnier. Eventually she had been sent out of the classroom until she got her giggling under control, and was then admitted back in after a stern rebuke from the teacher for laughing over nothing and disturbing the whole class. But it was not nothing – it was poor Mr Longman, the publisher . . .

She collected herself. 'I'm sorry, Mma. I understand. It's just that you and I are talking at cross-purposes. I have come here because I wanted to find something out, and you have imagined that I have come here because I am being mistreated by my husband.' She paused. 'Is that right, Mma? I take it that this is what you do – you help people with bad husbands.'

Maria visibly stiffened. 'What did you come to find out? Are you from the newspaper?'

Mma Ramotswe shook her head. 'No, I am nothing like that.'

This did little to reassure Maria. 'Then you have been sent by a man . . . by a husband?'

Mma Ramotswe held up her hands in protest. 'Definitely not.'

'Then why have you come?'

Mma Ramotswe spoke carefully. She knew that this was her chance to elicit the information she needed. At the same time, she knew that she should not deceive Maria; she would not lie.

'I am interested in helping Lakshmi. I suspect she has suffered much.'

All that she had said was true: she *was* interested in helping Lakshmi.

'She cannot be blamed,' said Maria forcefully. 'How can anybody blame her for that?'

Mma Ramotswe nodded understandingly. 'I can't,' she said.

'No,' said Maria. 'She put up with it for a long, long time. For years. And then she strikes out – which is what most people would have done well before she did – and he goes to the police and accuses her of attempting to murder him! Can you believe it, Mma?'

Mma Ramotswe sighed. 'It is very hard to believe something like that, Mma.' She made a quick calculation. 'Those police over the border ... ow, they're corrupt. They were in her husband's pocket, of course.'

She had made the right assumption.

'Of course they were,' said Maria. 'He paid them, I believe. So they put her on their wanted list.'

Mma Ramotswe was thinking. Now the whole story made sense. 'It was good of her brother to shelter her,' she said.

'He is a good man, I believe,' said Maria. 'But actually, he is her cousin.'

'Of course. He is her cousin. Of course. Did I say brother?'

'Yes.'

'That is my mistake. I know he is her cousin.' That was true: she did know now.

'And you have been good to her too,' continued Mma Ramotswe. 'You have done so much.'

Maria looked down modestly. 'We try, Mma. The support groups are very important for people in her position. They let her know that she has sisters. That makes a difference, you know, Mma.'

Mma Ramotswe inclined her head in agreement. Yes, women who suffered had to know that they had sisters – it was this that made the difference between hope and despair. And there were always sisters; no matter how difficult your situation was, there were sisters, vast legions of them – an army, in fact – who would be ready to help you. But you had to be able to find them, to tell them of your troubles, before the help could materialise; and that was not always easy.

Maria went back to the tap to pour another glass of water, which she handed to Mma Ramotswe. 'But now, Mma, you said something about helping her. How are you helping that poor woman?'

Mma Ramotswe took a sip from the glass of water. 'It is a strange story, Mma. You see, I am Mma Ramotswe of the No. 1 Ladies' Detective Agency. I am a person who helps people with their problems. Lakshmi's cousin came to see me and told me about her, although he did not give me her name. He said he wanted me to find out who she is.'

Maria's expression was one of puzzlement, and Mma Ramotswe told her that the story was even more complicated. She decided to tell her everything, and over the next few minutes explained what she had been asked to do, and why. Maria listened intently; at the end she sat down heavily on a kitchen chair and sank her head in her hands. 'This is hopeless,' she said. 'If the immigration people find out who she is they will check her name against the list they get from the police over the border. Those police give them lists of people they're looking for, so they can check any residence permit applications from South Africa. If the immigration people find her name on that list, they will simply send her back over the border – into the arms of the police.'

'And of her husband,' added Mma Ramotswe.

'Exactly,' said Maria.

Mma Ramotswe put down the empty glass. 'We cannot let that happen, Mma,' she said. 'We cannot.'

## Chapter Thirteen

# The Dish of Yesterday

If Mma Ramotswe had Sengupta affairs to keep her busy, Mma Makutsi was almost entirely preoccupied with the Handsome Man's De Luxe Café. The work on the kitchen had been accomplished even more quickly than promised, as had the painting and the delivery of the tables and chairs. There was now a café, even if the paint was still not completely dry here and there, and despite the fact that some of the kitchen shelves had yet to be cut to size and put up. What mattered was that the public could be invited to begin using the café at eight o'clock the next morning. Breakfast would be available until eleven o'clock, at which point lunch would be on the menu until two. Dinner would be served from six o'clock onwards, and the café would shut its doors at nine. This was to be the pattern of the new business.

Phuti had warned Mma Makutsi about staff. 'That is going to

be your problem, Grace,' he said. 'There are plenty of people looking for work, but how many of these are the right person?' He shook his head sadly, as memories returned of his own experience at the Double Comfort Furniture Store. 'I can tell you, that's the problem every business faces – getting staff you can trust.'

She had taken the warning seriously: Phuti knew what he was talking about when it came to running a business. And when it came to unsuitable employees, his views were, of course, coloured by the fact that he had employed none other than Violet Sephotho in the bed department of the store. That had been a complete debacle, as he had eventually discovered that Violet's impressive sales record was entirely attributable to the unconventional and unauthorised inducements she put the way of male customers. That was a famous case, but there was also the equally awkward case of the employee who was found to be stealing furniture from the store. The size of furniture normally prevents its being stolen from under the noses of the management, but in this case the employee had been removing items of furniture piece by piece, disassembling tables and chairs and then removing them leg by leg, seat by seat, over a period of days.

'You have to be careful, Grace,' said Phuti. 'You never know.'

*You never know.* She had pondered the words. No, one never knew, but just as you never knew what difficulties you might encounter, you also never knew about the positive things the future might hold.

'I shall be very careful, Phuti,' she said. 'But I have a good chef, remember, and he is the one who has chosen the waiting staff. He has the contacts, you see.'

Phuti looked doubtful. 'But you are the boss. You should choose these people.'

'The chef is the one who'll be working with them,' she said. 'He must have a good relationship with them.'

Phuti remained sceptical. 'You are the manager, Grace. A manager must manage.'

'I shall manage,' she reassured him. 'I am getting ready to do a lot of managing.'

Phuti had another query. 'Have you planned the menu yet?'

'The chef is doing that. That is his department.'

'I see.'

She sought to reassure him further. 'He has been working on all of this, Phuti. He has found a good waiter and a good waitress. They are very experienced, apparently. And he has written out the menu. I am going to type it up.'

She handed her husband the sheet of paper that Thomas had passed on to her. There were greasy fingerprints down the side of it – 'That is because it is written by a chef,' explained Mma Makutsi.

Phuti struggled to decipher the chef's handwriting. 'Small mouth,' he said. 'What is this about mouths? Small mouth, and I see he has something called big mouth.'

Mma Makutsi smiled. 'That is the fashionable term, Phuti. *Small mouth* refers to the size of the portion. That is the first course, you see. You start with the *small mouth* and then you move on to the *big mouth.*'

Phuti shrugged. 'Why doesn't he say *first course* and *second course?*'

Mma Makutsi did not answer the question. 'What do you think about the dishes? They are very tempting, aren't they?'

Phuti read down the list. Under *Small Mouth* there were various items on toast: *Scrambled Eggs on toast. Sardines and Baked Beans on toast. Cheese and Pineapple on toast. Sliced Sausages and Tomato Sauce on toast.* 'There is a lot of toast,' he observed.

Mma Makutsi replied that this was quite normal. 'Many people will want a quick snack,' she said. 'They do not want to be sitting for a long time waiting for their food to be prepared. They want food they can eat quickly and then get on with their busy lives.' She paused. 'These people are busy executives, you see. They are the people who are going to want toast.'

Phuti moved on to the *Big Mouth* list. She watched his lips move as he read – a habit of his that she always meant to talk to him about but had never broached. 'This is a very interesting menu,' he said at last. 'This chef . . . '

'He has a lot of experience,' Mma Makutsi said hurriedly. 'He trained in these big hotels – the Sun, the Grand Palm – all those big, important places.'

Phuti did not argue. 'I'm sure he did, Grace. It's just that some of these dishes are . . . '

She finished the sentence for him. 'Unusual. Yes, they will be the talk of the town. I am quite sure of that, Phuti.'

Phuti returned to the menu. 'What is this *Dish of Yesterday?*' he asked, pointing to an item at the head of the list.

Mma Makutsi laughed nervously. 'Oh, he told me about that when he gave me the menu. It is the leftovers from the day before.'

'Usually menus have a dish of the day,' said Phuti mildly. 'I've never seen a dish of yesterday.' He glanced at her reproachfully. 'You shouldn't tell people that they're having leftovers, you know. People don't like that. It's as bad as saying "second-hand food".'

Mma Makutsi's eyes widened. 'Oh no, Rra! It is nothing like that.'

'I'm just expressing an opinion,' said Phuti. 'I am not one to judge these things, I am saying what I think.'

She considered this. It was a curious thing to say; anybody who said anything at all was making a judgement, and she did not see how claiming that you were only expressing an opinion changed that. There was no time for such discussion, though, as Phuti Radiphuti had moved on to the next item on the menu.

'Tomato Soup with floating pumpkin pieces,' he read.

'Yes,' said Mma Makutsi defensively. 'That is the soup.' She paused, and then added, 'Of the day.'

'Not the soup of yesterday?'

'Hah,' she said. 'No, it is not the soup of yesterday: it is tomato soup with pumpkin pieces.'

'They float?' asked Phuti.

'That's what it says, Phuti. You see, these days it is very fashionable to have things floating in food. There are things called *croutons*, which are really pieces of fried bread – or that's what you and I would call them – but they are *croutons* and they float on the top of soup. These bits of pumpkin will be like *croutons*.'

It was so far from Bobonong, she thought; so far. There had been no *croutons* in Bobonong.

'But does pumpkin float, Grace? I always thought that pumpkin was quite heavy. I do not think that it would float in tomato soup.' He waited for a reaction, but she remained silent. 'So perhaps this will be tomato soup with *sunken* pumpkin pieces.' He paused again. 'Perhaps it could be called *Tomato Soup Surprise* – the surprise would come when you found pieces of pumpkin at the bottom of your soup.'

Mma Makutsi was tight-lipped. 'I do not think so,' she muttered. 'I think that this pumpkin will float. The chef must have tried it out before.'

Phuti shrugged. 'Perhaps. Perhaps.' He pointed to the item below the soup. 'The Handsome Man's Hungry Sandwich,' he read. 'This says that it is a sandwich with beef, eggs, sausage, lettuce and ... and chips.' He was puzzled by the chips. 'Chips, Grace? Chips?'

'They are very popular,' said Mma Makutsi. 'Look at Charlie and Fanwell – what do they eat if they get half the chance? Chips.'

'They are boys,' said Phuti. 'They are young. They are not the sort of person you want to attract to the Handsome Man's De Luxe Café. They are suitable for ordinary, second- or third-class cafés.'

'Everybody likes chips,' said Mma Makutsi. 'I have heard that the British High Commissioner serves chips if you have dinner at that place.'

'I do not think so,' said Phuti. 'They will serve things that British people like to eat. And the same goes for the Americans.'

'They are always eating hamburgers,' said Mma Makutsi.

Phuti did not disagree. 'Yes, they like hamburgers. But the point I was trying to make, Mma, is that chips do not go with sandwiches. You cannot put chips in a sandwich. People do not do that, Mma.'

'But chips go with eggs and also with sausages? They go with those things, don't they?'

Phuti nodded.

'And there are eggs and sausage in the sandwich, aren't there? So the chips go with those.' She looked at him defiantly. 'That is why they are there.'

He handed the menu back to her. 'It is going to be a very interesting restaurant, Grace,' he said.

Mma Makutsi smiled at her husband. He was so generous, so encouraging. 'Yes,' she said. 'I have a very good feeling about it now.'

Phuti hesitated. Then he closed his eyes and said, 'So . . . s . . . s . . . so do I, Grace.'

His stammer rarely manifested itself now, but when it did come back, it was because he felt doubt or foreboding. It was as power-ful an omen as any of those signs that traditional people – people who lived all their lives in the bush, far from a town – could read in the way the wind moved in the trees, or the way a beetle scurried across a path, or a flock of birds rose up from a sheltering tree. Phuti knew that you should not ignore these signs, because as often as not they warned you of what was going to happen.

She told him that the chef would be cooking them dinner before the restaurant opened officially. 'It's to show us what he can do,' she said. 'He will do that tonight and I shall invite Mma Ramotswe and Mr J. L. B. Matekoni to join us.'

'That is very good,' said Phuti. 'I am looking forward to it already.' But he was not – he was merely being supportive, as any good husband should be when his wife insists on embarking on something that he feels is not a good idea and he knows that it is far too late to express reservations. That is the point at which wholehearted support is required, and he would give it.

Mma Ramotswe was pleased with the invitation that Mma Makutsi issued that day.

'I cannot remember when Mr J. L. B. Matekoni and I went out to dinner,' she said. 'Now, let me think . . . '

Mma Makutsi waited. 'It will be very good, Mma.'

'Yes, I'm sure it will. This new chef of yours . . . '

'Thomas. He is a very well-known chef. He has cooked in all the big hotels. Their standards are very high. We can expect some very good food.'

Mma Ramotswe nodded. She was still trying to remember when she and Mr J. L. B. Matekoni had last been out to dinner and was having difficulty in bringing the occasion to mind. But it was time for morning tea in the office, and Mr J. L. B. Matekoni and Fanwell would be coming through shortly from the garage next door. She could ask him; perhaps he would remember.

'This chef of yours,' asked Mma Ramotswe. 'What did you say his name was?'

'He is called Thomas.'

'Thomas who?'

Mma Makutsi looked out of the window. 'He doesn't use his other name, Mma. That is sometimes the way with . . . with chefs.'

Mma Ramotswe said she found that very odd. 'Is he ashamed of his name?'

Mma Makutsi shook her head. 'I don't think so. He is a very pleasant, cheerful man. He does not look like somebody who is ashamed of his name.'

'What about his *omang*?' asked Mma Ramotswe. The *omang* was the identity card that every citizen of Botswana had.

'I haven't seen it,' said Mma Makutsi.

Mma Ramotswe drew in her breath. It was a fundamental precaution to be taken before giving anybody a job. A person who did not have an *omang* was likely to be working illegally – and that had consequences; surely Mma Makutsi knew that.

'If you haven't looked at his *omang*, Mma Makutsi, then I'm afraid . . . ' She trailed off.

'He's not illegal,' said Mma Makutsi quickly. 'You can tell when somebody's illegal. Thomas is obviously a Motswana.'

'From the way he talks? That doesn't tell you much, Mma. Foreigners can speak Setswana very well. And English. You cannot tell just by listening to him.'

Mma Makutsi obviously did not want to discuss the matter further. 'Oh, well,' she said. 'I'm sure he's fine.' She had switched on the electric kettle and it was beginning to make its familiar whistling sound, which signified that the water was reaching boiling point. As she got up to fill the two office teapots – one for ordinary tea and one for redbush – the door was pushed open and Fanwell appeared, closely followed by Mr J. L. B. Matekoni. Both were wiping their hands on the rough blue paper that had replaced their traditional lint.

'This paper is no good for oil,' said Mr J. L. B. Matekoni. 'It does not absorb enough. We shall have to find some more of that lint, you know. That is what mechanics have always used. Now those people are trying to change everything.'

It was never made clear who *those people* were. They were referred to from time to time by Mr J. L. B. Matekoni when he had occasion to complain about the vagaries of bureaucrats, or the car-makers who produced complicated electronics for their cars, or for any of those people who made life difficult for a small business.

'It is the modern way,' said Mma Makutsi over her shoulder. 'We have to move forwards, Rra. It is all for the sake of progress, Rra.'

Mr J. L. B. Matekoni made a snorting sound and tossed his crumpled blue paper into the wastepaper bin. 'I am not modern,' he said. 'And there are many other people who are not modern. We do not want to move forwards at all. We want to stay exactly where we are, because there is nothing wrong with that place.' He looked at Mma Ramotswe, and then at Mma Makutsi, as if expecting a refutation of this defence of conservatism, but there was none. He decided, nonetheless, to repeat his position. 'That place is the place we have always been, and if you think that where you have been is where you should be, then why go to another place that you do not know at all and may not be as good as the place you were in before somebody came along and said to you that you must go forwards – which is not what you wanted to do?'

At first nobody answered, but then Fanwell, who had been listening intently, broke the silence. 'That is true, Rra,' he said, 'but sometimes there will be a reason to go forwards. If you think that it would be better to do things a different way, then surely you should say so – and people should listen to you.'

Mr J. L. B. Matekoni gazed into his mug of tea. '*If* it is better, Fanwell – *if* it is better. I am happy to change if it is really better to do things in a new way, but only if people can show me that. That is the problem. There are many people who want to change things for the sake of change. That is what I object to.'

Mma Ramotswe looked up. 'You are right, Rra. I think you are right. There is no reason to change things that we have simply because they are old. Old things can be very good at what they are doing. The fact that they are old does not matter.'

This caught Mma Makutsi's attention. 'I'm not so sure, Mma Ramotswe,' she chipped in. 'What about shoes?'

They all turned to look at her, and then their collective gazes moved down towards her feet. She was wearing a pair of blue open-toed shoes. Although they did not appear old, they were nonetheless clearly not new.

'I am very happy with my old shoes,' said Mma Ramotswe. 'As you know, I have very wide feet.'

Fanwell peered over the rim of his mug of tea at Mma Ramotswe's feet, which could be seen under her desk. 'It is not your fault, Mma,' he said. 'I have an aunt who has feet like that. When she walks in the sand people sometimes think that her foot-prints look like an elephant's. They say: *Look, an elephant has gone this way.*'

Mma Makutsi threw him a glance. 'Of course it's nobody's fault. Nobody can be blamed for their feet, and Mma Ramotswe's feet are not all that wide. They are very good feet.'

'Traditional feet,' said Mr J. L. B. Matekoni.

They all looked at him.

'There is nothing wrong with having traditional feet,' he said, rather nervously. 'They are the sort of feet that have done us very well for a long time.' He paused. 'It's as I was saying – there are things that have always worked well and do not need to be changed. We do not need to be trying to get these thin, modern feet that people talk about. They will be no use if things get difficult.'

There was an awkward silence. Now Fanwell spoke. 'What were you going to say about shoes, Mmaitumelang?' He used the traditional method of address: Mma Makutsi, as mother of Itumelang, her first born, might be addressed as 'Mother of Itumelang'.

Mma Makutsi smiled at the compliment. 'Thank you, Fanwell. I was just going to say that shoes are an example of things that do not need to be replaced if they are doing a good job. Those shoes of Mma Ramotswe's, those brown shoes—'

Mma Ramotswe interrupted her. 'They are not actually brown, Mma. They used to be cream-coloured. They have become brown.'

'That doesn't matter,' said Mma Makutsi quickly. 'Shoes will find the colour that suits them, and that is what they will be. And anyway it is more practical to have brown shoes in this country. There is a great deal of sand in Botswana, and brown is the right colour for shoes.'

'But yours are blue,' pointed out Fanwell.

Mma Makutsi gave a nonchalant shrug. 'It is also possible to wear blue shoes, or shoes of any other colour for that matter. All that I am saying is that those who wear brown shoes do so for a perfectly good reason. They are being practical. It is very important to be practical when it comes to shoes.'

Both Mma Ramotswe and Mr J. L. B. Matekoni looked up sharply at this. Of the many things for which Mma Makutsi had a reputation, the wearing of sensible shoes was not one. They would not say anything about that, though, as they knew all about Mma Makutsi's prickliness on some matters. Shoes certainly fell into that category. Fanwell, though, with the openness –

and perhaps the lack of discretion – of youth felt no such compunction.

'I do not think those shoes you're wearing are very practical,' he said.

The atmosphere immediately became tense, but Fanwell, who was not picking this up, ploughed on. 'You see,' he continued, 'those shoes of yours have heels that are far too high. And too thin, Mma. Surely there is a big danger that one of the heels will get caught in a hole. There are many holes in Botswana – wherever you look, there are holes.'

Mr J. L. B. Matekoni interrupted him. 'There are fewer holes in this country than in some other places, young man. There are many countries that are just one big hole, as far as I can make out.'

'Yes,' snapped Mma Makutsi. 'Mr J. L .B. Matekoni is right. You should not go talking about holes like that. You'll fall into one yourself if you're not careful.'

He did not appear to be discouraged. 'I was only saying that you could get one of your heels stuck in a hole in the floor, for example.'

'There are no holes in our floor here,' said Mma Ramotswe, trying to defuse the situation. 'I don't think the danger is all that great.'

'But what about outside?' challenged Fanwell. 'You should see some of the holes in that car park near Riverwalk. Have you seen them, Mma?'

'They aren't serious holes,' said Mr J. L. B. Matekoni. 'I think they've fixed them anyway.'

'I've got eyes,' said Mma Makutsi. 'I'm not going to go and walk into a hole, Fanwell.'

'Of course she isn't,' said Mma Ramotswe.

Fanwell shrugged his shoulders. 'I was just pointing something out,' he said. 'But there's another thing: those shoes go *click, click,* when you walk in them, Mma. They make this clicking sound. *Click, click.*'

'So?' said Mma Makutsi.

'They are not good shoes for a detective to wear,' said Fanwell.

Mma Makutsi stared at him uncomprehendingly. 'What are you saying, Rra?' she asked. 'What is this *click, click?*'

Fanwell put down his mug. 'How can you creep up on anybody, Mma? They will hear you – *click, click* – and they'll say: "There's somebody coming, we must stop what we're doing." That is what they'll say, Mma, and that will mean that you will never get close enough to hear anything. That is what I meant, Mma; that is why those shoes are no good for detective work.'

Mma Makutsi, Mma Ramotswe and Mr J. L. B. Matekoni were silent. Mma Ramotswe thought that it was time to change the subject; she had been thinking about dinner.

'We have been asked out,' she said to Mr J. L. B. Matekoni. 'Mma Makutsi has invited us to have dinner at her new restaurant this evening. It is not open yet, but this will be a special demonstration by the chef.'

'Oh,' said Mr J. L. B. Matekoni. 'That is very good news. Thank you, Mma Makutsi.'

Mma Makutsi acknowledged this graciously. 'That is all right,' she said. 'My chef is planning to show us what he can do.'

She cast her eyes downwards, in modesty, as she referred to *her chef.* But he *was* her chef, she thought, and she should not be ashamed of it. In due course she might get used to it, as people got used to changes in their circumstances. One might become president, for example, and feel, for the first few weeks at least, that it was strange that everybody should be opening the door for you and calling you 'Mma President' but then you would become accustomed to it and you would be president, even in your dreams. The world of dreams, of course, could take some time to adjust to where you were in life. She still dreamed that she was Grace Makutsi, writing her school examinations in that stuffy classroom up in Bobonong, where you had to close your eyes tight to remember the facts that you had committed to memory. *The main rivers of Africa are the following ... In the north, the land rises to make a plateau ... The three representatives of Botswana went to London to ask Queen Victoria ... A prime number is one that ...* Or she dreamed that she was at the Botswana Secretarial College, but, curiously, knew that she had already left it and should not be there; dreams could be like that – you knew that there was something contradictory, something that did not make sense, and yet everything seemed so real. So you could be at the Botswana Secretarial College and find that there was Violet Sephotho in the front row, paying avid attention to what the lecturer was saying, and you wanted to tell everybody that she did not really mean it, that she did not really care about shorthand or filing, and that it was men she was thinking of. But you could not speak, you were mute, just as you sometimes cannot run in a dream when you really need to get away from something, and Violet Sephotho rose to her feet and stepped forward to receive the prize for the most attentive student and you were struck by the sheer injustice of it.

Fanwell took a sip of his tea. 'I am sure it will be very good,' he said. 'You are very lucky.'

A silence descended. Mma Ramotswe glanced at Mma Makutsi, who had stopped thinking about dreams and was pouring a mug of tea.

'You can come too, Fanwell,' said Mma Makutsi. 'You are invited.'

Fanwell grinned with pleasure. 'I am already hungry,' he said.

Mma Ramotswe looked at Mr J. L. B. Matekoni. 'I was trying

to remember, Rra,' she said. 'I was trying to remember when we last went out to dinner together.'

Mr J. L. B. Matekoni frowned, and sat down on the spare chair near the filing cabinet. 'It must be a long time ago,' he said. 'I do not remember what we had to eat.'

'Or where it was?' prompted Mma Ramotswe.

He shook his head. 'I do not remember that either.'

Mma Ramotswe was silent. She had decided that they had never been out to dinner, but she did not want to spell it out. And looking across the room at Mma Makutsi, she could tell that she, too, seemed to be thinking: she had never been out to dinner with Phuti either. Well, thought Mma Ramotswe, all this was about to change.

'I have never been to a restaurant,' announced Fanwell. 'Ever.'

Mr J. L. B. Matekoni looked at his assistant and then threw an appreciative glance towards Mma Makutsi. He was grateful for her act of kindness in inviting the young man, who had had so little in his life, after all. He had always maintained that Mma Makutsi had a kind heart, whatever impression she gave of severity. 'We should not confuse strictness with unkindness,' he said. 'Sometimes they are both there at the same time.' Of course he had never been able to manage that himself; he had never been able to be strict with his apprentices. But that was a matter he would get round to addressing some other time – maybe.

'Time for work,' he said, and then trying to sound firm, he added: 'Work, then dinner, Fanwell – that is the rule, I think.'

Fanwell followed his employer out of the room, leaving Mma Makutsi and Mma Ramotswe exchanging expressions of bemusement.

'Sometimes I wonder what goes on in those boys' heads,' said Mma Makutsi. 'I do not think that their brains are organised in the same way as ours, Mma. They have different wiring, I think.'

Mma Ramotswe smiled. 'It is sometimes difficult to understand them,' she said. 'But that is often the case, isn't it, Mma? Men and women look at one another and wonder what the other is thinking. And I believe you're right – we do have different brains from them. I think that is well known, Mma Makutsi.'

Mma Makutsi nodded her agreement. 'It is very sad for men to have these strange brains,' she said. 'We must not be unkind to them.'

'Or to anybody,' said Mma Ramotswe.

'I agree, Mma.'

Mma Makutsi collected the teacups and mugs, stacking them on the tray for washing before returning to her desk, where a pile of correspondence awaited her. She looked first at the letters, then across the room to Mma Ramotswe's desk. They were partners in the business, although she accepted that Mma Ramotswe was the senior partner and she was the junior. Yet, even taking that into account, should a partner have to do secretarial work? She thought not. She should have a secretary herself; why not?

Of course she knew what Mma Ramotswe would say if she raised the matter. She would point out, quite reasonably, that the business did not make enough money to employ another person. And she would nod and agree with that, but then she would say: 'And Charlie?'

Now the idea occurred. There was not enough work for Charlie to do as a detective – that was clear enough, whatever tasks were cooked up for him – but if he was going to be around the place, and paid, then why should he not perform secretarial duties? Charlie could type – like many young men he could operate a computer keyboard – and that meant that he could type out letters and even do some filing if he received a bit of instruction. She would have to be careful about that, of course, as incorrect

187

filing could have severe consequences. 'Put a letter in the wrong file,' said one of the lecturers at the Botswana Secretarial College, 'and you can kiss goodbye to it.' That was true, she thought – it was absolutely true – and if she were to teach Charlie to file she would drum that into him right at the beginning.

Yes, she thought, Charlie could be a secretary. It would do him good to learn that there was nothing undignified for a young man to take on a job normally performed by a young woman. People had to learn not to be sexist about these things; if there could be female managing directors and engineers, then there could be male secretaries and nurses, and Charlie might as well get used to that sooner rather than later.

She would put the idea to Mma Ramotswe later – over dinner, perhaps.

That evening, shortly after six-thirty, when the sun had sunk into the Kalahari and the sky had turned the pale blue that comes at that hour, Mma Ramotswe, Mr J. L. B. Matekoni and Fanwell drove across the town to the Handsome Man's De Luxe Café, now almost ready to welcome the public. As Mr J. L. B. Matekoni parked his truck they admired the newly painted sign – the work of the same hand that all those years ago had written *The No. 1 Ladies' Detective Agency* above Mma Ramotswe's own premises. If one were to look for omens, then this might surely be one: since Mma Ramotswe's sign had presided over a business that prospered (or, at least, stayed afloat), so too might Mma Makutsi's sign announce a successful undertaking.

Or so Mma Ramotswe thought. 'Very good,' she said as she surveyed the newly restored building. 'That is a very welcoming sign. People will want to go in.'

'That is what a sign must do,' agreed Mr J. L. B. Matekoni. 'If a sign is unfriendly, you will get no business.'

Fanwell was concerned about the name. 'And if you're not handsome?' he asked. 'Where do you go then?'

'You are very handsome, Fanwell,' said Mma Ramotswe. 'So that is not your problem.'

Fanwell appeared embarrassed, but at the same time pleased. 'I am not,' he said modestly. 'Charlie is handsome. I am just average. The girls always look at Charlie. If they look at me, they shake their heads and turn away.'

'Nonsense!' exclaimed Mma Ramotswe. 'And if they look at Charlie, then they are very silly. We know that Charlie is dangerous to girls.' She paused, as if to consider an interesting possibility. 'In fact, there are some young men who should wear a sign round their neck saying "Beware".'

Mr J. L. B. Matekoni laughed. 'That is true, I think. Maybe a sign saying "Girls beware – and cars beware too".'

'He is not that bad,' said Fanwell. 'And now he is a detective, anyway.'

'Then there should also be a sign saying "Clients beware".'

'We must not be unkind,' said Mma Ramotswe. 'Charlie is learning. He's becoming more mature.'

'Yes,' said Fanwell. 'Soon the young girls will think he is too old. He will not like that, I think. Hah!'

The subject of Charlie was dropped as Phuti Radiphuti's car had drawn up beside them. They all went in together, Mma Makutsi proudly announcing as they entered the café, 'Here we are, Mma Ramotswe – this is my new place.'

It was an important moment for her. She had not forgotten – nor would ever forget – how Mma Ramotswe had given her that first chance and was responsible, therefore, for everything that had flowed from it. Had she not found that job in Gaborone, then she might have ended up in Lobatse or somewhere else, and would then never have gone to that dance class and met Phuti

Radiphuti. And then there would have been no fine husband, no new house, no baby, no Handsome Man's De Luxe Café – all of this she owed to Mma Ramotswe. And here she was welcoming her, that kind woman who had changed her life, who had taught her so much, into a business that she had created herself. It was a proud moment indeed.

'It is a very good café,' said Mma Ramotswe as she looked around. 'Those red tables, Mma – they are very smart. And the lights! They are very bright. Everybody will like those.'

'Yes, they will,' said Mr J. L. B. Matekoni. 'There will be big crowds coming here, Mma; very big crowds.'

Mma Makutsi made a modest gesture. 'Word will take time to get out,' she said. 'Rome was not built in a day. I have read that.'

'Rome took many weeks to build,' said Fanwell. 'There were no bulldozers in those days.'

'That is true,' said Phuti. 'Bulldozers were not invented until . . . '

They looked at him expectantly.

'. . . until much later,' he finished.

The chef appeared through a door at the back of the café. 'So,' he announced in a booming, confident voice. 'So, welcome everybody. Welcome to dinner.'

Introductions were made and they sat down at the table nearest the kitchen area. In the background, the two waiters, one a young man of extremely muscular build, and the other a young woman in a blue dress, stood at the ready.

'What have you prepared for us, chef?' asked Mma Makutsi.

'I have prepared steak,' he said. 'Steak with a special sauce. Potatoes in butter. Green vegetables and cauliflower with cheese on the top. It is called *The Steak No. 1 Special* in honour of Mma Ramotswe.'

This was greeted with delight – and laughter.

The waiter came to take the orders for drinks. Mr J. L. B. Matekoni ordered a Lion Beer, as did Fanwell, after Phuti Radiphuti had explained that there would be no charge for either food or drink. Mma Makutsi and Mma Ramotswe, neither of whom drank, ordered lemonade, and Phuti asked for water with a slice of lemon and some sugar.

'You should drink beer, Rra,' said the waiter. 'That is the best drink for men.'

Phuti frowned. 'I do not like beer,' he said.

The waiter's jaw set. 'Most men do,' he said.

Mma Ramotswe glanced anxiously at Mma Makutsi.

'He says that he wants water with lemon and some sugar,' said Mma Makutsi. 'That is what he wants.'

The waiter shrugged. 'Beer would be better,' he said. 'But if that's what you want ... '

'It is,' said Phuti, adding, 'If you don't mind.'

The waiter turned on his heels and disappeared into the kitchen area.

'I'm going to have to talk to that young man,' said Mma Makutsi.

'Perhaps it's his first job,' said Fanwell. He looked thoughtful. 'I think I may have seen him somewhere before.'

'Where?' asked Mma Makutsi. 'Does he live near your place?'

Fanwell shook his head. 'I don't think so. It is a long time ago maybe. His face looks familiar – you know how it is.'

'There are some people like that,' said Phuti Radiphuti. 'You think that you know them, but you don't really. They have the sort of face that looks familiar.'

Phuti and Mr J. L. B. Matekoni now struck up a conversation about a new van that Phuti had ordered for the Double Comfort Furniture Store. Fanwell joined in; he had views on the make of van and the conversation soon became quite technical. Mma

Ramotswe was examining her surroundings, taking in the details of the décor and watching the activity in the kitchen.

'It's a very good idea to let people see what's going on in the kitchen,' she said. 'That will stop them becoming impatient while they are waiting for their food.'

'Exactly,' said Mma Makutsi. 'They will like that.'

The waiter returned with the drinks.

'Here's your sugar water,' he said dismissively as he put a glass down in front of Phuti Radiphuti.

Phuti's politeness prevailed over the waiter's surliness. 'Thank you, Rra,' he said.

Mma Makutsi bristled. 'You do know who we are?' she muttered.

The waiter glanced at her. 'You're that woman,' he said.

'Yes,' she said quietly. 'I'm that woman.'

A few minutes later the food arrived. It was preceded by its aroma – a delicious waft of beef and gravy that would gladden the heart, thought Mma Ramotswe, of any citizen in Botswana. Cattle – and beef – were at the heart of the culture, and she imagined what her father, the late Obed Ramotswe, would have made of the sight of the large steak on the plate before her, surrounded by its steaming vegetables and pool of sauce and gravy.

Mma Makutsi felt a mixture of pleasure and pride – pleasure at the anticipation of the succulent steak; pride at the thought that she had chosen a chef who could so engage the senses. She leaned forward slightly to savour more fully the delightful smell arising from the plate of food, and it was at this point that she heard the small voice from below.

*I wouldn't touch that, Boss!*

She froze where she was, her head tilted forward above the plate, furtively glancing at Mma Ramotswe beside her at the table. Had she heard anything? There was no reaction from her friend, who was gazing at her own plate with undisguised delight.

*It's a word of warning, Boss. You don't have to listen to us, of course – you often don't.*

Mma Makutsi caught her breath. She leaned back and looked down at her shoes. She had changed out of the blue open-toed pair and was now wearing a pair of red shoes with white cloth rosettes on the toes. In the centre of each rosette was a small glass button that now looked upwards, for all the world like an eye upon her. On the side of each shoe was a diamante clasp. It was one of her best pairs, if not her very best, and she had only worn them a couple of times before. This occasion, she had decided, was sufficiently auspicious to justify taking them out of the drawer they shared with the special shoes that she wore to weddings and funerals.

These shoes had never said anything to her before. The sh oes that seemed to speak were those who did the most work – the everyday, working shoes that had what she considered to be something of an old-fashioned union mentality: they were quick to complain about the slightest inconvenience, highly sensitive to questions of status, and quick to remind her of the rights of footwear. Her more formal shoes spoke less frequently, and tended to make comments that were obscure or highly allu- sive and not at all complaining. Perhaps these new shoes had picked up bad ways from the everyday shoes – had learned to make the sort of streetwise, cheeky remarks that working shoes made.

*Don't say we didn't warn you, Boss!* continued the high-pitched voice from below. *This sauce is made of lies. That's all we've got to say, Boss. That's it.*

She looked about her. Mr J. L. B. Matekoni had already sliced off a piece of meat and had it on his fork. Phuti Radiphuti's mouth was already full and he was rolling his eyes in an exaggerated gesture of gastronomic pleasure.

*Oh dear, Boss,* came the tiny voice. *Too late!*

She tried to put the shoes out of her mind. Her shoes often said things that proved to be untrue and if she started to heed everything they said, then life would become unduly difficult. No, she would enjoy the meal, just as everybody else seemed to be doing.

It did not take them long to finish as there was little conversation between mouthfuls. At the end, Fanwell sat back in his chair and rubbed his stomach. 'I would like to eat in this restaurant every day,' he said to Mma Makutsi. 'This is really good, Mma.'

Mma Makutsi acknowledged the compliment with a nod of her head. 'I'm glad you enjoyed it, Fanwell.'

Mma Ramotswe suggested that the chef be called over to their table. 'We must thank him properly,' she said.

Thomas came out of the kitchen, wiping his hands on a piece of paper towel. 'Everything met with your approval?'

Phuti took it upon himself to be the spokesman. 'Very much so,' he said. 'That was first class, Rra.'

'Good,' said Thomas.

'May I ask where you are from, Rra?' said Mma Ramotswe. As she posed the question, Mma Makutsi glanced at her anxiously.

Thomas shrugged. 'Where is any of us from?' he said. 'We start this life as little, little children, and we are always running around. Here, there, everywhere. Then we get bigger and we are still looking for the right place for us in the world. Later on, we ask ourselves: where am I going?'

'That's very interesting, Rra,' said Mma Ramotswe. 'But where are you actually from? Where is your village?'

Thomas crumpled up the piece of kitchen towel and tucked it into the pocket of his apron. 'My village is the world,' he said. 'That is where my heart is – in the world.'

194

'But where in the world?' persisted Mma Ramotswe. 'The world is a big place, and most of us have one small place in that big place. That is where we are from, I think.'

Mma Makutsi now tried to change the subject. 'I am from Bobonong myself,' she said. 'And I am proud of that place, even if it is far away from everywhere. But this meal, Rra, was so good! I think people will be lining up to eat here.'

'I hope so,' said Phuti.

Thomas smiled and returned to the kitchen – with relief, mused Mma Ramotswe, as she watched him go.

'To think that he produced that meal all by himself,' said Phuti. 'Sometimes it seems as if these chefs must have ten or twelve hands to keep all the pots and pans going at the same time.'

'But he's got a person helping him,' said Fanwell. 'I thought I saw a woman,' he explained. 'There was a woman back there when we came in. Then she went out.'

'Was there?' asked Mma Ramotswe. 'I didn't see anyone.'

'No, there wasn't anyone,' said Mma Makutsi.

*There was*, came a small, almost inaudible voice from below.

## Chapter Fourteen

# Tiny Points of Light

Households do not run themselves, Mma Ramotswe had often observed: there is shopping, cleaning, repairing and organising to do – and all of these, for some reason, seemed to be the responsibility of women, or almost always.

She thought that only one of these functions could not be described as a chore. No matter how much one tried to take a positive view of cleaning – no matter how frequently one told oneself that sweeping and dusting had their moments, it was difficult to see the whole business as anything but a use of time that could be more profitably and enjoyably spent doing something more satisfying. Even organising, which sounded as if it could be interesting, was really all about telling other members of the household what to do, checking up to see that they had done it, and asking them to do it when it transpired – as it usually did –

that they had not got round to doing it yet. No, shopping really was the sole item in the positive column of these household accounts.

Mma Ramotswe liked to do her shopping weekly, usually on a Friday afternoon. She knew that this was far from being the best day to pay a visit to the supermarket, as it was inevitably full of people buying provisions for the weekend. When a Friday coincided with the end of the month, and therefore with payday, the supermarket was even more crowded – this time with people whose kitchen cupboards had grown empty as money ran out. It was not hard to spot these people as they tended to help themselves to snacks from the contents of their trollies as they went around, to compensate for the short rations of the previous few days. That was perfectly all right, she felt, as long as the food from which they took these advance helpings was already measured and priced for the cashier. All that was happening there was that people were eating food that they were going to pay for anyway.

But this was not always so, and there were those who ate without paying. Mma Ramotswe had witnessed one particularly bad case only a few weeks earlier. She had been in the fruit and vegetable section of the supermarket when a woman – traditionally built, as Mma Ramotswe herself was – had come into sight, pushing a trolley and surrounded by five young children. This woman had stopped, looked over her shoulder, and then whispered instructions to her charges. The children waited for a moment or two and then fanned out across the supermarket floor, grabbing pieces of fruit from the counters and stuffing them into their mouths. They were, Mma Ramotswe thought, rather like a swarm of locusts descending on the land, picking the best of what they saw, munching hungrily as they marched across the landscape.

Almost too shocked to speak, she had stood there with her

mouth agape at the sheer effrontery of the behaviour on display. When she eventually recovered, she called out to the woman, now only a few yards away from her, 'Excuse me, Mma. Excuse me.'

The woman looked up, as if surprised to be addressed. 'Yes, Mma? What is your problem?'

'Problem? I have no problem,' said Mma Ramotswe. '*You* have a problem, Mma.'

The woman had stared at her with undisguised irritation. 'Why do you say I have a problem, Mma? I have no problem that I can see. If there are any problems, they must be *your* problems, not mine.'

Mma Ramotswe pointed at two of the youngsters, one of whom was halfway through a banana while the other gnawed at a large apple. 'Your children, Mma, are eating the fruit.'

'So,' said the woman. 'So, they are eating fruit. That is good for them, is it not? Does the government not say, *Eat lots of fruit and you will be very healthy?* Do they not say that, Mma?'

Mma Ramotswe marvelled at the woman's brazenness. 'But the government doesn't tell you to eat other people's fruit.'

The woman's irritation increased. 'This fruit does not belong to anybody yet. It has not been bought. We are not taking fruit from anybody.' She paused before delivering her final shot. 'So please mind your own business, Mma.'

With that, the woman had marshalled her brood of children – some still with their mouths full – and drifted away in the direction of the bread counter. Mma Ramotswe had stood quite still, hardly able to believe what she had seen. Mind her own business? But it was her business. When other people behaved dishonestly it *was* the business of others, because if we did not react to the bad behaviour of others, then we weakened the whole of society, and that was definitely part of everybody's business.

She hesitated. There is an inbuilt human reluctance to inform on other people; nobody likes to be thought of as a sneak, as somebody who runs to the authorities. And yet it was her duty, she felt, to warn the store that this woman and her little band of locusts were eating food that did not belong to them. So she went to one of the desks and told the young woman there what was happening. 'Now they have gone to the bread counter,' she said. 'They will be helping themselves there, too, unless you stop them.'

The young woman shrugged. 'We know that woman. She is always bringing her children in here.'

Mma Ramotswe waited for something further to be said, but the young woman simply shrugged again.

'You should stop them, Mma,' said Mma Ramotswe.

'Can't prove anything,' said the young woman. 'They never do it when we're watching. They are very clever.'

Mma Ramotswe stared at her in disbelief, but this merely elicited another shrug. And with that, the incident, it seemed, was closed. But she thought about it – both there, in the supermarket, as she did her own shopping, and afterwards, as she drove home in the white van. She thought of what her father, the late Obed Ramotswe, or even Seretse Khama himself would have said about this. They would have said: *This is not what Botswana needs.* And they were right, she felt, although she was relieved that, being late, they had been spared the sight of what she had witnessed.

On this occasion there was no such shocking incident at the supermarket, but there was nonetheless a meeting. This was with Mma Potokwani, whom Mma Ramotswe encountered in the supermarket's sauce and condiment section. Mma Potokwani was examining a jar of extra-strong pickle with the expression of one who is doubtful as to whether her palate will be able to bear the heat.

'Ah, Mma Ramotswe,' she said. 'Do you know whether this sauce is as hot as the jar claims? The label has a picture of a man with fire coming out of his mouth. Look.'

She handed her friend the jar for scrutiny. 'I believe this is very hot,' said Mma Ramotswe. 'But the picture is an exaggeration, I think. I do not think it will set you on fire.' For a moment she pictured Mma Potokwani with flames coming out of her mouth. She imagined herself reaching for a fire extinguisher and covering her friend in white foam, or pushing her down to the ground and covering her head with a fire blanket. It would be an undignified end to a meal.

The jar of sauce found its way into Mma Potokwani's trolley, and the conversation moved on from sauce to the possibility of a chat after they had both finished their shopping. An arrangement was made: they would meet in forty minutes at the café near the outside stairs. 'There is something I need to talk about, Mma,' said Mma Potokwani. 'It is quite a serious matter, I'm afraid.'

Mma Ramotswe did not relish spending the next forty minutes worrying, and so she asked Mma Potokwani what it was about.

'It is rather hard to explain,' said Mma Potokwani. 'It is to do with Mma Makutsi. I shall tell you once we sit down and can chat.'

To do with Mma Makutsi? This hardly helped, and by the time she found herself with Mma Potokwani at the Equatorial Café she was feeling thoroughly anxious. But even then, the conversation did not go straight to the subject of Mma Makutsi, but meandered gently in that direction, by way of a discussion of orphans, cake and guilt, and one or two other subjects of equal importance.

The subject of orphans was triggered by Mma Ramotswe's enquiry as to whether any new children had arrived at the Orphan Farm.

'There is a young boy,' said Mma Potokwani. 'He has recently come in. It is very sad. He lost his parents in a mining accident up at Selebi-Phikwe.'

'Both parents?' asked Mma Ramotswe. 'The mother as well as the father? Did they both go down the mine together? At the same time, Mma?'

Mma Potokwani waved the question aside. 'There are many women who go down mines,' she said. 'Women are always going down mines these days.'

Mma Ramotswe looked dubious. 'Are you sure, Mma?'

Mma Potokwani was sure. 'I could tell you some very sad stories,' she said. 'But what is the point? The fact of the matter is that the poor child has no parents. That is what we have to deal with. It does not matter how the parents were lost.'

'But it's unusual for two parents to be lost in the same mining disaster, don't you think?'

'The Lord works in strange ways,' said Mma Potokwani, closing down the discussion. 'That is all I have to say on the subject.'

They had moved on to cake, having ordered a slice each to eat with their tea. Mma Potokwani had told the waitress that she wanted a large piece, and she was sure that Mma Ramotswe felt the same. 'None of your thin slices,' she warned. 'I have seen you serve some very thin slices here. We do not want any of those, if you please.'

Mma Ramotswe had nodded her agreement. 'I see no reason why we should not have a large slice,' she said. 'Or even two. I do not feel guilty about eating cake any more. I used to, but no longer.'

'You are very wise,' said Mma Potokwani. 'How did you do it, Mma? Did you stop thinking about the things that made you feel guilty?'

Mma Ramotswe shook her head. 'I read an article in a magazine.

I was at the dentist and there was a magazine for the patients to read. I read an article under a headline that said: *Why you shouldn't feel guilty any more.* I started to read it but then the dentist called me in and I had to leave it in the waiting room.'

'It's always very annoying when that happens,' said Mma Potokwani. 'Sometimes I'm listening to something on the radio – something interesting – and one of the housemothers calls me for one emergency or another. It is always the same – you miss the ending.'

Mma Ramotswe was silent. 'I have a confession to make, Mma.'

Mma Potokwani raised an eyebrow. Had Mma Ramotswe been eating too much cake? Was that weighing on her? *Cake can weigh on people* . . . She smiled at the thought: it certainly could, and it weighed heavily on her, perhaps, as on other traditionally built people.

'After the dentist had finished,' Mma Ramotswe went on, 'I went back into the waiting room . . . and took the magazine.' She paused. 'It was very old, and I was just going to borrow it.'

*Is that all?* thought Mma Potokwani. If that was all that troubled Mma Ramotswe, then hers must be an unburdened conscience indeed; although small things could always exert an undue influence on those whose lives were otherwise largely spotless. She had known a man, a cousin of her husband, who had been tormented by an ancient act of minor dishonesty and had dwelt on what he had done until he had made himself sick with guilt and worry. And it was such a small thing: a matter of a neighbour's chicken that had wandered into his hen-coop and, rather than being sent back, had been allowed to stay. That was all, and yet he had dwelt on the incident for years and the neighbour could not understand why he kept being given chickens as a present on every conceivable occasion – Christmas, Botswana

202

Day, Seretse Khama's birthday, and so on. 'What have I done to deserve such a kind neighbour?' the recipient of this continued largesse had asked – a question that only made it worse for the donor, who thought: *If only he knew that I am not kind – I am a stealer of chickens.* Eventually he had confessed his torment to Mma Potokwani's husband, who had simply laughed and told him to forget the whole matter as he had more than made up for his wrongdoing. Rra Potokwani told the neighbour, in fact, who went round to see the cousin and told him that he should give the matter no further thought, as he himself had done exactly the same thing with one of his chickens that had wandered across the boundary between their properties. And this, it seemed, had been the absolution that the cousin had wanted all along, and he was released from self-reproach, although he distrusted his neighbour thereafter on the grounds that he seemed so unmoved by his own wrongdoing. If he could so easily overlook something like that, what else could he overlook?

'People are always taking magazines from waiting rooms,' said Mma Potokwani. 'Dentists don't mind about it – they know that it happens all the time.'

'I intended to take it back.'

Mma Potokwani was sure that Mma Ramotswe had done exactly that, but no, it appeared that she had not. 'I lost it,' she said. 'I read the article about guilt and it made me feel so guilty that I decided to take the magazine back the next day. But then I lost it, Mma. I don't know what happened to it.'

Mma Potokwani laughed. 'I thought it told you not to feel guilty.'

'But I did.'

'So what happened next?' asked Mma Potokwani.

'I bought a new magazine and took it to the waiting room. I told the receptionist that I had bought a present for the waiting room. It was so that other people could enjoy the magazine while they waited to have their teeth looked at. I said that it would take their minds off what lay ahead.'

Mma Potokwani thought that this would have been a great comfort for those facing the dentist's drill. Mma Ramotswe, though, had more to tell.

'The receptionist laughed,' she continued. 'She said: you must be another of those people who take our magazines and then regret it.'

'Oh,' said Mma Potokwani. Then she added, 'That lady is not very sympathetic, Mma. That was not a kind thing to say to somebody who had stolen a . . . borrowed a magazine and then felt bad about it.'

With orphans, cake and guilt all disposed of, it was time for Mma Potokwani to broach the subject of Mma Makutsi. 'Mma Makutsi,' she said simply, 'has, I believe, some café or other.'

Mma Ramotswe nodded. 'She is very proud of it,' she said. 'We went there for a meal the other day. She has a chef—'

Mma Potokwani interrupted her. 'A chef called Disang.'

Mma Ramotswe was cautious. 'I think he's called Thomas.'

'Yes, Thomas Disang.'

Mma Ramotswe looked down at her cup. She feared where this was going. 'Isn't Mma Makutsi's lawyer called Disang?'

'Yes,' said Mma Potokwani. 'That is his name. But it's also the name of the chef. And of the waiter. And the waitress, for that matter.'

A fresh pot of tea arrived, and Mma Potokwani raised her cup to take a deep draught. She was a quick drinker of tea, and always managed two or three cups to Mma Ramotswe's one. 'Yes. They are all Disangs – and they are all relatives of that lawyer of hers.'

'It is a common name,' said Mma Ramotswe. 'There are hundreds of Disangs.'

'It is certainly a common name,' agreed Mma Potokwani. 'But I can tell you this, Mma – those Disangs in that restaurant are all one family. The chef is the lawyer's brother. The waiter is the chef's son, and the waitress is the son's wife.'

Mma Ramotswe reflected on this. It was not uncommon for people to look after their relatives – it was a very African thing. If your cousin was in need, for instance, why not help him? Surely it was wrong, according to the old traditions, to let somebody close to you suffer need. Yes, but ... and that *but* was a very big one. That desire to help was one of the roots of the vine of corruption that had smothered so much of Africa.

'Does Mma Makutsi know all this?' asked Mma Ramotswe.

Mma Potokwani shook her head. 'I do not think she knows. And there is another thing she doesn't know: that Disang man cannot cook.'

Mma Ramotswe remembered their dinner. 'But he can cook, Mma. He's very good. He cooked for us the other night.'

Mma Potokwani shook her head slowly. 'He did not cook, Mma. That meal was cooked by somebody else.'

'But he was there in the kitchen,' protested Mma Ramotswe. 'They served it to us directly from the kitchen. He was there. I saw him.'

Mma Potokwani poured herself another cup of tea. 'It was cooked by one of my housemothers,' she said. 'She told me.'

Mma Ramotswe stared at her friend. She remembered what Fanwell had said about seeing a woman in the kitchen. She groaned inwardly. 'You may as well tell me everything, Mma,' she said.

Mma Potokwani put down her cup. 'She mentioned it to me casually,' she said. 'She wasn't trying to hide anything. I had gone to inspect her kitchen and had complimented her on her cooking. Then she said that she had recently cooked a meal for some people in a restaurant. She is the aunt of that chef. She said that she was very surprised that he had found a job in a restaurant as he is one of the worst cooks she knows. She also said that he is a good-for-nothing who never sticks at any job.'

'Oh,' said Mma Ramotswe. It was all she could think of to say.

'So I'm afraid those Disangs are taking advantage of Mma Makutsi,' continued Mma Potokwani. 'It will end in disaster, I'm afraid.'

Mma Ramotswe sighed. 'I'm afraid it will, too.'

'And it gets worse,' said Mma Potokwani.

'How can it get worse, Mma?'

Mma Potokwani refilled her teacup. 'That waiter – the chef's son – he's even more hopeless than his father. Apparently he spilled a whole plate of stew over one of the customers yesterday. I heard about it from our infant teacher, who was there. She said there was a terrific row and the waiter stormed off without apologising. The poor customer was covered in stew and had to clean himself up as best he could.'

'That is not good,' sighed Mma Ramotswe.

'And it gets even worse than that,' said Mma Potokwani. 'Did you see the *Botswana Daily News*? They had something on the front page. It said: *Read our restaurant reviewer's assessment of a new café – in tomorrow's* Daily News.'

Mma Ramotswe tried to be positive. 'That can help sometimes,' she said. 'Often these places really want a review. It can be an advertisement.'

'Except for one thing,' said Mma Potokwani. 'Do you know who has recently become their restaurant reviewer?' She did not wait for an answer. 'She signs her reviews with her initials: VS.'

'VS?'

Mma Potokwani let her friend work it out for herself. A louder sigh came, and that sigh was more of a groan. 'Violet Sephotho?' ventured Mma Ramotswe.

Mma Potokwani nodded. 'I'm afraid so,' she said.

'Oh my goodness,' said Mma Ramotswe. 'That is *very* bad.' She paused. 'What does that woman know about restaurants?'

'Nothing,' said Mma Potokwani. 'But then many people who write about things know nothing. As you yourself might say, Mma Ramotswe – that is well known. How does Violet get any of her jobs, Mma?'

Mma Ramotswe knew the answer but did not want to spell it out. The two women looked at one another – they understood.

'She must know a journalist,' said Mma Potokwani. 'She must know one of those journalists very well.'

Nothing more needed to be said. Violet Sephotho, sworn enemy of Mma Makutsi and graduate of the Botswana Secretarial College with barely fifty per cent in the final examinations, was incorrigible. There was no low to which she would not stoop in pursuit of her ambitions, which were money and men, in either order. The two goals, in fact, were intertwined: men brought money, or if they did not, they were not the sort of men in whom Violet was interested.

Mma Ramotswe stared out of the window of the Equatorial Café as this new piece of information sank in. Gaborone, although a city, was really a small town, as most cities were. Everybody read the *Botswana Daily News* and bad publicity in that quarter would kill Mma Makutsi's restaurant stone dead. People believed what they read – for the most part – and few, if any, of them would know that the initials VS stood for Violet Sephotho. And even if they did, not everybody knew about Violet's track record and would assume that a restaurant review would be written by somebody who had all the necessary experience and judgement to write such a thing. VS ... that could stand for *Very Suspect*, thought Mma Ramotswe, or perhaps *Very Spiteful*.

Mma Potokwani shook her head sorrowfully. 'She will be writing something very bad, I think.'

Mma Ramotswe was deep in thought. There had been no indication from Mma Makutsi that things were going wrong, although now that she came to think about it she had seemed a bit subdued over the last day or two since the restaurant opened. She was not sure how hands-on Mma Makutsi was planning to be with her restaurant – she had many other things in her life, after all. It was possible that she was intending to leave the whole thing to Mr Disang, and if that were the case, she might not have heard of these disturbing incidents and might be assuming that everything was going well. That was unlikely, though: what was the point of having a restaurant if you were not going to take a reasonably active interest in it? It was not as if Mma Makutsi needed a business purely to make money; since her marriage to Phuti she had been in the fortunate position of not having to worry much about money – the Double Comfort Furniture Store was doing well, by all accounts, and then there were all those Radiphuti cattle. No, the restaurant had not come into existence simply to make money.

She turned her gaze away from the window and back to Mma Potokwani. 'This is a big disaster, Mma,' she said.

Mma Potokwani nodded gravely. 'It is not at all good. In fact, it is bad, Mma. It is very bad all round.'

More tea was poured. They were both thinking the same thing: how would Mma Makutsi be told? It was not Mma Potokwani's responsibility – Mma Makutsi was Mma Ramotswe's friend and colleague – but when you were a matron the problems of others tended to be your problem too. Mma Ramotswe knew that she would have to raise the subject with Mma Makutsi, but she was not looking forward to witnessing the distress that her friend would feel when she found out. The Handsome Man's De Luxe Café was not only a café – it represented more than that in Mma Makutsi's mind: it was her own business, her own creation, the emblem of everything she had accomplished. It was about having achieved ninety-seven per cent; having struggled against all the odds; having acted on her initiative. Mma Ramotswe closed her eyes and sighed. She would find a time to speak to Mma Makutsi, but that time had not yet arrived.

Mma Potokwani, full of sympathy for this difficult situation, took it upon herself to move the discussion on.

'It's one of your cases that's worrying you, isn't it?' the matron said.

'It is, Mma.'

Mma Potokwani reached out and patted Mma Ramotswe's arm. 'Friends can always tell.'

There had been numerous occasions, Mma Ramotswe now reminded herself, when Mma Potokwani had not only been able to tell but had been able to help as well, though she was not sure whether even Mma Potokwani could do much about the complicated circumstances in which she now found herself.

Clasping her teacup in both hands, Mma Ramotswe related how Mr Sengupta had approached her, how Charlie had pointed out Maria's house, and how Maria had inadvertently provided the key to the whole situation. 'That poor woman,' she said. 'She must have suffered so much and then she hits back and the police come after her.'

'In South Africa?' asked Mma Potokwani. 'Not our police – the ones over the border?'

Mma Ramotswe nodded.

'It is very difficult for them,' said Mma Potokwani. 'Some of them are honest – maybe many of them – but there are some who are real *skellums*.' She used the word that was popular over the border: a *skellum* was malevolent; there was no reasoning with a *skellum*.

'Yes,' said Mma Ramotswe. 'I really only know one of them. He is quite senior now, I think. He is a good man.'

Mma Potokwani was interested. 'He is the one who used to be over at Mmbabtho in the old days? The one you told me about?'

Mma Ramotswe nodded. 'His mother is from here. The father was born over there, but he is Setswana-speaking. He is over in Johannesburg now.'

Mma Potokwani sipped at her tea. 'I know that man's wife. She's from Tlokweng. You say he's senior now?'

'Yes,' answered Mma Ramotswe. 'He's a police colonel now. But he's the same old Billy Pilane to me. You never change the way you look at people, you know. Your friend can become president, even, but to you he'll just be your friend.'

'As long as your friend doesn't change,' cautioned Mma Potokwani. 'There are some people who change as they become more important. Imagine if . . .' She paused. She had entertained a possibility that was too horrible to contemplate.

Mma Ramotswe was interested. 'If what, Mma?'

'Imagine if Violet Sephotho became president.'

It was a possibility too painful to contemplate. 'We should not think about such things,' said Mma Ramotswe.

'No, we should not.'

Mma Potokwani wiped her lips with a blue handkerchief she had tucked into the sleeve of her blouse. 'Your problem, Mma, is that you cannot be dishonest. You have always been like that.'

Mma Ramotswe said nothing, but Mma Potokwani was right; she could not be dishonest.

'So here you have a client who is using you, Mma. He is not telling you the truth.'

'No, he is not.'

'But you still feel you must tell him that you have found out what he already knows?'

'Yes, because if I don't, he will tell the authorities that every step has been taken to find out the identity of this Lakshmi lady.'

'He will then ask the authorities to exercise their discretion in her favour as an unidentifiable person,' said Mma Potokwani.

Mma Ramotswe agreed. 'I think that is what he wants to do.'

'While all the time,' went on Mma Potokwani, 'he knows exactly who she is.'

Mma Ramotswe could not think of that as anything but dishonest, and yet, and yet . . . 'It isn't her fault,' she said. 'Lakshmi is only here because of her violent husband.'

'That's right.'

'So,' continued Mma Ramotswe, 'is there nothing we can do for her?'

'We could keep quiet,' suggested Mma Potokwani. 'Or rather, *you* could keep quiet. You could say nothing. You could say that you have found out nothing.'

'But then I'd be misleading our own government people,' said Mma Ramotswe. 'Or at least I'd be part of a plot to mislead them.'

They both saw the problem, and were both silent for a few minutes. Then Mma Potokwani spoke. 'Go and see him,' she said. 'Go and speak to them – Mr Sengupta and Lakshmi. Tell them that you know everything and that you cannot continue to be involved in the case. That way you will not be doing anything illegal. You will not be misleading our own officials.'

Mma Ramotswe considered this. What Mma Potokwani proposed sounded reasonable enough: she had no duty to report the crimes of others – simply being a citizen did not impose on you a duty to turn in everybody who was up to no good. Certainly, if she were ever to find out about anything really serious – a murder or something of that sort – she would go straight to the police, but this was . . . what was it? It was a misleading of the authorities by one who was desperate; by one who was faced with persecution by both an abusive husband and corrupt police officers. What chance did an ordinary woman have against such a combination? To whom could such a person turn for justice?

That last question remained with her as she drove home from her trip to the supermarket and her meeting with Mma Potokwani. She imagined what it must feel like to be falsely accused of a crime. She imagined what it must be like to be terrified of going home. The world was a hard enough place as it was – how much harder it must be to have nobody to turn to, no friends, no allies, and only a cousin who was prepared to take you in and do the things that sometimes needed to be done if the weak were to be given shelter, if some semblance of fairness was to be achieved in a world that often paid no more than lip service to the idea of justice. The world was not perfect – it never had been and never would be; it was full of pitfalls and problems, of fear, of regrets and of bitter tears. Here and there, though, there were tiny points of light, hard to see at times, but there nonetheless, like the welcoming lights of home in the darkness. The flames that made these lights were hard to ignite, but occasionally, very occasionally, we found that we had in our hands the match that could be struck to start one of these little fires.

## Chapter Fifteen

# He May Sell Stationery, But He Is Really a Hero

A t first Charlie did not take his change of duties well.

'A secretary?' he asked. 'Me, Mma? A secretary?'

Mma Ramotswe had urged Mma Makutsi to be gentle in her approach. They had discussed the matter and decided that since there really was so little for Charlie to do it made sense for him to take some of the secretarial burden off Mma Makutsi. Now, as they explained to him the basis of his future employment in the agency, Mma Ramotswe could not help but notice that Mma Makutsi was showing every sign of satisfaction.

'Not a real secretary, of course,' Mma Makutsi said pedantically. 'The profession of secretary normally calls for attendance at the Botswana Secretarial College. It also requires examinations. So you'll be a sort of para-secretary, Charlie.'

Charlie's mouth dropped open. 'A para-secretary?'

Mma Makutsi warmed to her theme. 'Yes, you'll have heard about paramedics, Charlie. They're the people who give first aid before you get to hospital. Then a real doctor takes over.' She smiled. 'Or a real secretary – in the case of a para-secretary.'

Charlie glowered. 'Mma Ramotswe,' he muttered, 'you said that I could be a detective . . . You promised—'

Mma Makutsi interrupted him. 'No, she did not promise. She said that she would *try* to find things to keep you busy, Charlie. *Try to.* And she did try, and now there are no more things for you to do as a detective.' She paused. 'But when one door closes, another opens. That other door, as it happens, is marked *secretary*, or *para-secretary* perhaps.'

Charlie took a deep breath, seeming to puff up in indignation. 'She did—'

'No, she did not,' said Mma Makutsi. 'I was here – remember?'

Mma Ramotswe glanced discouragingly at Mma Makutsi. The other woman had many talents, but an ability to deal tactfully with young men like Charlie was certainly not one of them. 'I think you should give it a try, Charlie. We can call you a clerk rather than a secretary, if you like.'

Charlie considered this. 'Clerk?'

'Under-clerk?' suggested Mma Makutsi.

Again Mma Ramotswe looked across the room sharply. 'No, clerk, I think.'

'A clerk is junior to a secretary,' said Mma Makutsi. 'A good secretary normally gets paid more than a clerk.'

Charlie frowned. 'Is that true, Mma?' he asked Mma Ramotswe. 'Is a clerk really junior to a secretary?'

'I'm not sure about these things,' answered Mma Ramotswe. 'And I'm not sure whether it matters all that much, Charlie.'

Mma Makutsi intervened. 'I can answer that, Charlie. A clerk is definitely junior to a secretary. I have a friend who works in a bank and when they take on school leavers – these are sixteen-year-olds, remember – they call them clerks (fourth class). They have tea in a separate room from the secretaries and they do not get the same annual leave entitlement. They get less.'

'Less tea?' asked Mma Ramotswe.

'No, less leave. They all get the same amount of tea, I think.'

'I am glad to hear that,' said Mma Ramotswe. She had known, of course, that the reference was to leave rather than to tea, but any diversion to defuse the tension between Mma Makutsi and Charlie was worth making.

Charlie, though, had reached a decision. 'If a clerk is junior to a secretary, then I want to be a secretary rather than a clerk. I am fed up with being junior all the time. Apprentice. Assistant detective, and so on. I would prefer to be a secretary, even if it is a job just for women.'

'Para-secretary,' chipped in Mma Makutsi. 'And what do you mean *just for women*? Where have you been for the last twenty years, Charlie? Have you not heard that women will no longer put up with that sort of sexist talk?'

'Sex, Mma?' shouted Charlie. 'You're talking about sex now? Is that what you want to talk about?'

'Sex*ist*, Charlie. Can't you tell the difference? A sexist is somebody like you – who thinks that women are nothing.'

Charlie turned to appeal to Mma Ramotswe. 'I never said that, Mma Ramotswe. You see how she accuses me of saying things I never said. I can't help being a man – it is just what I am. I can't help thinking like a man ... '

'I think that para-secretary is too long a description,' said Mma Ramotswe, eager to avoid further escalation of the discussion.

Mma Makutsi offered a compromise. 'Assistant secretary, then.'

'Why assistant?' protested Charlie. 'If we do not have any secretaries here any more ...' He looked at Mma Makutsi and then back at Mma Ramotswe. 'If we do not have any secretaries because certain people who used to be secretaries are now something much more important – managing directors, or whatever – then how can I be an assistant secretary? Where is the secretary I'll be assisting, Mma? Where is she?'

Mma Makutsi sighed. 'You do not have to have an actual secretary to be assistant to. You are not assistant *to* a secretary – you are *an* assistant secretary. There is a difference. In the army you have assistant generals even if you don't have a general.'

Charlie was not about to let this pass. 'I have never heard of that rank. I know somebody who is in the Botswana Defence Force and he has never spoken of assistant generals. You get sergeants and majors and then you get generals. You don't have assistant generals – never!'

Mma Makutsi hooted with laughter. 'Sergeants, majors, then generals? Is that how you think it goes, Charlie? One, two, three: three rungs to the ladder. What about captains? Yes, what about captains? And what about colonels? Where are they in your army, Charlie?'

'We do not need to talk about the army,' said Mma Ramotswe. 'The army has got nothing to do with detective agencies.' She gave Mma Makutsi a particularly intense look before continuing. 'I think that this is settled, now. You could start showing Charlie how the filing cabinet works, Mma.'

For some reason, the prospect of teaching Charlie rather appealed to Mma Makutsi and she took the young man over to the double filing cabinet on the other side of the room.

'This is the memory of the business, Charlie,' she said. 'This is where you will find all the correspondence, all the bills, all the everything. It is all filed away. Any questions?'

'Why?' asked Charlie.

'We file it so that we can retrieve it if we want to find out who wrote what and when,' said Mma Makutsi.

Charlie opened a drawer and peered in. In spite of himself, he was intrigued, and they were soon immersed in a discussion of the filing system that Mma Makutsi had created for the office. From her desk, Mma Ramotswe watched them fondly. At heart, Mma Makutsi and Charlie were probably rather more alike than either would care to admit: they both had the same sort of personality for which there must be a special name in a book somewhere. *Makutsian*, perhaps: marked by a tendency to be a bit prickly and wear fancy shoes ... The sight of them working together, rather than arguing, pleased her. Why can't we all be like that? she thought. Not just this office, these two people, but everyone, everywhere – the whole world? She gazed out of the window. One day, she hoped, peace would break out, and friendship, too. It would break out and ripple across the world, ending corrosive enmities and hatreds, bringing men and women together across the globe. Muslims and Christians and Hindus and people who said that there was no God at all. And they would hold hands and hug one another and realise how small we were and how little time we had, and how silly it was to spend that time fighting and arguing and destroying the trust that otherwise exists between people. Oh, let that happen one day, she thought; let that happen. And perhaps it might even start here in Botswana, where there had always been so strong a desire for peace, since the days of that great and generous-spirited man, Seretse Khama, whose example to the world had been such a good one, and even before him. It could start here, in Gaborone itself, rippling out across the acacia-studded bush like one of those warm winds that seem to come from somewhere you cannot see but are strong and insistent. Then it would fan out to all those distant and busy places that might never even have heard of Botswana but would stop and listen and marvel that such a loud message could come from so quiet a country.

Mma Ramotswe had intended to take Mma Makutsi with her on her next visit to the Sengupta house but Mma Makutsi had excused herself from the office and was unable to come.

'I have to go to the café,' she said. 'I have had a telephone call.'

Mma Ramotswe had heard her answer her telephone but had not been able to work out what the call was about – Mma Makutsi had lowered her voice and cupped her hand round the receiver.

'I hope everything is all right, Mma.'

Mma Makutsi, gathering her things and stuffing them into the shoulder bag she liked to carry, was non-committal. 'There are always things happening in a business,' she said.

'Not bad things, I hope,' said Mma Ramotswe.

Mma Makutsi half turned round, but obviously thought better of pursuing the conversation. 'I shall see,' she said. 'I'm sure that everything will be fine.'

Mma Ramotswe lowered her eyes. She had decided that she would tell Mma Makutsi what she had heard from Mma Potokwani, but wanted to wait a while before she did so. It was possible that things might work out, and she did not want to sound negative; she was only too aware of Mma Makutsi's sensitive nature. To that list of institutions in the Makutsi pantheon of which seemingly innocuous discussion could cause a slight, there now had to be added the Handsome Man's De Luxe Café.

'If you need anything,' muttered Mma Ramotswe, 'never hesitate to ask, Mma.'

Mma Makutsi was tight-lipped. 'I'm sure that everything will be perfectly all right, Mma,' she said. 'But thank you, anyway.'

Mma Ramotswe judged the moment right for a further remark. 'If I had a business that was getting into trouble, then I would go straight to my friends and discuss it with them. I would not suffer in silence, Mma.'

Mma Makutsi hesitated again, but then nodded politely and left the office.

Now, turning into the Senguptas' road in the newly repaired tiny white van, Mma Ramotswe thought of the encounter ahead. It would not be easy, she felt, and it would have been good to have Mma Makutsi there to support her, but that was not to be. She would take a deep breath and say what she had to say: she could do nothing but that.

Miss Rose answered the intercom and bade the electric gate slide open for her. Mma Ramotswe was careful; it would not do to sustain yet another dent in the bodywork of the van. Sooner or later, Mr J. L. B. Matekoni had hinted, vehicles just fell to bits if you bumped into too many things in them.

Miss Rose greeted her warmly. 'I am very pleased that you came, Mma,' she said. 'We have been wondering about how things were going. You have news for us, is it?'

*Is it?* It was what people said – a general question mark that they added at the end of any enquiry.

'I have some news and then I . . . then I have no news.'

Miss Rose raised an eyebrow. 'That is very good, Mma . . . or maybe not?' She ushered Mma Ramotswe into the formal sitting room. Mma Ramotswe sat down gingerly on one of the large ornate armchairs, almost reluctant to lower herself onto the gold-coloured upholstery. Miss Rose seemed to pick up on her hesitation and was quick to reassure her. 'Make yourself comfortable, Mma. Do not worry about the chairs. They are meant to be sat upon.'

Mma Ramotswe managed an embarrassed smile. 'These chairs

would not be out of place in Buckingham Palace,' she said. 'They will have many chairs like this at the Queen's place. She will always be sitting on chairs like this.'

Miss Rose was pleased with the compliment. 'It is good to think that the Queen would feel at home if she dropped in.'

'Yes, she would like these chairs.'

There was a short silence that was broken by the sound of somebody approaching along a corridor.

'That will be Mrs,' said Miss Rose. 'She must have heard you arrive.'

Mrs came into the room. Her eyes went straight to Mma Ramotswe, and for a moment anxiety passed across her face. It was soon replaced, though, by a guarded smile of welcome.

Mma Ramotswe looked at Mrs. 'How are you, Lakshmi?'

The other woman began to answer. 'I am very well, thank you, Mma. I am …' And then she became silent. Now she looked sharply at Miss Rose.

'Why did you call her that?' asked Miss Rose. 'Have you found out what her name is?'

'I think you know that already,' said Mma Ramotswe. 'I think both of you know it.'

'She does not,' said Miss Rose. 'She does not know who she is.'

Lakshmi sat down heavily on the chair nearest her. 'See,' she said. 'She knows. This lady knows.'

Miss Rose turned to her quickly. 'You cannot say that. She knows nothing. You know nothing either. You don't even know who you are. Remember?'

'She is called Lakshmi,' said Mma Ramotswe evenly. 'And I must tell you that I know what happened.'

Miss Rose eyed her suspiciously. 'How can you know that? You are just telling us that – it's not true.'

'It is true,' countered Mma Ramotswe. 'Lakshmi is from over

the border – that way.' She waved an arm towards South Africa. 'She had a very bad husband who beat her. She tried to defend herself and he went to the police. He had a corrupt policeman charge her with attempted murder.' She paused, watching the effect of her words. 'That is why she is here. She is running away.'

Lakshmi now spoke. 'You see, Rosie? You see. It's all over now.'

'It is not over,' snapped Miss Rose. 'You have no proof of all this, Mma. We shall just say that it is all lies.'

'But it is the truth, Mma. I do not like to lie.' She put her hands together and then opened them, palms upward, in a gesture of openness.

Miss Rose closed her eyes, as if to shut out the obvious. She drew a deep breath. 'You don't know what it's like, Mma Ramotswe ... '

Mma Ramotswe did not let her finish. 'But I do, Mma.'

Both women looked at her.

Mma Ramotswe held their gaze. She did not like to talk about this; she never mentioned it, in fact, because it was something very personal, and painful too. But now she felt that she had to.

'When I was young I married a man called Note Mokoti,' she said. 'My father did not want me to marry him – I could tell that – but you know how it is when you are young: you think that you know better than everybody else. So I ignored him when he said that he thought that Note would not be a good husband for me and that he could not be trusted. I think he knew, too, that he would be violent, but he did not want to spell that out to me.'

They were silent.

'I think that you may know what I'm talking about, Lakshmi.'

Lakshmi did not say anything, but the slight movement of her head showed her agreement. She knew very well.

'I went ahead and married Note, although it must have broken my daddy's heart. And then, shortly after we were married, he began to hurt me. He began to hurt me in many ways – in my heart and in my body. He struck me with a belt. He made me cry and cry and that only seemed to give him more pleasure. He taunted me for being too weak to stand up to him.

'I thought: I must run away from this man. I thought that, but there is a big difference between thinking something and being able to do anything about it. Sometimes it is difficult for women to get away, even though they know they must . . . '

Lakshmi nodded vigorously. 'Yes, Mma. Yes. That is exactly right.'

Mma Ramotswe continued with her story. 'At last I got back to my father and he never said anything like *I told you*. He said nothing like that; he took me back and the nightmare was over.'

'Yes,' muttered Lakshmi. 'It is like a nightmare. It is just like that.'

'So, you see, Mma,' concluded Mma Ramotswe. 'I do know what it's like. I know very well.'

Miss Rose exchanged glances with Lakshmi. It was clear that she did not quite know what to do. 'So now you have found out,' she said at last. 'So, what now?'

They were both staring at Mma Ramotswe. For a few long minutes there was silence, eventually broken by Lakshmi.

'Maybe I should tell you, Mma,' she said.

Mma Ramotswe nodded. 'Yes, of course, Mma. I do not know everything about what happened.'

Miss Rose raised a hand in a gesture of warning. 'Lakshmi, I don't think you should.'

But Lakshmi was not to be dissuaded, her voice gaining strength as she began. 'My husband said that he loved me. This was after we were introduced by our parents – you know how it is with us, Mma: we like families to have a hand in the marriage.'

Mma Ramotswe knew all about this. As a younger woman she had been offended by the thought of arranged marriages and wondered how anybody could enter into one: how could one accept the choice of others in such a private matter? But then, as she saw more of these, she increasingly realised that they tended to work, at least where the arranged marriage was consensual. Perhaps one of the reasons for this, she thought, was that compatibility was something that families could judge, perhaps even better than the man and woman themselves.

'And I thought I was very lucky to have this nice-looking man who might have been a bit older than I was but who seemed well established. We had a good house outside Durban, Mma, and he was earning a lot of money in a firm that brought things in from India. Many of my friends said that they would have happily changed places with me. I thought I was very lucky.

'But then I began to see another side of him. If anything went wrong in the house – even the smallest thing – he would shout at me. Then he started to hit me. I remember the first time it happened I thought that it had been an accident; I thought that he had raised his hand to make a point and that he had slipped. But then it happened again, and again after that.

'He became suspicious. He said that I should not go out of the house because there were men around who would flirt with me and he said that I would flirt back. I told him that I would never do that, but he laughed and said that all women were the same. He said that it was always women who led men on and that there were no exceptions. He said that if he caught me looking at another man he would make sure that I never looked at a man again.

'He told me that I was not to mix with other women – the wives of his friends. He said that these women would lead me into bad ways and that they probably all had lovers. He said that

223

he would be able to tell if I tried to see these people secretly. He had people who would report back to him if they saw me out in the town.

'And all the time the beatings went on. Sometimes he did it because he was angry with me for something to do with the house, but on other occasions he said that a beating was to remind me not to step out of line. He also used to shout at me and mock me for not having children. I told him that I was doing my best and that maybe the problem was with him, but that drove him into a frenzy. It was in one of these frenzies that I tried to defend myself. I ran into the kitchen and picked up the only weapon that I could find, which was a bread knife. I shouted to him that he should keep away and that I would use the knife to defend myself, but he mocked me. He said that I couldn't even cut bread properly, let alone use a bread knife to defend myself. Then he threw something at me and rushed towards me. I held out the knife, and it went into him – not very far, because it hit a rib. It stopped him, though, and he shouted and squealed like an animal in the slaughterhouse. Bullies are like that, I think, Mma: they are not very courageous when they are hurt – they become like little boys.

'I ran out of the house and went to one of my friends. She took me in and she was the one who drove me all the way over here the following day when we heard that he had gone to the police and I was now wanted for attempted murder.

'I could not go through any of the border posts because I would be stopped on the South African side. I also didn't have a passport and Botswana would not have let me in. So my friend drove to one of those game ranch places where you can go on safari. We pretended that we were there to admire the animals, but we were really interested in the border, which ran down one side of the game reserve. My friend paid one of the staff at the reserve to guide me across at night and to walk with me to a road on the Botswana side. They had been in touch with my cousin. He said that he would pick me up at a certain time, and he was there waiting for me when I got to the road. He brought me here and talked to me about what to do. And the rest, Mma, I think you already know.'

Miss Rose shook her head. 'It's a mistake to tell anybody this,' she muttered. 'It is a big mistake.'

Mma Ramotswe waited until it was clear that Lakshmi had finished. Then she folded her arms. 'You need not worry, Lakshmi, I am not going to tell anybody.'

Miss Rose looked at Mma Ramotswe disbelievingly. 'And how much do you want for your silence, Mma?'

Mma Ramotswe remained calm. 'I want nothing, Mma.'

'You see,' said Lakshmi. 'This is an honest lady.'

Mma Ramotswe brought up the fact that Mr Sengupta had asked her to take on the case. 'He wanted me to say that I have found out nothing, but I cannot do that. I cannot make any false statement that I know will be given to the Botswana authorities. I cannot do it, Mma.'

'So what will you do?' asked Miss Rose.

'I will do nothing,' said Mma Ramotswe. 'I will withdraw from the case. You will not claim that there has been any investigation by me, and I shall say nothing about what I know. I am sorry if that is not what you really wanted from me, but I do not think that I have much choice.'

Miss Rose and Lakshmi looked at one another for guidance. 'Maybe that will be all right,' said Miss Rose eventually.

'And you will explain the whole matter to Mr Sengupta?' asked Mma Ramotswe.

Lakshmi replied: 'I will tell him, Mma. He will understand. He is a good man. He may sell stationery, but he is a very big hero underneath.'

'I think I can see that,' said Mma Ramotswe.

Miss Rose had something to add. 'Yes, Mma Ramotswe – my brother is a very big hero indeed. You may not know it, but he was even prepared to ignore your assistant crashing into him in order not to cause you inconvenience. He thought that since you were being kind to us he would be kind to you.'

Mma Ramotswe was baffled. 'I beg your pardon, Mma?'

'Your assistant . . . that young man. He was following our car and he collided with my brother. Your young man was not paying attention to the traffic. That young man and his girl were lucky.'

'His girl?'

'There was some floozy with him in the van, my brother said.'

'I see,' said Mma Ramotswe.

She rose to take her leave. She would walk out of the house and out of the tragic life of this poor woman. Her fate would be decided by others now, and there was nothing Mma Ramotswe could do to influence the direction of that decision; she wished that there were, but it was not the case. One could not set all the wrongs of the world right; one could not do anything about even a tiny proportion of those wrongs. It was a hard conclusion to reach, and she did not feel happy about it. But she could hardly make a report that she knew would be used to mislead the officials of her own government. Botswana was a well-run country – such things belonged to the corrupt side of Africa, and that, she was determined, would never gain a toehold in her Botswana. Never.

As she left, Lakshmi came up to her and took her hand. 'Thank you, Mma,' she said.

Mma Ramotswe returned the pressure on her hand. 'I hope all goes well for you, my sister,' she whispered.

She meant it. Sometimes such words are uttered as a matter of course; we wish people well when we have not really reflected on it and may even be indifferent to what happens. But she meant this – with all her heart she meant it. And even now she was thinking of what else she could possibly do to help, having declined to give her assistance in one respect. She wondered whether she would come up with something. Sometimes ideas came at totally unexpected times – when you were walking in your garden looking at Mr J. L. B. Matekoni's beans, or when you were sitting on your veranda watching the sun sink over the tops of the acacia trees, or when you were simply looking up at the sky, so high, so pale, so empty. Ideas could come to you completely unbidden; suddenly they were there, ready to be invoked, ready to solve a problem that you thought was quite intractable. So it might be that an idea could come to resolve this rather sad situation; an idea that might seem improbable but might just work – such as getting in touch with Billy Pilane over in Johannesburg and saying to him: 'Billy, would you be able to get somebody off the wanted list if you knew the true story and you knew that she did not deserve to be there . . . ?'

## Chapter Sixteen

# You Don't Want Handsome Men

When Mma Ramotswe arrived at the office the following morning, Charlie was already there, sitting on the empty oil drum at the side of the building, his eyes closed, sunning himself, humming a tune that she had often heard him hum before – an annoying little tune that had wormed its way into her mind too and would not be shooed away.

He opened his eyes when he heard her open the door of the tiny white van. 'You see, Mma,' he called out, 'I am first here. I am Mr Keen, first class, one hundred per cent dedicated.'

She laughed. 'I am glad that you are enjoying being . . . ' She was about to say 'a secretary', but she stopped herself. And anyway he said it.

'I like being a secretary, Mma. It is a very cool thing to be.'

'Oh, yes? Cool?'

Charlie lowered himself from his drum, dusted off his trouser legs, and joined her at the office door. 'I have discovered that girls like men who are secretaries,' he said. 'I was speaking to one last night at a dance and when I told her that I was a secretary, she said, "Ow, you must be one of these new men." So I said I was, and she said, "New men are very sexy – everybody knows that." And so I said, "Yes, that is true. Everybody knows that."'

Mma Ramotswe rolled her eyes. 'I see. So you're pleased.'

'Very pleased.'

They entered the office together.

'I have something to discuss with you, Charlie,' said Mma Ramotswe.

'Any time, Mma. A filing problem? Let me sort it out. A letter to dictate? I can write quite quickly even if I can't do those stupid signs with a pencil that Mma Makutsi goes on about.'

'Shorthand.'

'Yes, shorthand. I do not need that rubbish. I can write quickly.'

Mma Ramotswe sat down at her desk and reached for a pencil. It was easier to talk about difficult things, she found, if she had a pencil in her hands. The pencil could be twirled between fingers and, if necessary, tapped on the desktop. She cleared her throat, gesturing for him to sit in the client's chair in front of her desk.

'Charlie, I wanted to talk about that accident the other day.'

Charlie's eyes narrowed. 'What accident?'

'You know what I'm talking about. The dent my van received. That one.'

'Ah,' said Charlie. 'That accident.' He paused, concern passing over his face. 'Has the van not been repaired properly? Do you want me to take it back?'

'It's fine,' said Mma Ramotswe. 'You can't tell that it has been damaged.'

'Good,' said Charlie, and then added quickly, 'So, no problem then.'

He was about to get up, but she signalled for him to remain seated. 'You never really told me exactly what happened.'

Charlie shrugged. 'There's not much to say, Mma. The other driver didn't stop at a stop sign.'

'Yes, but it would be interesting to hear your report on it. Why don't you tell me what happened? In your own words, of course.'

He clasped his hands together. She could see him squirm.

'My words, Mma?'

Mma Ramotswe looked into his eyes. He looked away, his gaze falling to the floor.

'Yes, Charlie?'

He drew in his breath. 'I was driving along ... '

'Yes?'

'I was driving along, you see ... '

'By yourself?'

He hesitated. 'Maybe,' he said. 'Maybe not. No, maybe I wasn't by myself.'

'Ah.'

'I think I was with a friend. Yes, I remember now: I was with a friend. I was giving him a lift somewhere.'

'Him?'

Charlie's hands tightened their grip on each other. 'Maybe it wasn't a him. Maybe it was a lady. Yes, I think it might have been a lady.'

'Or even a girl?'

He frowned. 'Ladies, girls – all the same, Mma. One word covers both.'

'So you had a girl in the cab.'

'I was trying to help her, Mma. She had a long way to walk.'

Mma Ramotswe conceded the point. 'That was kind of you,

Charlie. And then what happened.'

He stared up at the ceiling, as if trying to dredge information from the furthest recesses of his memory. 'It was a long time ago,' he said.

'Five days?'

'That's a long time when so much is happening, Mma. Five days is almost a whole week.'

She tapped the pencil on the desk. 'Try to remember. I know it was a long time ago.'

He turned his gaze to meet hers. 'I came to an intersection,' he said flatly. 'Then Mr Sengupta didn't stop, and he hit me. So ...' He hesitated. 'So, I lost sight of where the other car went. I didn't really see the exact house.' He lowered his voice. 'I had picked up that girl, you see, Mma, and I was showing off to her.'

They looked at one another in silence. She noticed that his lower lip was quivering, and she made up her mind.

'Then that's all right, Charlie. You've told me the truth, and now we can forget about it.'

He had not expected this. When he spoke, his voice faltered. 'You're not angry, Mma?'

She shook her head. What was the point of anger? There were occasions when Mma Ramotswe, like all of us, could feel angry, but they were few – and they never lasted long. Anger, Obed Ramotswe had explained to her once, is no more than a salt that we rub into our wounds. She had never forgotten that – along with the things he said about cattle, and Botswana, and the behaviour of the rains. 'I was, Charlie,' she said quietly, 'but not for long. I wanted to give you the chance to tell me yourself that you weren't on your own, and now you have done that.' She paused, allowing herself the faintest of smiles. 'And as for accidents – there are so many things in Botswana that are in the wrong place. So we can't help being involved in accidents, can we? And we can't help being nice to young women, can we?'

The young man was almost too astonished to speak. But he just managed, 'Yes, Mma, that is true.'

'And now you can take a letter, Charlie. I shall dictate and you can write it down – then you can type it up.'

Charlie rapidly busied himself with his preparations. 'Fire away, Mma,' he said. 'I am ready.'

And he thought: I would do anything for this woman – anything.

If the day started well for Charlie, it did not for Mma Makutsi. She was late arriving at work; Mma Ramotswe had dictated her letter and Charlie, inordinately proud of his handiwork, had typed it, handed it over for signing, and addressed the envelope by the time she came into the office.

She lowered herself dispiritedly into her seat. 'It is all over,' she said, her voice flat and without emotion. 'Everything is finished now.'

Mma Ramotswe, who had been examining a set of suspect receipts passed on by a client, pushed the papers aside. 'Mma?' she said with concern. 'What is it, Mma?'

There was defeat in Mma Makutsi's voice. 'This. The paper. Today.' She held out the folded newspaper, which Charlie took and passed on to Mma Ramotswe.

She knew what it was before she read it. This would be the review of the Handsome Man's De Luxe Café by the self-appointed restaurant critic and markedly undistinguished graduate of the Botswana Secretarial College, Violet Sephotho. Mma Makutsi was right; this was the end.

*Our renowned restaurant critic visits a new establishment!* shouted the headline on the front page. *See page 6 for the full story.*

With the air of one who dreads what she is about to read, Mma Ramotswe turned to page six.

*De Luxe?* the review began. *Not in my dictionary! Of course anybody can call a business anything these days and get away with it. Anything at all. There's a place in town that calls itself the No. 1 Ladies' Detective Agency. Says who? What about the CID? What about the FBI? They may have something to say about that claim. So when an outfit sets up calling itself the Handsome Man's De Luxe Café, the warning bells sound loud and clear. Who are these handsome men? Where's the luxe? When I went there, there were certainly no handsome men – and I even looked under the tables to make sure. There were a few men around, but even their mothers would not have described them as handsome. So that was a bad start – in my view, at least.*

*And then it got worse. The waiter appeared and took my order. I'm not sure if you can write things down correctly when you're drunk, but at least he tried. I had to help him to spell sausage, which is not a good sign. If there's one thing a waiter should be able to do, it's to spell s-a-u-s-a-g-e.*

*I looked around the place. The less said about the décor, the better. Next time I go there – not that there's likely to be a next time – I'll take a tin of paint with me and try to sort out the places where the painter forgot to go: all part of the service!*

*My food took thirty-eight minutes to arrive – I timed it. I was hungry by then, but not hungry enough to eat what was put before me; you'd have to be starving to eat anything at this place. Better to go hungry than to spend the next few days sick, I always say!*

*I looked at the food and smelled it. Ladies and gentlemen, don't go there – just don't go there! So here are my scores (out of ten) for the Handsome Man's De Luxe Café: atmosphere: zero; décor and cleanliness: zero; service: minus one; food: minus ten. Believe me – give this place a very wide berth (five miles, to be on the safe side)! VS.*

233

Mma Ramotswe finished reading and laid the newspaper down on her desk. She looked at Mma Makutsi, whose large round glasses were flashing out a message that was hard to interpret but could hardly be cheerful.

'Not a good review?' asked Charlie.

Neither answered him. Then Mma Ramotswe said, 'That woman is full of venom, Mma. She is like a snake.'

'Snakes do not write in the newspapers,' muttered Mma Makutsi. 'That is the difference. Snakes cannot harm you by what they write.'

Charlie had now picked up the newspaper and was working his way through the review. 'Ow!' he exclaimed. 'This is one big lie, Mma. People will see that. They'll know who this VS is.'

'No, they won't,' said Mma Makutsi. 'They won't know who she is and they'll believe every word of it.' She paused before continuing. 'I am finished now. I have wasted all that money of Phuti's and for nothing. I have discovered something about the chef and the waiter. And the waitress, too.'

Mma Ramotswe suspected what was coming, but waited to hear it.

'They are all related,' said Mma Makutsi. 'He dropped his *omang* on the floor when he went out to the stores and I picked it up. I saw his real name. I asked the waiter, and he told me everything. He was drunk and had had a fight with his father. He told me everything. He is not a real chef. My lawyer is his brother and always tries to help him, but it never works . . . And now they have all handed in their notice and said that they have had enough, and so there is nobody to run the restaurant. It's the end, Mma Ramotswe – it's the end.'

Mma Ramotswe grimaced. It was difficult to see what could be done and she felt at a loss as to what to say to Mma Makutsi. Should she recommend that she simply walk away from the business; that she close it down and cut her losses rather than letting them mount up? What if she advertised for replacements and found another set of these types, every bit as bad as the last lot?

Mma Makutsi needed help, and she could not provide it. Her thoughts turned to Mma Potokwani. Catering was something she knew about, and was good at. Was there a chance – just a chance? She glanced at her watch. It would take them twenty minutes or so to get out to the Orphan Farm and when they arrived she imagined Mma Potokwani would be ready to serve tea and fruit cake. Mma Makutsi and Mma Potokwani had had their differences in the past, but there was no doubt of Mma Potokwani's ability to deal with a crisis.

'I think we should go for a drive,' she said to Mma Makutsi. 'There's no point sitting here and brooding.'

'I'm finished,' said Mma Makutsi. 'There's no point in doing anything.'

Mma Ramotswe rose to her feet. 'Never say that, Mma.'

'But it's true,' said Mma Makutsi. 'I am a big failure, Mma.'

Charlie, his sympathy engaged by the outrageous review, shook his head vigorously. 'No, Mma, you are not a failure. Ninety-seven per cent – remember?'

'That was a long time ago,' she muttered. 'This is different. This is a . . . a whole new area of failure.'

There was no point in wallowing in misery, thought Mma Ramotswe. 'Come on, now, Mma,' she coaxed. 'Let's go somewhere where we can look calmly at what you might do.'

Mma Makutsi rose from her desk. 'A big failure,' she muttered, to nobody in particular. 'That's me.'

Nobody else heard it – but she did: from down below, at floor level, came the voice of her shoes, a voice that was at the same time tiny and crowing.

*We warned you, Boss. Did you listen to us? You did not. Result? Failure – big time!*

The children were singing when they arrived. That's something, thought Mma Ramotswe – the sound of children's voices was a reminder that however bad things might look, they were not as bad as all that. Children's singing is like the light; or like the much-needed rain at the end of a drought. It is the thing that will comfort us and remind us that there is good in the world, and hope, too.

'Listen to that,' said Mma Ramotswe, as they got out of the van. 'Listen to that lovely song, Mma Makutsi. That is one that we sang ourselves, isn't it? All about a bird that looks after the fields when the people are away and warns them when the locusts try to eat the crops.'

Mma Makutsi made a non-committal sound.

'Yes,' said Mma Ramotswe breezily, 'it is the same song. That was a very helpful bird, that one.'

'Maybe,' said Mma Makutsi. Then she muttered: 'There are no helpful birds – not in real life.'

They walked over to the block where Mma Potokwani had her office. When they knocked, they could hear voices within. Mma Potokwani's assistant came out to greet them. 'She's busy right now,' she said, 'but she will be ready to see you in a few minutes. I can fetch you tea, Mma Ramotswe – or you can wait until Mma Potokwani is ready.'

'I shall wait, Mma,' said Mma Ramotswe. 'It is not too hot and I am not thirsty.'

They took a seat in the small waiting room. There were pictures of children on the walls, including a photograph of one of the orphans who had done particularly well in the recent school-leaving examinations. The assistant, noticing that Mma Ramotswe was looking at the photograph with interest, said, 'That is a very clever girl, Mma. She came to us when she was three and has been with us since then. She won one of the scholarships to Maru-a-Pula School and now Mr Taylor is getting her something that will take her to university. She wants to be a vet. Think of that, Mma – one of our children becoming a vet. She will be able to take care of the few cattle we have here – and the goats, too, I think.'

'It is a very good thought,' said Mma Ramotswe. She turned to Mma Makutsi. 'That's good, isn't it?'

'Maybe,' said Mma Makutsi, barely audibly.

The door to Mma Potokwani's office opened and a woman dressed in a flowery dress stepped out. She smiled benignly at Mma Ramotswe and Mma Makutsi before making her way out of the room. Behind her, framed in the office doorway, stood the familiar, generous-sized figure of Mma Potokwani.

'You must come in, *Bomma*,' she said. 'I have finished interviewing.'

This warm greeting drew a smile from Mma Ramotswe, even if Mma Makutsi gazed down at the floor. Mma Ramotswe saw Mma Potowkani glance at Mma Makutsi in a concerned way. She had picked up that something was wrong; of course, she would – if you were responsible for the welfare of two hundred people, children and housemothers, cooks and cleaners, then you learned to read moods.

They sat down while Mma Potokwani's assistant put on the kettle.

'I was interviewing a new housemother,' said Mma Potokwani brightly. 'That lady who went out – I think she'll get the job. She had ten children of her own, you know, and now ... well, she says that since the youngest has grown up she doesn't know what to do with her time.'

'Ten children is too many,' said Mma Makutsi.

237

Mma Potokwani caught Mma Ramotswe's eye; a silent message was exchanged.

'Children are good for Botswana,' said Mma Potokwani evenly. 'We still have a lot of room in this country.'

Mma Makutsi said nothing.

'Mma Makutsi,' said Mma Potokwani, 'I can tell that something is wrong.'

'I am fine,' sniffed Mma Makutsi.

'No, you aren't, Mma. I can tell that you are not fine. You are very unhappy about something.' She hesitated for a moment before continuing, 'It's this new café, isn't it?'

Mma Makutsi looked straight ahead of her. She took off her glasses and began to polish them. Mma Potokwani signalled to her assistant to fetch the fruit cake tin.

'It is very difficult running a business,' began Mma Makutsi.

'Of course it is,' said Mma Potokwani. 'Probably even harder than running an orphan farm.'

The implicit compliment winkled a response out of Mma Makutsi. 'I have had trouble with my chef,' she said.

Mma Potokwani nodded her head in agreement. 'That man is very troublesome. He is not really a cook, you know. That business about having worked in the Grand Palm – complete nonsense.'

Mma Makutsi seemed surprised to hear that Mma Potokwani knew about Thomas Disang. 'You know of him, Mma?'

Mma Potokwani looked sympathetic. 'Many people know about him,' she said. 'He is what they call a chancer, I think.'

'And the waiter?'

'He is his son, I believe,' said Mma Potokwani.

Mma Makutsi turned to Mma Ramotswe. 'Everybody will be laughing at me,' she said. 'My name is going to make people laugh and laugh. They'll say: "Mma Makutsi", and then people will start laughing.'

'They will not,' said Mma Ramotswe. 'They will not laugh.'

'No,' said Mma Potokwani. 'Not if you ...' She trailed off.

'Not if I what?' asked Mma Makutsi.

'Not if you change everything,' said Mma Potokwani.

Mma Makutsi pointed out that after Violet Sephotho's review it would make no difference. 'The Disangs have handed in their notice and gone,' she said, 'but people will still remember that Sephotho woman's warning. That is what this place is like, Mma. It is a village. You do not forget things in a village.'

Mma Potokwani was not discouraged. 'You change the name,' she said. 'You change the clientele. You get a new chef. You change everything.'

'I don't see how you can change the clientele,' objected Mma Makutsi.

The assistant had now prepared the tea. There was fruit cake, too – generous, therapeutic slices appeared on plates.

'You don't want handsome men,' explained Mma Potokwani. 'You don't want that crowd.'

Mma Makutsi said nothing, but was listening intently.

'You want women, Mma. Women like places where they can go and talk to other women.'

Mma Ramotswe began to smile. 'Of course they do. Of course.'

'So, instead of the Handsome Man's De Luxe Café, you have the Ladies' Afternoon Café.'

There was a long silence. In the distance, the children had stopped singing while Mma Potokwani had been speaking. Now there was only the sound of cicadas screeching outside. Somewhere, far away, a car's engine whined.

Mma Makutsi was the first to speak. 'The Ladies' Afternoon Café,' she intoned, giving each word its full weight. 'The Ladies' Afternoon Café.'

Mma Ramotswe clapped her hands together. 'That will be very popular, Mma! Everybody will go ... or, rather, all ladies will go.'

'Not all,' conceded Mma Potokwani. 'But enough. And you needn't have a full menu – they're always lots of trouble. You will just have scones and cake.'

'And tea,' interjected Mma Ramotswe.

'Of course.'

'Redbush tea *and* ordinary tea.'

Mma Potokwani repeated the formula. 'Redbush tea *and* ordinary.'

Mma Makutsi was thinking. 'I'll need people to do all this.'

Mma Potokwani lowered her eyes modestly. 'I can manage it to begin with,' she said. 'Later on we can get a manager to take over from me. I have a retired housemother in mind who would love to do it. She is a famous baker of scones.'

Mma Makutsi looked enquiringly at Mma Ramotswe, who signalled that this was clearly a good idea. 'Mma Potokwani is good at getting people to do things,' she said. 'You can count on her.'

'So I needn't worry about anything?' asked Mma Makutsi, her tone now distinctly more cheerful.

'Nothing at all,' said Mma Potokwani. 'In fact, you can forget about everything. You can go back to doing what you do so well, Mma, which is being one of the best detectives in the country.'

This flattery had an instant effect. 'You're very kind, Mma Potokwani,' said Mma Makutsi.

Mma Potokwani made a self-effacing gesture. 'I do not like to see my friends in difficulty.' She paused. 'Which is why I have a piece of news for you, Mma Ramotswe.'

Mma Ramotswe raised an eyebrow. 'News, Mma? Good or bad?'

Mma Potokwani laughed. 'Have a piece of fruit cake first, Mma. Fruit cake goes with ... '

They waited.

'Fruit cake goes with good news,' concluded Mma Potokwani.


That evening, Mma Ramotswe and Mr J. L. B. Matekoni sat out on their veranda later than usual. It was a Friday evening, and Motholeli and Puso were both away on sleepovers with friends. As a result, the house was quieter than usual, prompting Mr J. L. B. Matekoni to turn on a radio, which Mma Ramotswe immediately switched off. 'If you don't mind, Rra,' she said, 'it will be more peaceful without music.' He did not mind; Mma Ramotswe was right – they did not need any distraction: there was so much to talk about.

'So,' said Mr J. L. B. Matekoni, 'you went out to Mma Potokwani's place?'

'We did,' said Mma Ramotswe, sipping from the glass of guava juice she had poured. 'She was on her usual good form.'

'That woman,' he mused. 'She's like a ... ' He searched his mind for a way of describing their formidable friend. A railway engine? A bolt of lightning? A determined cow? No, that was uncomplimentary, and he did not mean to be disrespectful. A stately hippopotamus, then? No, that was worse.

'She is like a matron,' said Mma Ramotswe. 'Don't you think?'

'Of course. Yes.' That was it. She was like a matron and she *was* a matron. And we needed matrons, he thought – we needed them. He had read that hospitals were getting rid of matrons and appointing all sorts of people who were not matrons to run them – people who did not wear matrons' blue and white uniforms and did not have watches pinned onto their fronts. How would such people know how to run a hospital – or a children's home, for that matter? Who were these people to imagine that they could do the things that matrons had always done? No wonder hospitals were full of infections and people lying in unmade beds; matrons would never have tolerated that – not for one moment.

'So what did matron say?' he asked.

They both smiled at the question. Mma Ramotswe took another sip of guava juice and told him about her renaming – and effective takeover – of Mma Makutsi's café. 'Actually,' she said, 'Mma Makutsi was rather pleased. I think she had realised that running a restaurant or a café may sound exciting but is really extremely hard work; I would never try to run one, Rra – never. She seemed pleased to be handing over the responsibility to Mma Potokwani.' She paused. 'And the terms were good, too – from my point of view.'

He did not see what she had to do with it, and so she explained. She had previously told him about her financial arrangement with Mma Potokwani – he had been tight-lipped about it, but pleased that something had been done for Charlie – and she had also told Mma Makutsi, who had disapproved of it strongly. 'Well, it was Mma Makutsi who came up with a plan. She said that the profits from the café, if there were any, would be shared by the two of them, but she – Mma Makutsi, that is – would use her share to pay off the loan that I took from Mma Potokwani.'

Mr J. L. B. Matekoni gave a whistle of surprise. 'Her own share? Mma Makutsi's own share? That's very generous of her, Mma.'

'It is,' said Mma Ramotswe. 'She told me that she feels that Charlie's pay should come from her, since he is helping her with the secretarial side of things.'

'I suppose I can see that,' said Mr J. L. B. Matekoni. 'But still ...'

'Yes. But then Mma Makutsi does have a softer side, you know. She's really quite fond of Charlie – underneath it all.'

'So everybody's happy?'

Mma Ramotswe thought for a moment. 'I think so.'

'Well, that's good.'

She picked up her glass. 'It gets better.'

'What?'

She let her gaze rest on her garden. The evening sun, weak now in its final moments, had crowned the large acacia tree in the front garden with its golden, buttery light. Individual branches of the acacia were outlined against the sky. It was a thorn tree and only moderately hospitable to birds, but a Cape dove had settled on it and was looking anxiously about, surveying the world that birds see – the world of leaves and twigs and air. *I hope you find your wife*, she inwardly wished the bird. *I hope you find her.*

She turned to Mr J. L. B. Matekoni. 'I decided on a way of sorting out the Sengupta affair,' she said. 'You remember Billy Pilane?'

He did. He had liked Billy Pilane and had often thought that it would be good to see him again.

'I was going to see if I could persuade Billy to get that woman off their list.'

Mr J. L. B. Matekoni's expression clouded over. 'You don't want to get involved in that sort of thing. You don't want to go about asking people in the police for favours.'

'Even if there has been an injustice?'

He shook his head. 'Where would it end?'

'I don't have to do it anyway,' she announced. 'It's done.'

He sounded displeased. 'You got in touch with him?'

'No,' said Mma Ramotswe. 'Mma Potokwani got in touch with his wife – of her own accord. They talked and now, well, Lakshmi is no longer on that list. She shouldn't have been on it in the first place, of course, but now she's off it.'

'Mma Potokwani did all that?' He thought it quite possible;

nobody argued with Mma Potokwani, and that included senior police officers, and their wives.

'She's a matron,' said Mma Ramotswe. It was sufficient explanation, she felt.

'And so?'

'Well, since she's not wanted by the police, she can make a regular application to be allowed to stay in Botswana. They can tell the truth and explain to the authorities that she has been abused by that man back there. It will be a strong case and if Mr Sengupta sponsors her, they're likely to give her a residence permit.' She paused, and thought: *there are so many people who would love to be able to live in peace, but there are so many others who do not want to let them.*

Mr J. L. B. Matekoni stood up. 'Let's go for a walk in the garden,' he said. 'While there's still light.'

They left the veranda. The light was fading quickly now, but there was enough to see the things they wanted to see – the progress of the next crop of beans, the state of the Namaqualand daisies that Mma Ramotswe had recently planted along the side of the house, the new shrubs put in by the *mopipi* tree.

There was also enough light, Mma Ramotswe reflected, to see that the world was not always a place of pain and loss, but a place where our simple human affairs – those matters that for all their pettiness still sometimes confounded us – were not insoluble, were not without the possibility of resolution.

She held her husband's hand. No further words were exchanged, or needed.

Alexander McCall Smith is the author of over eighty books on a wide array of subjects. For many years he was Professor of Medical Law at the University of Edinburgh and served on national and international bioethics bodies. Then in 1999 he achieved global recognition for his award-winning series The No. 1 Ladies' Detective Agency, and thereafter has devoted his time to the writing of fiction, including the 44 Scotland Street and Corduroy Mansions series. His books have been translated into forty-six languages. He lives in Edinburgh with his wife Elizabeth, a doctor.